REQUIEM

CHARLES D'AMICO

Cover & Interior Design: Blue Handle Publishing, LLC

ISBN: 978-1-7347727-5-3

To everyone that has helped me along this journey, I thank you. From the criticism, closed doors and a blind eye turned to the praise and acceptance of what I'm doing. I thank everyone for their role in this process.

Here's to hitting 1 Million words before my 40th birthday.

Sis, thank you for continuing to be my literary inspiration. Thank you to my wife for all the support and belief in this crazy dream.

To all the fans and supporters, thank you.

Thank You, Bryan, Mike, and Joe. Without your early support, none of this would have happened.

REQUIEM

1

AS IF I WASN'T SPEEDING ENOUGH ALREADY, NOW I NEED TO DEAL WITH THIS SHIT.

Initially we were supposed to go on a trip to Costa Rica for missionary work with Father Roberts, but that never came to fruition. He made his way down and did the job to great success, according to him. He went shortly after Gaines's arrest and transfer to FCI. It was hard for me to get free time. Maria and I spent the months after Gaines's detention continuing the case, working through as much of the paper trail we could find. Maria focused on Erin and her web of cons and name changes. This took her all over the country following up on old cases now pinned with her MO. I spent most of my time working with Cappelano, continuing our work on his cases. The problem is that Gaines was getting into Frank's head and mine. We would drift off-topic for hours at a time. I'll catch up on that shit show more, but for now, let's just enjoy the breeze as Father Roberts sleeps in the passenger seat.

Maria and I were unable to make the Costa Rica trip with Father Roberts a few months ago. We planned a new trip, not nearly as far as Central America. Still, a fulfilling getaway allowing us to relax but also give back. Instead of helping Father Roberts build a community center in the slums of Costa Rica, we are working with a soup kitchen that needs support and some work done. At the same time, they have staff out of town. Father Roberts knows I like using my hands, doing carpentry work, making this trip a win all around.

We are staying in a small house I rented for the three of us for a few weeks. I might stay longer; we'll see. I'm pretty burned out; it's been a long, rough couple of years. I also have an endless supply of footage to review and type. This gives me a chance to review it all. We're driving from Detroit to Santa Fe, New Mexico, not flying. I thought it would be relaxing, as well as giving Father Roberts and me time to talk and catch up. Maria is flying down in a couple of days. Since she continues to be active in the bureau she still has some rules to follow on vacation. As I'm the owner of my own company, I can set up a shop there if I want and never go back.

"Neil, how far until the next stop? I could use a break, maybe something to drink." Father Roberts was waking up.

"We're a little past halfway into the trip, somewhere in Kansas. The GPS says we have a little over ten hours left in the trip, and we're about six hours from Amarillo, Texas."

"What's in Amarillo? I didn't know that was a stop." Half-awake Father was still lost.

"According to the last fifteen billboards in Kansas, the biggest steak in Texas is there. Figured we would stop and grab a bite."

"I'm always game for a big steak, but that sounds pretty far still. Can we pull off somewhere to get gas, use the bathroom, and stretch our legs?"

"No problem, Father. I'll hit the next stop we see."

"Neil, are you doing OK? I know the first couple of hours all we did was talk about Cappelano and Gaines. Have you finally gotten that out of your system?"

"I wish, Father, but I hope this long drive can deal with that. I want to have as clear a mind that I can when we get there."

Since closing the Cappelano case, and recently the Gaines case for the second time in a week, I have been drained. It's not surprising that I would be running on fumes after all this chaos. Still, I haven't slept a decent night since Cappelano and Gaines became acquainted at FCI Milan. The boys and I at BCI started a war room with Gaines on the wall. "Why?" you might ask. He's locked up, yes. He still has significant influence on what goes on outside of prison with his company and his enterprise.

We've been able to connect Gaines to local politicians and power players in the community. TJ is confident there is another stash of money that we have yet to find, allowing Gaines to keep up his influence. I agree that the way someone of Gaines's stature controls others starts with cash. We thought we had given Gaines's empire a blow with the financial moves but looks as though we merely stunted his growth. Gaines is still making moves. The board even reinstated him with a temporary leave while he finishes dealing with his court case and prison time.

Enough about Gaines for now; this trip is about unwinding from that stress. Driving across the country in my navy blue Challenger has been fun. Ken made sure and bought me an excellent radar detector for the trip down, to minimize the tickets. It's been fun to mess with Father Roberts and punch it over 115 now and again. My favorite part has been driving in the middle of nowhere. The calmness out here has been just what I needed. Similar to the ways a shower, or the rhythm I get when punching a heavy bag, the road is hypnotizing me.

"Father, according to the GPS we have a gas station coming up in a few miles. We can pull off, stretch our legs, then head into Amarillo for dinner."

"Okay, sounds great. Are you sure you're still good driving? I was able to get a nap, so I'm refreshed." Father Roberts yawned as he woke up.

"Right now I'm doing great. The drive is calming for me, I'll be fine. Especially with us stopping soon, I'll be good to go."

As we finished driving through the plains of Kansas, I began dreaming of the giant steak I keep seeing billboards for; it's insane. I feel like I started seeing those billboards a few states ago for a small town in the middle of nowhere, Texas. I guess it's working because I really want to go there for some reason. I can assume that Father Roberts is the same, since he is licking his chops every time we pass one.

"Neil, if we pass another billboard talking about large steaks, but don't eat soon, I might start eating your arm."

"Father, calm down. We're only a few minutes from a truck stop. We can fill up the car, get you something to eat, and get back on the road. Before you know it, we'll be in Amarillo."

"I never thought I'd be looking forward to Amarillo, Texas. What does that say about the past couple of hours of driving?" Father has a point.

"I'm with you. We can pull off, get something to eat, and then it's a short four-hour drive to Santa Fe, where we can relax."

"Neil, you know we aren't going to relax. We have a ton of work to do, starting in two days. You'll get tonight and tomorrow, when Maria lands to settle in. Then it's working at the soup kitchen. You've got to help us build a new storage shed."

"I think we'll be able to manage. Compared to the life I usually lead. It will feel like a vacation just the same."

After witty back-and-forth banter, we made it to the truck stop. Luckily, we arrived when we did because Father Roberts was close to dying of starvation and dehydration. Then again, he is a bit melodramatic when he's hungry, like Carol Lynn when she was five. She used to throw the biggest tantrums when she was hungry. You would have thought we were the Gestapo starving her. Father Roberts is doing his best impersonation of his five-year-old self.

"Neil, thank you for stopping. That was needed, not just getting out and stretching my legs, but also getting something to eat."

"I know, the car is comfortable, but sitting stationary for eight hours is brutal regardless."

"You have a point there. How long is it until Amarillo?"

"Just over five hours from here. We should be pulling into Amarillo between four and five. Perfect for a quick dinner, then back on the road to get into Santa Fe around nine or ten at night. With the time change, it won't be too bad."

"That has been crazy, I would have thought by now we'd be past Central Standard Time and into the others by now." Father Roberts has a point; it's nuts how big CST is.

"Let hop back in the car, get rolling, and grab that big-ass steak. Although something tells me, we are going to be drastically underwhelmed."

My theory is that any restaurant that has to advertise from three states away to drum up interest might not have the best food in the world. It may just be great advertising, but it's also something to think about. For now, I'm going to set the speed at ninety, and we might get there a bit sooner.

"Let's get to move on. If you need me to drive, just let me know."

"Father, I'm not sure my car can allow it after the few hours you drove this morning, doing the speed limit or slower. I could feel my car weeping on the underperforming your driving was."

"You've been an ass since we were kids. Great to see nothing else has changed."

Father Roberts was right. Our relationship hasn't changed much over the decades, just the way we lead our lives. He is still my best friend, the person I go to, and the best euchre partner a bro can have. If you're not from the Midwest, I'll take a minute and let you Google it. Having a primo partner for a skill game such as euchre made my teen-through-twenty years quite profitable. However, Father Roberts's priestly conscience can get in the way from time to time. I tried to get him in on a company euchre tournament. He wouldn't, knowing we'd probably smoke everyone.

The rest of the drive was a beautiful one. Father Roberts began his daily meditations. At the same time, I started reaching out to Ken and Maria to check in on everyone. I had been texting with Sheila and Carol Lynn most of the trip. If you're wondering about the girls, I have one of the guys staying at my place in the spare bedroom, keeping an eye on them.

"Hey Ken, how's it going? Have we made any progress on anything? I saw your text a few hours ago to call, but the signal has been spotty at best."

"We have some news about Gaines and the case overall. I'm not sure you're going to like it, though. It's the kind of information that might make you slam on the breaks or the gas pedal and do over a hundred."

"Ken, I'm not that easily thrown off. unless you're about to tell me he's getting released on a plea deal, I think I'll be okay."

"It's not that, Neil, so we're good there. I think he likes it there with Cappelano. Gaines already feels comfortable in prison; hell, he converted his cell, damn near upgraded it all."

"Yeah, that shit pissed me off, but what are you going to do? There are loopholes in every system. Not to mention money talks. Get to it. What's the crap news?"

"Remember how the warden was an assistant filling in? After you got the other one arrested? Gaines pulled some strings and got a former member of his board as the replacement warden of the prison. TJ is working on the connections needed to pull it off."

I punched the gas, just like Ken thought I would. The speedometer went up, reading 90, then 95, and eventually settling between 120 and 130. Father Roberts began breathing heavily and punching me in the arm.

"Isn't that just great, Ken? Gaines gets to handpick the person who oversees his incarceration. Maybe they can just give him a key and let him come and go as he pleases."

"Hey Neal, is everything okay over there? It sounds like Father Roberts isn't too happy with your driving. Are you speeding?"

"Of course I'm speeding. It was either that or slamming on the breaks going almost ninety."

"I'm not sure either is a good way to take the news. Ken was raising his voice.

"Neil, are you going to slow down?" Father Roberts asked excitedly.

"I'm down to one-ten, but I guess I can keep slowing down for you. Since you look like you're going to throw up."

"Thanks, Neil, very friendly of you." Father Roberts looked worn out.

"Neil, I knew I should have waited to tell you, but I'm not a fan of lying or withholding information from you. You know that."

Yes, he should have waited to tell me. Now we're going to get to Amarillo in record time. I'm slowly increasing speed without Father Roberts noticing, and I'm back up over 110. This car rides so smoothly. It's hard to tell, especially under 130. Thinking through the news Ken just dropped on me, I quickly said 'bye and hung up. My car ride companion didn't even bother to ask me what was wrong.

Gaines has picked his captor, in essence. He has a personal connection that will allow him to move with even more ease in the walls of FCI Milan. I'll see how bad the scenario is going to be once I get the breakdown from TJ of how the guy is and how he's tied to Gaines. Think of it in terms of being punished as a kid. If you were told to sit in a corner and stare at a wall, it was a real punishment. If you lived on a ranch, you might have to mend fences and spend the day working tirelessly. If your punishment were to go to your room and think about what you did with your favorite video game system, computer, and TV, it's not quite as bad.

With this sour taste in my mouth, I don't want to call Maria; I don't want to talk to anyone. I'm going to crank up the radio, drive fast, and get to Amarillo. As I was speeding, in my own head, and enjoying some loud Frank Sinatra, I saw a text come through. I didn't pay any mind to it since my signal has been so bad.

"Neil, want me to read it to you? Seeing as you're driving fast as shit?"

"Sure, Father, lay it on me. Who's it from?"

"It's from Maria, and it says, 'Don't be alarmed, but I'm pretty sure someone is following me! Also, neither one of us has any signal whatsoever.'"

Isn't this just great? As if I wasn't speeding enough already, now I need to deal with this shit.

2

IT'S NOT LIKE MARIA TO BE SWAYED EASILY; SHE IS OFTEN SKEPTICAL.

For the next three hours I kept trying to make a call, send a text, or get any semblance of service, but no luck. For almost three hours, I'm driving fast as shit, thinking about what Maria might have spooked. Father Roberts just sat there, quietly waiting for me to open up and respond. He's known me long enough to wait, and he doesn't push. It's also in his nature to wait, be patient, and simply pray on it.

"Father, I know she'll be okay. I know she was just giving me a heads up in case something happens so we can better look into it, but it's got me worked up."

"Neil, it's not surprising you're worked up a bit. Following her recent run-in with Gaines and getting kidnapped. She's also on edge and hypervigilant because of it. All of that mixed together makes for a volatile cocktail."

"The worst part is that I'm partially thinking she is overreacting. Since the kidnapping, she claims she's fine, but she has been on edge more than normal. She also took losing Erin and her trail harder than most of us. Which I can relate to."

"At least you're trying to be measured about it. Except for the part where you tried to drive over a hundred and fifty miles an hour. Making my testicles move to my throat."

He has a point there. Once we get to a place where my signal works, I can settle in and reach back out to Maria. I probably should have called her first. Then again, I didn't think I would be without a strong enough signal for a call. My cell phone is only able to grab enough signal to let me know I have messages; it's not even sending out. Luckily, I'm not neurotic in any way, or I would be going slightly insane right now. Oh wait: I am neurotic as shit.

The next three hours were a mix of anxiety-driven conversations with Father Roberts. Me driving close to nearly double the speed limit, and eventually just giving up on my cell phone. I had checked it so many times you would have thought I was a teenage girl waiting for a guy to ask her out for the prom; it wasn't pretty. Eventually we saw a sign saying that Amarillo was only thirty miles away. I decided to grab my phone, with the signal strength ready to call Maria.

"Hey Maria, sorry, but my signal has been nonexistent. Is everything okay?"

"I figured that's why you didn't respond. I'm okay, just shaken up. I swear I saw someone tailing me a few different times today, and not just anyone, but Erin."

"Maria, are you sure? Her trail went cold somewhere in the Southwest. What makes you think she's back in Detroit?"

"You mean, other than me seeing her with my own two eyes? I know I've been getting worked up lately, but I'm telling you I saw her today. Two different times. The first time was when I got my coffee; she was there waiting for me. Then again, when I went to the gym, I saw her."

"I'm assuming you told Mike already. Since your flight leaves early tomorrow morning, are you going to have someone sit on your place to be safe?"

"Neil, I appreciate you taking me somewhat seriously, but I can still tell that you don't believe me. Then again, I don't believe myself all the way." I could hear Maria's uneasiness.

"If you need me to have Ken send some guys, or if you want to stay at my place, Christian is staying in the guest room. At least for tonight, it might make you feel a bit better."

"Good idea. I'll run back to my place and finish packing, then head over to your place. I can text Christian." Maria was calming.

"I'll give him a heads up as well. Call me if you need anything; we'll be in Amarillo shortly, grabbing dinner, and my signal should be fine there."

"Okay, Neil, I'll talk to you later."

Off the phone and pulling into the restaurant, I felt like we were about to eat at a carnival. I turned to Father Roberts and told him I'm not sure it was a great idea. I decided to look up a few other places to eat in the area that might better suit us. In the meantime, we got out and stretched our legs. We still went inside, to feel out the place, especially since it looked like an old Wild West carnival shit show more than a restaurant.

Please don't take my crass attitude to say it was a dump. It was more like a pretty girl that doesn't know how to wear makeup. It may be worthwhile, but there is just something off-putting about the presentation. Walking through, there were sideshow antics, crazy things to take photos with, and gift shops galore. The restaurant looked like a massive cafeteria, with a stage for the steak competition. That was enough for me; once I saw the stage, I was out. It was also around then that I saw a list of restaurants on Sixth Street and decided to eat at a place called Golden Light. It looks like it's one of if not the oldest place in Amarillo.

After fifteen minutes at the carnival, we made our way back to the car, grabbed some gas, and made our way over to the Golden Light. As soon as we walked into the small bar, we both looked at each other and knew we picked the right place.

"This is more of our style," Father Roberts said with a smile.

"I'm with you, want to sit at the bar area, next to the grill. It reminds me of some dive bars back home. What do you say, Father?"

"I'm down. After driving for nearly nineteen hours, I'm happy for anything, though."

"Fair point."

As we walked up to the quiet and noticeably empty bar, I glanced at my watch. It was only four in the afternoon. It felt so much later to me, and I'm assuming to Father Roberts as well.. We left yesterday at 9:00 p.m., driving through the night. I took the first shift, making it to about three in the morning, then Father Roberts drove until eight. I've been driving ever since. I know it's a long time, but my car hugs you, rides smoothly, and makes it effortless.

"Hey guys, what can we get you two to drink for starters? A beer? Water, perhaps?"

The bartender/waitress/manager/bouncer, since she was the only ones in the building that we could see, was just what one might expect in this establishment. She looked to be in her early thirties, arm tattoos, and her hair had some purple in it. She looked like she walked out of a 1930s pinup, with a modern flair to it.

"I'm just in need of some water right now, I've had a ton of coffee and been driving for hours. How about you, Father?"

"Water is perfect for me."

"You guys really are out for a fun evening; two glasses of water it is." She was a sassy one.

"Hey now! We have been driving for nearly twenty hours. I appreciate the attitude, but a beer would put me to sleep, and we still have a few more hours to go."

"Calm down there. I just like giving anyone shit that gets water in a bar. It's an old habit, and it's hard to break. Here's a menu."

"Any recommendations?" Father Roberts wanted a steak, but he was open to anything at this point.

"Burgers are a fan favorite around here, but I'm a big fan of the Frito pie."

"Count me in for the Frito pie. How about you, Neil?"

"I'll go burger and fries. Want to split them?"

"Sounds good to me. I have no shame, not after sharing nineteen hours of farts with you in your car."

"I finally begin to think of you wholeheartedly as a priest, but comments like that remind me we've been friends since birth."

"Maybe it's a good thing the two of you are drinking water. I'm not sure I'd want to see you guys drunk." She has a point; we can get a bit childish.

Dinner hit the spot: greasy burger, excellent bar atmosphere, and a bartender with a rocking attitude consistently putting me in my place.

If the last place was a girl with too much makeup, this place was the hot girl rocking a hoodie and a baseball cap. It was exactly what we needed and got us back on the road.

Thanks to a quick dinner, no drinking, and a led foot, we made our way into the mountains just outside of Santa Fe by seven, just in time to see the sunset. The drive from Kansas, through Amarillo, then along into New Mexico, was something out of a painting. It is hard not to think that some form of divine intervention didn't play a role in the visuals one gets to enjoy along the way. I made sure and checked in via text with the usual crew one last time before we headed out just in case my signal was lacking, as it had been before.

Maria informed me she was still shaken from the encounter with Erin. The way she is certain makes me believe she did see Erin. It's not like Maria to be swayed easily; she is often skeptical. After speaking to Ken, I made sure to have another one of our guys keep an eye on the house and Maria until she gets on the flight. Call me overprotective, but something just doesn't seem right.

The drive up US 84 was particularly fun, not and just because I was playing hopscotch with slow drivers. As we climbed into the mountains, the skyline was changing, and it was majestic. I had never seen anything like it before. The air even smelled different, and there was a crispness to it. I know we were getting close; the drive had been a long one, going on twenty-five hours by the time we will be pulling in, but I just needed to pull over.

"Neil, why are we pulling over? Is everything okay?"

"Yeah, it is, Father, I just really wanted to enjoy the sunset. I can't remember the last moment I took the time to enjoy one. This view just seems like it's worth taking the time to enjoy it."

"I can appreciate the wonders of the Lord as much as the next guy. It's about time you started to slow down. It only took twenty-plus hours of driving across country to do it. Hopefully, it lasts."

"I have a feeling it will be a mixed bag of relaxing and getting rewound up. I'm hoping that I can find a rhythm with Maria and the projects you have us doing at the soup kitchen. When I work with my hands, it tends to calm me down."

"That's true. You've been that way as long as I can remember."

It was odd because we just stopped talking. We simply watched the sun go down, and the sky turns from blue to a burning red. It was like watching Bob Ross paint smiling clouds turn to a fiery red sky on TV, live in front of us. After the sun disappeared behind the mountains, we still sat there in the dark, just quietly enjoying the moment.

"Neil, it's getting cold without that sun out here. Why don't we get going? We're almost to Santa Fe."

"Sounds like a good idea."

The drive into Santa Fe was a quiet one. No music, just the windows down, the wind ripping by, and the sounds of the mountains filling the car. Father Roberts and I were simply enjoying the ride, quietly driving into Santa Fe, cruising through the night. Lit by the moon, the mountains were merely shadows playing hide-and-seek with the road as we made our way into downtown Santa Fe.

The place I rented for us was a bit over the top. Though we were working in a lower-class soup kitchen that needed help, I was renting a two-bedroom condo in downtown Santa Fe. I had plenty in the bank to waste on a much-needed vacation. Thanks to the book deal I signed and the caseload the company has been carrying since the Cappelano closing, I could splurge. Little do Father Roberts and Maria know, but I'm already planning on staying here longer than the ten days initially expected.

I spoke to the person renting out the condo, ensuring it would be available for the entire month if I needed it. It's a two-bedroom condo, walking distance from the plaza, or square. That's the central area downtown, according to the sites I researched. The soup kitchen we are working at is also walking distance from there; that way we don't always have to drive.

"Neil, twenty-five hours with you has been fun, and I know we are going to do it on the way back, but it's time to get some rest. How do we get into this place?"

"There's a lockbox on the house; they texted me the code this morning. We can get in, unpack, and crash."

As we made our way into the house, I realized my phone had been dead, not sure how long. I plugged it in, next to the bed, and made my way back out to the car to grab my favorite hat. That's when I noticed that the charging plug had come loose. I guess twenty-plus hours in the car had me off my game of observation.

"Neil, I'm exhausted and need to do some prayers before bed. Have yourself a good night. Thank you for getting us here safely."

"Night, Father Roberts."

I made my way into the bedroom, turned my phone on, and noticed I had several missed messages and calls from Ken and Maria. A few from Sheila with some pictures of her and Carol Lynn wishing me a safe trip. I got back to the messages from Ken and Maria, and that's when it got a bit crazy.

Maria said she was going to bed, and told me to call her in the morning before she got on the plane. Her flight was early out of Detroit, into Dallas, then Albuquerque, where I'll have to pick her up. Which, according to the GPS, is about a forty-five-minute drive from Santa Fe. That was ordinary, standard stuff, but it was Ken's message that threw me off.

"Call me ASAP. We're pretty sure Maria isn't seeing things!"

3

I COULDN'T TAKE THE SHIT WATER PRESSURE ANYMORE.

Ken wasn't up; I called him three different times. It was only nine locally and almost eleven back home, but Ken is usually up. He also often answers his phone late when I call. Sifting through his messages, it looks like the person sitting for the house noticed someone matching Erin's description circle the house a few different times, scouting it out. You may ask yourself how Erin, a professional from what we understand, didn't notice someone watching my place. That's quite easy. There is a house for sale across the street. We occasionally reach out to the owner, pay him a fee, and use it.

I was about to give up hope, take a long shower, and pour myself a drink. I may have reached out to the owner of this place and sent him a list of items to stock the place with before we got here along with some cash to do so. One being some high-end tequila as well as a shit ton of coffee. I digress: I was making my way to the shower when my phone went off. Ken was calling me back.

"Neil, sorry I couldn't answer a moment ago. I was on with Mike. We were coordinating for the rest of the night, as well as tomorrow. It seems Erin has resurfaced for some reason, and she's got her sights set on Maria. We're not sure why."

"Well, I'm dead exhausted, traveled by car across the country, and need some rest. I guess that shit is shot, similar to my golf game." I know, not the time for jokes.

"Hilarious, Neil. You know we have her covered, we won't let anything happen to her. She has your system armed. Christian is aware of the situation, Terrance is across the street, keeping an eye and TJ is running surveillance through your camera system."

"I know she's in great hands, but that doesn't always make the anxiety go away. I also know she is an excellent agent. However, that doesn't take the fear out of my mind. Hell, if she had the same right hand as Mike Tyson in his prime, I'd still be worried about her."

"I know; that's why I called Mike, looped in the FBI to get others involved and get the trail going for Erin. I'm not sure why she resurfaced, but I want to make sure Maria gets on that flight safely first thing in the morning. Then we'll worry about Erin out here."

"Thanks, Ken. I'll do my best to get some sleep."

"You mean drink until you pass out."

"Pretty much. Talk to you in the morning unless something bad happens."

"I promise I won't call before nine your time unless something bad happens. Sound good?"

"Perfect. Thanks, Ken."

After I got off the phone with Ken, I backtracked to the kitchen, in nothing but a towel and my Tigers hat. I know the cap is unnecessary, but it was on. I have really let my hair go over the past couple of months. It's down to my shoulders, a bit of a mess. I was going to get it cut, but Maria said she likes my Samson's hair. In the kitchen, I found some exciting clay cups—more like chalices than cups. Dropped a few ice cubes into one, then filled it with tequila. I'm not sure what the brand is, but I can tell you it is smooth.

Walking back to the shower, I noticed that the routine of having my girls roaming the house was missing. It wasn't merely the lack of familiarity with my surroundings that threw me off, but of the things that make it home. Maria, Sheila, my daughter, and my dogs truly make that house my home.

Finally, in the shower, carrying a buzz, I let the hot water run over me, but something was lacking. The water pressure seemed off. It almost felt like someone had turned the water pressure down by half. I had read in a few articles and blogs about things to be aware of. There was water conservation that has water pressure lower than average, no plastic bag usage, as well as some other liberal hippie stuff. I'm not right or left, but it was new to me, so I'll use the generic left-right moniker to distinguish for now.

Okay, it's time to get down to mental business. What the fuck is Erin doing back in town? Why is she working her way back into the scene? Erin has to know we are going to keep an eye on our own people and that she is going to be spotted if she tracks someone such as Maria. My guess is that she isn't trying to harm Maria, though that is an option. Often if someone is working to set up a plan to hurt someone, you stake out one location you feel is advantageous.

This means that it's more than likely that Erin is trying to find a way to contact Maria. But why? That is the six-thousand-dollar question, not a million dollars. Its important, but not that important. Erin wouldn't be tracking her down, looking for an in to talk to her, if she were trying to hurt her. She would pick one spot, sit on it, and make her move.

After twenty minutes of debating with myself what Erin's intentions were, I couldn't take the shit water pressure anymore. Somehow a place with a beautiful sunset and mountain view has ruined my favorite past time of showering. Off to bed—I need some sleep if I'm going to function tomorrow when I get up. I'll try to call Maria, then fall back asleep only to drive to Albuquerque to pick her up at about noon. Side note: am I the only one that immediately goes to Bugs Bunny when I hear Albuquerque? There's no way. My guess is that at least 40 percent of you thought that. Now that I brought it up, more than 80 percent will think of it when I mention Albuquerque.

Most of the night, I spent struggling to sleep. Tossing and turning thinking of Maria, Erin, and how the puzzle fits together. This trip was supposed to be about relaxing and letting go of all those distractions. I guess life, as usual, had different ideas. I rolled out of bed to find the smell of coffee in the air, and Father Roberts in the kitchen ready to go for the day.

"Morning, Neil. Are you going to want company today? Or can you drop me off at the soup kitchen?"

"I'll be good; It's not a far drive. I'll drop you off. Do you want to grab breakfast somewhere? Or do you want to make something here?"

"I'll make some breakfast and get moving. I'll get eggs and bacon going on the grill. The kitchen in this place is awesome."

"That's one of the reasons I rented it. It had a grill in it; thought it would remind us of the old days when you and I had that summer job working at the beach. Cooking burgers and fries."

"Oh yeah. I almost forgot about that job. They should never have let fourteen-year-olds operate fryers and grills." Father Roberts was right.

"We had so many burns and cuts from that summer job. Hey, memories to last a lifetime and wounds heal."

"Neil, those are called scars."

"Fair enough. I'll get ready."

Under normal circumstances I would shower again, but this water pressure has me turned off from showering. I can't believe that thought has crossed my mind, but it's true. I can hear Maria already giving me shit about my lack of showers over the next couple of weeks, but some things just can't be helped. It took only a few minutes to throw on my favorite jeans, worn-in, a T-shirt, and that trusty Tigers hat, with my hair tucked back. With Father Roberts making breakfast and the rental owner setting us up with groceries ahead of time, we turned our breakfast to burritos on the go.

As we hopped in the car, I saw a text from Maria saying she had made it to Dallas already and was about to get to her gate and to give her a shout. Good old DTW and DFW, what shit show airports. Then again is any airport that's not some small three-gate airport, not a shit show? That being said, I should probably stop worrying about how much we all hate flying out of Detroit or Dallas and just call my girlfriend.

"Hey Maria, glad you got through security; it's usually easy in the morning. How'd you sleep?"

"Since I was at your place with some people keeping an eye on me, I feel better. Thank you for that."

"No problem; that's what we're here for. Anything for you."

"I'm just glad I didn't have to deal with her again, or what I thought I saw. I'm going to grab some breakfast here, settle in, and I'll see you in a little bit. This flight is a short one. Should be there quick."

"See you soon, Maria. Be safe."

I dropped off Father Roberts and made my way out to the airport. By this time Ken had plenty of time to call me; it was well after nine in the morning. I can only assume something changed, or he was waiting for me to reach out in case I was sleeping after a day of traveling.

"Hey Ken, what gives? Anything change? Or was the night status quo?"

"It was weird. We had a good trace on her heading out of town, then we lost her. She was heading south of Detroit, either out of town or toward the airport. TJ tried tracking her through security and other means, but we lost her. Sorry, Neil."

Something doesn't seem right with Erin, on so many fronts. At first we thought she was some helpless girl, activist, social lite. Now she's got a trail of a con artist killer. What gives?"

"I'm with you; it just doesn't add up. I'd say international spy, but I reached out to contacts, and no one is talking or confirming anything, not even off book." Ken has contacts all over, so this would usually hit for us.

"I guess we'll just have to see where the trail takes us. I'll let you know if Maria has any insights by the time she lands. See if she sees Erin somewhere on flights. It seems Erin is trying to make contact with her for some reason."

"Sounds good. Be safe, and enjoy yourself. You're wound so tight you need this time to relax. You know, if you need a few more days or a few more weeks, we got you."

"I know, Ken. We'll see."

My plan is to stay out here longer than expected. I just don't see how a week to ten days are going to be enough for me to decompress. I wouldn't be surprised if this ends up being a monthlong trip for me. As I made my way from Santa Fe to Albuquerque, I couldn't help but realize how straight a drive it is. I'm used to Detroit, where I-94 East runs north. Yup, that's correct.

The drive was straight out of the mountains downhill, which made it easy to get the car above 140. I had to keep catching myself and slow back down, but I figured out quickly that the local police didn't care. Most of the cars were doing more than 100 themselves, so I wasn't going to stand out very much. Making my way through the decline, I noticed that the small towns, casinos, and tracks along the way were all that seemed to be between Santa Fe and where I was headed.

As I pulled into the big city out here in New Mexico and made my way to the airport, I couldn't help but notice that there were a few signs for a balloon museum and a balloon park. It seemed a bit odd at first, but once I made it to the airport waiting lot, I took a moment to look it up. That's when I found out the largest collection of hot air balloons every year during the balloon fiesta. If you've ever seen a photo with hundreds of hot air balloons, chances are you've seen a picture of Albuquerque.

Just got a message from Maria that is a little strange. I guess I'm going to find out when she walks out here.

"Don't be mad. I made a new friend on the plane; we're going to have company. Also, this vacation became a work trip."

As I saw her walking out of the airport, I noticed she was talking and smiling with a familiar face. There's no way—what are the odds they were on the same flight from Dallas to here? I mean, that would take some planning and organizing to pull off on her part. Right then I texted Ken:

"I FOUND ERIN! SHE'S WITH MARIA! APPARENTLY THEY'RE BESTIES!"

4

I COULD SIMPLY PULL OFF AND FLIP THEM THE BIRD, WHICH WOULD BE EPIC.

Some days I wonder why I get out of bed. I just don't see the point. I spent a whole day, more than twenty-four hours, in a car, driving out to New Mexico for a way to unwind and disconnect. Knowing I couldn't disconnect if I simply flew out, I spent that day driving, relaxing, unplugging, and enjoying the vastness of this remarkable land. I know it seems like I'm describing a modern version of the Oregon Trail from your youth, but don't worry, Tommy won't die of a broken leg on this trip. I might kill Erin, but that's a different ailment altogether.

As I watched, Erin and my girlfriend walked toward my car, laughing and chatting like old high-school friends playing catch-up. I started flipping through the different reactions I could have as they approached. I could play it cool, not react at all, and see what they say. I could simply pull off and flip them the bird, which would be epic. Without the proper witnesses, it's not worth it. I could lay into Maria, asking her what the hell is going on. I could talk under my breath and grinding my teeth the whole time and driving like a maniac but acting like nothing is wrong.

So many options to choose from; I guess we'll just play it by ear and see what they have to say when they roll up. I had a feeling that Erin was trying to get a handle on Maria, make a connection, but not like this. I thought it was for something else, to ask her for leniency, not for what this seems. From my vantage point, it looks like Maria has already warmed up to her. She has already committed us to help her, which means she believes whatever she is selling. I stepped out, opened the trunk and door. I tossed everything in the car and was a gentleman and opened the door for them as I greeted Maria with a smile.

"Hey honey, I guess we solved that mystery." I leaned in and kissed Maria.

"I wasn't losing my mind after all. It's great to see you, honey. I see you made the trip down in one piece." I guess Maria is playing the denial game too.

We piled in the car and acted like nothing was going on. Just some small talk about the drive down from Detroit to Santa Fe. How Father Roberts was doing, what the plan was for the day and the rest of the week with the soup kitchen; you know everything but the colossal elephant in my car named Erin. At this point I think it's a game of chicken to see who is going to break the ice. I'm not going to. I decided since I couldn't flip them off and drive away, I would play it cool and ignore the situation.

We were almost back to Santa Fe, making our back into town. No longer on the freeway when you could feel the tension increase. Maria stopped talking with me and directed her conversation to Erin, talking about a spa day and some shit. I was starting to lose it mentally. I just wasn't going to show anyone, but I was getting close to teetering. That's when Erin finally broke; she couldn't do it anymore.

"Okay, you two are crazy. I already knew that from scouting the two of you, but this takes the cake. With my history and you two, the fact that Neil is just acting like everything is perfect. I mean, what is wrong with you? Aren't you curious?" Erin was a bit hyper.

"Erin, I trust Maria. Simple as that." No, it's not; this shit is getting to be fun.

"I can't speak for Neil; I just wasn't going be the first to break. Plus I was caught off guard when he didn't lose his shit on the two of us. Maybe Santa Fe and this drive actually mellowed him out?"

"I heard there is excellent weed out here. Neil, are you high?" Erin has jokes.

"You two are something else. I figured we had a long drive back, no reason to pick a fight. Definitely no reason to get worked up in the car. If Maria trusted you enough to have that reaction to you as you walked to my car. The least I can do is trust her. Will I help you two? That's another question altogether."

"Fair point. You came out here to relax, and we dropped this shit in your lap." Maria is wising up.

We pulled into the condo and made our way upstairs, where I poured myself an afternoon drink. Quite a large one, then covered it with some black coffee. I've never been a fan of stale black coffee and high-end tequila, but I might start drinking it. It's not half bad. I might call it the Cluster-Fuck. Maria and Erin came out of our room and made some wiseass comment in unison.

"If we share this room, Father Roberts is in that room. Where are you sleeping?"

"Hilarious, ladies. As far as I'm concerned, Erin made it as far as she's getting. The front door for a cup of coffee. If she thinks hospitality is going beyond that, she can chip in with a couple of grand toward the cost or rent the place down the street. I'm helpful, but I'm not a schmuck."

"That's the Neil I've come to know and love," Maria chimed in.

"Neil, Maria, I don't want to intrude any more than I already have, but I need help. As I informed Maria on the plane, my situation is a bit complicated. I have played too many sides over the past couple of years, and it's coming back to haunt me. I know I don't deserve help, but I'm still asking for it." Intruders can be shot. Is that an option?

"Erin, just tell Neil what you told me. Start from the beginning." Maria gave me that thousand-mile stare, telling me to be helpful.

"Erin, let me start with this question, to you too, Maria. Did you two start being friendly on the flight from Detroit? Or Dallas?"

"Why does it matter, Neil?" Maria wasn't happy.

"I'll take that as a yes to Detroit. And judging by the looks you shot each other, you have confirmed it. Erin, go on with your story."

Erin went on for the next hour, going into detail about her past. What has gone on over the previous year and how she ended up in her current situation. I guess I can start by giving you the details of where this all started. Erin is actually from a small town in Georgia, where she excelled in a few sports, especially track and field. Being young, intelligent, and aggressive, she went to college at Georgetown University.

It wasn't long into her sophomore year when she was getting recruited by a few different agencies. The one that got her attention the most was the CIA. She said that coming from a small town, being able to see the world became an easy sell. She focused on her studies at Georgetown, majoring in economics and several European languages. I realized halfway through her story that she isn't nearly as young as we initially thought. She's actually in her early thirties, not twenties. She has the look to pull off a range of ages, that's for sure.

Back to the mess she's in. While working for the CIA and specializing in East European languages, she apparently was working on getting intel related to a family in Poland. I may have messed that lead-up when I was out there looking into Andrew's mother and upsetting his mother's applecart. According to Erin, Marie Choike was working with a Russian mob family on a designer form of heroin. Some research tech found a way to minimize the addictive nature of the drug while maximizing the effectiveness in small doses. They nicknamed it Requiem, which is Latin for rest. I think it's a bit far fetched. Still, I can't forget Russia is a country where their literary masterpieces are dark and twenty thousand pages.

Okay, maybe not that many pages, but you get my point. It's not surprising that a country known for its cold, hard winters named a drug rest, in Latin, to encourage people to take it. Not to mention, most kids taking the drug are going to think the name is cool, more than anything. Imagine a twenty-year-old asking for drugs. They aren't asking for weed or coke; they're asking for a hit of Requiem.

Now comes the fun part. What the hell do Erin, Marie Choike, and a designer drug have to do with Neil Baggio and his vacation? Absolutely nothing that's what. They have nothing to do with me, except for the part where my girlfriend already offered my services to said CIA agent. Well, former agent—that part is coming up in the story. Sorry I got sidetracked because I'm still a bit pissed about all of this, and my Cluster- Fuck needs a refill.

Erin, while trying to get intel on all this, was sidetracked because of my shit. It became a blessing in disguise. I messed up everyone's plans so badly it made them change course. Opening up a piece of intel previously unknown. The scientist who found this bit of information out. The process for Requiem and the place they were making the drug as none other than Gaines Chemical. That's right. This is where my life gets flipped the fuck upside down.

Erin was really trying to stir the pot with Gaines Chemical because of the drug they were manufacturing. We pulled him off the street, but not for the reason that the CIA or Erin may have wanted. Erin supposedly went rogue in what she was doing with Gaines Chemical. For example, the CIA is not supposed to work on US soil; they are an international agency. It doesn't mean they can't; it just means they are supposed to play nice and work with people such as the FBI when they do ops in the United States. Since she went off on her own, operated without proper authority, the CIA has cut ties with her.

"Let me get this straight. I have been single-handedly screwing up and helping your case all at the same time without even knowing it for almost two years and in two different countries?"

"Pretty much, Neil. That's why I came to you. You're already tied to this case more than you know, and no one has more skin in this shit show than I do. Other than you and Maria." Erin has a point.

"So Neil, does this mean we're going to help her?" Maria interjected.

"I still don't know what she needs help with."

"Oh, good point. She's only given you the backstory so far."

"Exactly, Maria. I've gotten a lot of information, but none of it explains why I need to give up my first vacation in nearly a decade for this."

"He has a point, Maria. This is my mess. I created it going off on my own. My bosses told me, I can't go out on a limb, it would end poorly. Just like they told me it would, it's a shit show."

"I understand anything related to Gaines, Choike, and an international drug trade can't be clean, but how does this come back to you? What did you steal, or who did you kill? We did enough research and tracked enough movements to know that you and Bond have some things in common."

"I have taken my fair share of lives over the years in the line of duty, as have you. That isn't why we're here. Neil, you've already figured out that I need your help because I did something, and someone is coming after me."

"People are always coming after people like you and me, Erin. The question is, Why does it involve me? Why am I involved at all?"

"Once Gaines figured out everything and what I had done to gain Bryan's trust. How I used him to gain access to his company, he approached me with a way to make amends and start a new relationship with him and Gaines Chemical."

"You mean the part where you drove a Pontiac Fiero into a prisoner transport killing a few people including Bryan, his former head of security. Let's not forget a few of our colleagues. Side note, Maria: how the hell doesn't that part alone not piss you off?"

"Neil, I don't know why, but I've thought of the things you and I have both done that might have caused others pain, in the name of justice. I guess I found a way to forgive her, in the name of taking down Gaines and his empire even more."

"I can't think of us intentionally harming other law enforcement agents to get in good with a criminal. It's just a hard one for me to wrap my head around. Even when I drove that truck into a building in Poland, there was no intent to kill or harm. It was a distraction to save a life."

"Neil, I'm not going to argue with you over this point. Hear her out, then make your decision."

"After I got on Gaines's good side, I was able to convince him that the scientist who created Requiem has too much control. Gaines needed to digitize the process, the formula, so he didn't need the scientist anymore. This way, it would make me more accessible for me to steal it, hindering his ability to make the drug and impact our streets."

"I'm assuming then at this point you have it on you? Or are you going to give me some bullshit line that it's somewhere safe?"

"Actually, I don't have it. It is somewhere safe, but I think you'll be happy when you find out where I put it." Erin had a smile on.

"Where?"

"She gave it to me, Neil. That's how she gained my trust. I loaded it up on my laptop. I'll send it to TJ to verify if I get your okay."

"At this point I feel like I'm already being pulled in regardless. My question is, if Gaines is in prison, and you have the formula on a thumb drive, he can't make the drug. What's the issue? Are you hiring us to be your bodyguards? It's not my specialty."

"I need you to help me close the Gaines case, get me back in good with the CIA so they'll protect me."

"How the hell do we do that from here?"

"Funny story. Remember your old friend Marie Choike?"

"Yeah. What about her?"

"She owns an art studio here in Santa Fe. It's a great way to launder drug money, Gaines owns one too. I'm surprised you didn't know that when you decided to come out here." FUCK ME!

"I came out here because I thought it would be relaxing, and Father Roberts knew a soup kitchen and church that needed help."

"You mean the Sisters of St. Francis Soup Kitchen?"

"Yeah. How do you know about them?"

"I may have called them, called him, and started this whole process a few weeks ago."

"Get the FUCK out of here! I'm done with you."

"Neil, wait."

"Nope, get out, it's my vacation. You can help her. I'm done."

5

NEIL, FOR SOMEONE AS GOOD AT FIGURING SHIT OUT AS YOU ARE, SOMETIMES YOU FORGET HOW MUCH PEOPLE LOOK UP TO YOU.

I was so close to relaxing, so close to feeling like I might be able to decompress. I've never been much of a runner, I'm a big fan of hitting a heavy bag to work up a sweat, but for this trip, I figured working with my hands will be all I need. That mixed with some runs and hiking, and I would be good to go. Maria and Erin left, which isn't surprising, I told them to get the fuck out, I just couldn't handle it. I pulled out my phone, Googled hiking paths in Santa Fe, and found a group on Facebook. I know it's a bit of a cliché, but I'm new to the area, and any intel would be great.

From what most of the posts stated, I think I'm just going to head toward St. John's College and hit the Dale Ball trail out there. It looks like it goes for miles, and it's a great trail for someone like me who is new to the area. It's also pretty close to where I am, only a five-minute drive. With some beat-up but comfortable Puma running shoes, my Tigers hat, and running shorts, I made my way from the car to the trail. I took out my oversized noise-canceling headphones and started jamming out. I needed to disappear for a little bit.

As I was beginning to run, I saw that Ken and others had started blowing my phone up. I turned off the cell signal, enjoyed the music, and just took off running through the dirt trail. I needed a moment, some time to grasp what was going on. Maria dropping this shit in my lap, Erin thinking if I would just forgive her killing FBI agents and our informant in the case of bringing down Gaines to help save her skin.

I wished they would have had a little bit more tact when asking me to help in this case. Don't get me wrong; keeping a designer drug off the street is huge. Especially one to the level of Requiem as described by Erin, but it's just not that simple. If Maria already has the intel, the formula that Gaines needs, we merely need to sit on it and lock it up. The thing I'm struggling with is that Maria knows this. Hell, Maria had friends in there, she had friends die from that car crash. What is she thinking? Erin came out and laid her cards down, showing she is manipulating us, manipulating the whole circumstance, and Maria is still bought in.

Running through the hills and trails out by St. John's is gorgeous, I know I keep saying it, but it's true. For someone who hasn't grown up around mountains, this view and environment are breathtaking. The air, the overall surroundings take your soul on a journey that clears your mind. I may have been played a bit to get out here, but this is just what I needed. The case is not what I needed, but being here in these mountains, working with my hands to help someone, those will help me.

It took me a good forty-plus minutes to make it far enough into the trail to find myself atop a peak and look over everything. I turned my phone back on, let the messages come rolling in, but there was only one that I needed to see. It was from Maria, and it simply said,

"I'm sorry. I could have done that better."

That's the understatement of the year. I know I could have handled it better, but I tried to. It just kept getting worse, eventually leading to me at the top of a peak in the mountains somewhere. Ken reached out to me, asking me what's going on since I left him in the dark since I told him Erin was here with Maria. Lately, the way I'm handling stress is poor. I have been leaving people in the dark. I can't stand it when someone doesn't return my call or text; for me to do the same is jacked up.

"Hey Ken, sorry for not returning your call and messages. It's been a shit show out here."

"Is everything okay with you and Maria? What's this shit about them being Besties?"

"Apparently Erin got to her on the first flight out of Detroit, convinced her not to shoot her, then on the second flight they became best friends."

"I'm assuming that's the Neil notes version." Kind of like the *Cliff's Notes* version, only shorter.

"Yup. It looks like she stole something vital from Gaines, regarding some new drug he was going to push, something that was going to make him billions. That's why he didn't care about being in prison. She wants our help getting back in with the CIA and not getting killed by Gaines and his crew of merry men."

"How are we going to be able to get her back in with the CIA? And no wonder I couldn't get anyone to confirm who she worked for. She had been burned. Almost like a bad action flick on cable or something, only real life." Ken has jokes.

"I may have handled the situation poorly, very poorly, with Erin and Maria. I overreacted, screamed a bit, and told them to fuck off in so many ways. However, one good thing came out of it."

"What good came of it?"

"Actually, a few different things. I came up with my vacation drink, and I realized something that I'm going to focus on for this trip."

"Well, you already stopped smoking for good this time, drinking has been cut way back with Cappelano behind bars, and you've been in the best shape in the time I've known you. So I'm lost with what you're going to work on. Also intrigued on your vacation drink."

"I'm going to stop ducking calls and messages. If I'm going to run or work out, I'm going to give the critical people in my life a heads up. As for the drink, I call it a Cluster-Fuck. It's top-shelf tequila and cold coffee."

"First of all, the drink is messed up, but it fits your idea of a vacation to a T. Second, I don't think you duck call that much. You just like to focus at certain times and work through things. You're good at what you do, and the key people around you understand that. We'll support you either way. That being said, how are you going to handle Erin and fix your shit response to Maria?" Ken is always supportive.

"Well, Maria already feels horrible for the way she approached me and dropped it on my plate. That means we can meet in the middle and compromise this shit somehow. As for Erin, I'm not sure what I'll do. I'll probably end up helping Maria and Erin. Just like I did with the last case that got me involved with Gaines and Christian."

"Fair enough, at least you're aware of your shortcomings. Call Maria and figure it out. You need to enjoy some of this trip. It can't just be the view that will wear out quickly if you're stressed." Ken has a point.

Off the phone with Ken, working up the courage to call Maria, I thought of what to say. I know she already apologized, but that didn't take away from the fact that I was wrong. If someone punches you, then you hit them with a bat, you're still wrong for going overboard with the bat. I understand they shouldn't have hit you in the first place. It doesn't make it okay to haul off and swing a bat.

"Hey Maria, you and Erin go grab a bite to eat?"

"Yeah, we're walking around downtown, the plaza, and seeing the galleries. Just sitting down for a coffee right now. Are you finally calmed down?"

"I'm doing a little better. I'm sitting on top of a peak somewhere enjoying the view, thinking about all this shit. It's got me wondering why she chose us, why she came into our world to figure this out."

"Well, Neil, for someone as good at figuring shit out as you are, sometimes you forget how much people look up to you. You have a reputation of sticking your neck out for the long shot and figuring it out. She came to us because she felt we were the only option." Maria is laying it on thick.

"Tell you what, let's meet up for dinner. It'll take me about an hour to get out of here, then back to take a quick shower, and we meet downtown. Just text me a place, and I'll meet you there. Say around five? We can talk a bit more civilly about all of this mess Erin has gotten herself into and needs our help getting out of."

"I'd appreciate that, Neil. Thank you for coming around on this. She needs our help, and we all want to see that asshole's empire crumble." Fair point.

"I'll see you soon, Maria. Why don't you start by reaching out to TJ and having him get to work on that thumb drive, see what he needs from you to get started? Do you have your laptop with you?"

"Yes, Neil, I do as usual. I'll reach out to him and text you a place for dinner. Talk to you in a bit."

Off the phone and running down the hill, I felt better. I had clarity on what was in front of me with Erin's issues. All I needed to do now is sprint back to the car, get back to the condo, clean up, and get to the restaurant and make nice with the two ladies I had massively pissed off earlier. Not surprising—going downhill and heading back down a path I had gone down once before was much quicker than uphill. I made it back to the condo in thirty minutes. I quickly ran into the condo and jumped into the shower, knowing it was going to feel like someone pouring a warm glass of Gatorade over my head.

Just as fast as I got in, I got out. Though I did take a few minutes to shave, I like to shave in the shower. I've been growing in some form of stubble. Keeping it trim under a quarter of an inch. I also shave the area around my lips and under my jawline, only along my face. I know I'm an odd bird, but we've established this before, remember my vacation drink of choice. As I walked out into the condo, dressed and ready to grab a C-Fu for short, hey, I can't be running around screaming "Cluster-Fuck!" I noticed Father Roberts was home.

"Hey Neil, where's Maria? And what's up with the extra bags? Even I know she didn't pack that much." Father Roberts is picking up some stuff from being around me.

"You are correct, sir. They are Erin's bags. The one and only—she made friends with Maria on the plane, and we are going to help her."

I went through everything that happened with them, how I overreacted. Father Roberts pointed out that I may have reacted appropriately and that it was good to see me coming around on the shit show that was coming my way.

"I guess my biggest concern is, what does this mean for the work we are supposed to do for the soup kitchen?" Fair point.

"We are going to meet up for dinner at a place called the Cowgirl, according to the text from Maria. I'm going to devote my time to working at the soup kitchen. I need the therapy, working with my hands, and helping someone without it being attached to a murder or a crime is needed for me, for my soul."

"I'm glad you understand the importance of this trip, Neil. I'm worried about you."

Father Roberts and I decided to walk down to the restaurant. According to the GPS, it was only a two-mile walk. Plus I planned on drinking a few C-Fu's. Since I made good time to the condo with Father Roberts, we arrived at the restaurant before Maria and Erin. We were able to get a table outside to enjoy the crisp night air coming down from the mountain, along with the band playing music outside.

"Hey guys, while you wait for the other two, would you like something to drink?"

"I'll take a beer, Stella, if you have it." Not sure when Father Roberts started that one.

"I'll take a cup of cold, stale coffee if you have one laying around, and a top-shelf tequila neat."

"I'm sure we have some coffee in a pot somewhere. I'll find some for you. Patrón or Cuervo for the tequila?"

"Your choice; I'm not a connoisseur yet."

"You got it. I'll say I'm intrigued."

"Me too." As she walked away, Father Roberts shot me a look.

"What the hell is the cold, stale coffee for?"

"I'm going to mix it with the tequila. It's my vacation drink. I call it a Cluster-Fuck. C-Fu for short."

"I've known you long enough not to ask. That seems nasty, but I'm sure it'll work out some way. You know there's already coffee tequila, Patrón Café?"

"Yes, Father, I do. You also know I'm not a fan of sweet drinks, and that shit is too sweet for me. I like the bitterness of the stale coffee. It mixes well with the smooth tequila. I might try it next with lime over ice; it'll be a progression. Tomorrow it might be in a thermos with multiple limes."

"Here come the ladies. I see them walking up the street now."

As Maria and Erin walked up, it was weird still, seeing her hug Father Roberts. The pleasantries, after all the shit that has gone on. Internally I continued to be a mess. At least Maria still looked terrific. Something I overlooked when I picked her up. I may have been focused on the psycho CIA agent killer that she was hanging out with.

"Hey Maria, how are you two doing? Ready to eat? I know I am. After the long run and hike, I'm ready for something filling."

"Yes, we walked all over and ate very little. Plus I've known you long enough; it's not like I need to impress you anymore; I'm about to chow down." Maria cracks me up.

"How about you Erin? You ready to get your eat on?"

Before she could answer, the server brought over my drink. As I began to mix it, the look on all three of my compadres at the table was priceless. You would have thought that I started lining up cocaine on a mirror I had just pulled out of my pocket in front of them. They were in disbelief with what was going down at the table.

"I'm ready to eat, but what did you just do to that tequila? You know they have Patrón Café?"

"Yes, Erin, as I told Father Roberts earlier. I'm not a fan of the sweetener added to it."

"Okay, I get it being too sweet, I can understand that, but that coffee smelled flat. Did you order it that way?" Maria was chiming in on her judging.

"Yes, it's my vacation drink. I'm going to try different versions of it. It will always be cold, stale coffee, and top-shelf tequila. How I drink it will change. You can stop giving me shit now, 'cause it's not going to change it."

"He didn't even tell you, two ladies, the best part of this atrocity to the palate. Ask him what he named it."

"Father Roberts is alluding to the name. It's called the C-Fu. Short for Cluster-Fuck." The three of them enjoyed a good laugh.

"Well, I guess I can't say anything. I need your help so you can count me out of the ribbing game." Erin caught on quickly.

"I need your help, but you like having sex with me, so I'll give you a hard time, but I'll have to watch it." Maria has a good point there.

"Father Roberts, what say you?"

"I've known you forever, so you know I'm giving you shit. Tirelessly and without reprieve."

"Fair point, duly noted to all."

As I sat there sipping on my drink, I couldn't help but notice the judgmental eyes. It was okay because I was drinking a Cluster-Fuck; it takes all that ails away. The tequila takes the edge off, and the caffeine from the coffee gives you the kick needed to power through the shit you have going on. As for dinner, everyone tried some form of BBQ or another, except me. I kept up the crazy train and ate breakfast for dinner. I've always wanted to try *huevos-rancheros*, over easy and runny. Slopping the eggs on the plate with the red and green sauces was a flavor to enjoy.

The girls split a brisket plate; yes, they shared a meal like best friends. Father Roberts went for a rack of ribs and probably would have had more if there were fewer witnesses. He may be a man of the cloth, but Erin is a pretty woman, and he's still human. Father Roberts was lightly flirting with her, watching how Father ate, never should have ordered ribs. It was funny watching him realize he had a big plate of ribs to eat in front of a lady he was suddenly smitten with. Anyone who knows a priest will tell you, especially the good-looking ones are chick magnets.

"Now that we're all good and full, I guess it's time to talk about the case. Review what we need to do for Erin. I'm going to be working at the soup kitchen first and foremost. I will help when I can after I finish what needs to be done over there."

"I'm just glad you're willing to hear me out. I know we dropped this shit on your plate like a poop parachute. It wasn't done right, and I apologize, but I didn't know who else to turn to."

"Erin, I get it. Maria made a good point earlier. She pointed out how I can forget why people come to me for the asinine cases. It can upset me at first, then I come around and get intrigued. Then I get an idea, get fixated, and the rest is Baggio history."

"I had a feeling you would come around, but that doesn't change how we could have done it better. The biggest thing I need help with is getting me back in the good graces of the CIA. I have no clue how to do it. As a burned spy, my resources are limited. The only things I have are my abilities and a few connections. As usual, intel and a case closed are the best ways I can do anything."

"We have resources up the ass, that's for sure. We can start looking into Gaines and Choike's art galleries, see if they're legit. Which we doubt since it's a great way to move illegal products. Even if they have legitimate artists, I'm sure they're selling dogs playing poker for three million along with a crateful of drugs."

Maria whispered into my ear, thanking me for jumping on board. Honestly, I'm a little drunk, a little intrigued, and Santa Fe has a bit of a trance on me. With a mix of coffee, tequila, and eggs in my stomach, I'm a happy camper. Although I just had a realization that I booked a small condo with Father Roberts across the hall from Maria and me. This is going to be like sneaking private time with your high-school girlfriend.

It might make for an exciting trip, or it might make for an uncomfortable friendship with Father Roberts for a few weeks following our vacation. The four of us started talking about ideas, coming up with different ways we could investigate the case. Since Father Roberts was involved a bit with the Choike case, he wanted to jump in and help. Maria and Erin wanted to run down as many leads as they could with Gaines and their operation out here. It looks like the old divide and conquer plan.

"I guess that settles everything. We have a starting point and what we need to do. Maria, did you get the info over to TJ?"

"Yes, I was able to upload it to him. He's reviewing everything and said we might have to call in an old friend to review it. He said you'd know who."

"Yeah. He's talking about Dr. Brown. He's a bit coarse, but he's great."

"Whatever needs to be done, let's do it."

"That reminds me, Father Roberts, I'm going to need your help with Ms. Choike if she's out here."

"Not sure what I can do, but I'm willing to help."

"Good. Make sure you're good to put out. This case will save lives."

"Wait. What?"

6

SHE PISSED OFF HER BOSSES, WENT ROGUE, KILLED FBI AGENTS, AND YOU SIT HERE AND SAY I'M THE PRICK!

I would never make Father Roberts do that. I might make him allude to it and tease her, but he has too much respect for himself and his devotion. The look on his face was worth the comment. I know he's going to give me hard-core shit for the C-Fu, I need to build up some licks. Don't let Father Roberts fool you, though. The man is and was a stone-cold lady-killer. From our teenage years to last year, he has always been able to grab the eye of the hottest girl in the room. I'm still not sure why he ended up down this path, but I'm sure his parish is glad he did. He is fantastic at fund-raising, and not just because he's a stud.

After dinner, we went for a walk around downtown, talking for a good couple of hours, trying to figure this whole thing out. Eventually we made our way back to the condo, where I realized we still had Erin's shit there. That conversation got awkward quickly because I am willing to help, but I'm not sheltering her too.

"Since I have committed to helping, that only means so much. Earlier, you two joked about sleeping here; that's not going to fly. This is still my vacation; we need to have some boundaries."

"Neil, you can't kick her to the curb like that. She has nowhere to go."

"Maria, ask yourself this. If she is so broke, how did she afford a first-class ticket to Albuquerque short notice from Detroit? That had to be fifteen hundred easily. She can afford a hotel stay somewhere. If not, there are hostels up the street. I read about them when I was at the gas station earlier."

"Maria, Neil has a good point. I can find a place to stay. It's late, though, so I should be going, so I can try to find something with a room available on short notice."

"Well, you're resourceful. I'm sure you'll do fine."

"Neil, don't be such a prick. Erin, crash here for the night; you can sleep on the couch. Then you can call around in the morning and find a place to stay."

"Neil, I have an idea if it might help. The church has a rectory, where I can stay. I told you that when you booked this place. If you want me to run interference during this case, it might help if I'm there anyway." Don't help this shit show, Father.

"I appreciate the offer, Father, but let's allow Erin to find her own place in the morning. She can use the love seat. My bag is already on the couch." I kid.

"Neil, do you always have to be a prick?"

"Not always, just trying to remind everyone of the situation. I'm willing to help, but I'm not on board with everything all of a sudden. Doing what's necessary and accepting the premise aren't the same thing."

"Guys, I already found a place to stay and have a cab coming to pick me up." Erin is used to life on the run.

"See, Maria? I told you she's resourceful." This might hurt.

"Neil, Jesus Christ, can't you just let it go?" Maria was about to lose it on me.

"Maria, I will drop it when you two realize this isn't open season. Be thankful for what I'm offering and learn when to stop asking. I came around pretty quickly; let's keep it at that. I didn't forget all the shit that she did. I'm just willing to do my part."

"Okay, I get it, but the attitude is wearing thin."

"Maria, I get it. So is the bullshit you two are doing. Acting like everything is perfect and you're old college roommates vacationing together for the summer. Pull your heads out of your assess and pay attention. Erin is a burned CIA agent who took shit from a crazy man who's damn near besties with a crazed killer who loves me. She pissed off her bosses, went rogue, killed FBI agents, and you sit here and say I'm the prick!" Too much?

"Neil, Maria, I think it's time you two go talk in your room. I can see Erin out, and you guys can talk with her tomorrow. Her cab is here." Finally Father Roberts stepped up.

As Father Roberts walked Erin out the door, Maria and I went into our room and started kissing. I guess we had some pent-up frustrations. It's not surprising, and we haven't had much quiet time together. Maria has been pent up and riled up with all the stress of this Erin Beddington case. Tie all that together with a little alcohol and the fact that she has Erin here and a little closure, and you have instant agent aphrodisiac.

After a good fifteen minutes of rolling around and doing our best to be quiet so our parents couldn't hear us downstairs, Maria and I finally started talking again.

"I'm still mad at you, but you know I needed that. Thank you."

"How do I keep getting the short end of this? Mad at me? You keep getting mad at me because I won't be a complicit puppy dog? When have I ever played that role?"

"Neil, you make an excellent point. The reason I love you so much is that you're a bit bullheaded. You're stubborn and can become so fixated on some things. It's insane. Those qualities are what make you remarkable at this job. It's those, mixed with your level of loyalty to your team. Not to mention those around you that make you one of a kind." Maria is making me blush.

"It's not about being stubborn; I can be swayed. I just like to see it through, stay focused. I've made plenty of mistakes from not sticking to my gut in the past. I've also learned you can never have too many amazing people around you. That means if one of them needs you, you run through a wall if you have to. It's how Momma Baggio raised me. Family matters, and you're all family."

"*La familia.* I'm very familiar with that concept. I know what it's like to be on the outside, taking considerable risks to try to get noticed. Erin messed up. She messed up bad. That's why I want to help her correct this wrong. I truly think she deserves a second chance."

"I hope you're right, Maria. I'll back your play, even if I do it reluctantly. One of us has to push back and question. If not, we can both get burned."

"I can agree to that. Call it a bit of a truce?"

"Yeah. Isn't that what the sex was about?"

"No. I just needed to take the edge off." Damn, I feel a bit used. I'll get over it.

"Maria used me for a piece of ass. You are one cold-blooded woman."

"Shut up. You know you liked it. Let's go back out there and try to save face with Farther Roberts. I still think it's weird that you call him that, but I get it. He's earned it, and after a while it grows on you."

"While you go out there, I'm going to give Ken and TJ a quick call, get some things going, and set up a budget for this fiasco. Maybe that's what we'll call this operation."

"What's that?"

"The Santa Fe Fiasco."

I spent the next thirty minutes on a conference call with Ken and TJ. We went over the file that TJ was breaking down. He was waiting for confirmation from our research fellow we bring in on cases above our heads like this, but it looks like what Erin said. The question is, how easily replicable is it? The other issue is, where is the scientist? Erin keeps leaving that part out, but that is a bargaining chip we can use for the CIA. They love assets, people they can turn, throw in a dark room somewhere, and put to work instead of jail time.

The next thing we covered was that of the art galleries here in Santa Fe. TJ is going to start pulling information and see where the money runs. Ken is going to start running down people we can use on the case. We're not sure if we can get away with bringing any of our top talents out here for this. Christian is tied up on an affair with Terrance down in Miami. Shortly after they helped Maria out, they followed Erin's trail to Miami then picked up a new case for a local contact of Ken's. Nicolette is undercover on an extended case helping with an extensive sexual harassment investigation. We have some other talented people, but we might be rocking this one solo and leaning on Father Roberts for help.

We have a good team with the three of us, plenty of trust there. The wild card is Erin. I know she is talented and capable. The issue lies in trust; I just don't know if we can trust her. I have an idea of who we can lean on if we need to, but we'll cross that path if we need to. For now, I have TJ and his team doing the digital dive while we work in the Santa Fe streets. I say "we" like I'm going to be doing much more than directing.

I'll be working with the sisters doing carpentry, cutting stuff, sanding stuff, and drinking a ton of C-Fu's. You may ask yourself, how are you going to build things and drink? I will tell you that's what laser-guided levels are for. With that thought, I hung up with Ken and TJ, and made my way out to find Maria and Father Roberts talking in the kitchen.

"Are you guys talking shit about me? More importantly, you didn't pour out my coffee, did you? I need that coffee for my C-Fu's."

"Neil, so you're serious about this drink, huh? Can we at least come up with a better name?"

"What's wrong with the Cluster-Fuck?"

"How about the drink formerly known as the C-Fu? Now known as the Santa Fiasco?"

"Maria, that's not bad. I'll sleep on it. Is this what you were talking about?"

"No, but now that you brought it up."

"Well, it been a long couple of days. I have a buzz and need some rest. I have a long day of work ahead of me, according to Father Roberts."

"We do have plenty of work to do, especially with the extracurricular that Maria has gotten you involved in." Score one for Father Roberts.

"Okay, boys, let's go to bed. It has been a long day."

"Good night, Maria. Night, Neil."

7

I LOVE THIS LADY ALREADY

Well, I'm starting off the day with a Santa Fe Fiasco. I've decided that the Fiasco is for the morning: it's nine parts coffee to one part tequila. The C-Fu is three parts coffee to two parts tequila. Yes, I really am fixating on this drink thing more than most, but I'm used to sinking my teeth into a case right now. I need to find something to keep my mind busy, and this is a start. If not, I'll be jumping in this case with Erin regardless of how I feel about the situation. I'd do it merely for the riddle to be solved; that's how my brain functions. It sees a problem and wants to figure it out; it's also how I get in trouble a lot.

Waking up early, knowing today was going to be a busy day of work, I wanted to get a run in. Maria, someone in way better shape than I am, doesn't need much encouragement for a run. A few nudges and the word "run" got her up and moving.

"Hey, Maria. Want to go for a quick run with me?"

"You mean a job for me, run for you? Yeah, I'm game. Let's make it quick."

The two of us got ready quickly, threw on our running shoes, and took off out the front door. Father Roberts was in the kitchen doing his morning prayers and didn't even acknowledge us as we went out the door. We didn't talk much, just ran around the city, enjoyed the views, and spoke of how beautiful it was out there.

I understand what Maria was saying last night about the differences she and Erin must go through in our line of work. I know it's not the same; they have to put up with an insane amount of bullshit just to get through the day. If that's not enough, they have to work twice as hard and often take greater risks just to get similar rewards, even though they are just as talented as any other agent. The run was a bit chilly, as it wasn't fully light out yet, but the view of the sunrise coming up over the city was breathtaking.

"Maria, slow down. Just stop for a minute."

"What's wrong, Neil?"

"Nothing, I just want to enjoy this with you. It's breathtaking just like you are. I'm not sure how many moments we are going to get like this. I'm going to embrace every one of them until they run out."

"You can be a sweetheart sometimes. Neil, I know this is going to be hard for you, but I know you'll be there when it matters most. That's one of your greatest qualities."

"What's that? Reluctantly doing what's needed?"

"YES! It's what makes you crazy on so many levels. You do the things most people can only dream of, only dare to. You do it bitching, like an old crank ass grandpa, but you do it. Where most of us would stop and sit on the sidelines. That's what makes you great."

Maria always has a way of making me feel special. Only one other person in my life has had this effect. That's my ex-wife, but we couldn't live together. Maria and I make it work. I think it's because we are always on the go, so we share only 30 to 40 percent of our week. With

Sheila, she was constantly home, needing something I couldn't give her. She felt like a prisoner to my career and my schedule, more so than me. At least I found joy in what I did; she merely had to be home alone because of it.

Back at the condo, Father Roberts had breakfast going and some fresh coffee for Maria. He was kind enough to keep some cold stuff left out from before we went on our run. He's a considerate guy; I guess it goes with the territory of being a priest.

"Hey guys, welcome back from your run. I have a fresh cup of coffee for Maria and a nice cold one for Neil sitting over here. How was it? The air seemed a bit chilly when I got up this morning. It's not something I'm used to back home."

"You should have been out there. Could you see the sunrise from here? It was something amazing coming up over the city and the mountains," Maria said with a smile.

"I could see a bit of it, but I wasn't brave enough to venture outside to the porch to catch all of it," Father Roberts said with a chuckle.

"Thank you for the coffee, Father. We're going to get ready, and then we can head out to start working with the sisters."

Maria and I switched off, quick showers and getting ready so that we could get out before eight. I didn't want to be late for the sisters. The last thing I wanted to do was piss off a group of nuns. Maria was going to meet up with Erin and get to work on scouting the art galleries. At the same time, TJ and his team started piecing the backchannel info over to us. I will be spending most of my mornings working on building a new storage shed for the soup kitchen. From what I understand, the foundation is there, and the framing is up with a roof. It's my job to finish the inside, build shelves, walls, etc. We even have an electrician lined up. I'm paying for that; it's a donation to the lovely ladies and the work they're doing.

As we walked up to the soup kitchen, I can't wait to meet these women and see what's in store. I had experience with the religious order in high school at St. Mary's Prep. I'm looking forward to the attention and devotion once again. As we walked up to the kitchen, it looked like an old house, with an unfinished large shed out back; I can see where I'll be working. I also see a staunch woman with broad shoulders and a grimace. She looks like a former professional wrestler turned spiritual leader.

"Good morning, gentlemen. Nice of you to join us this morning."

"I'm sorry, Sister, were we late this morning?" Father Roberts looked perplexed.

"We're always late to the Lord's work. We need to work toward being on time."

"Understood, Sister. Let me introduce you to my longtime friend Neil. He will be helping us."

"Nice to meet you, Neil. May I ask what's in the thermos?"

"Sure; it's called a Santa Fe Fiasco. I'm on vacation, and it's going to help me keep from assaulting people." Father Roberts's face dropped to the ground.

"If you're saying that coffee has a bit of a kick, count me in. This sister does the Lord's work but doesn't forget that life can be stressful. What's in it? Just remember, no shenanigans, need to keep it sane around here." I love this lady already.

"It's cold, leftover coffee, it can't be fresh, with top-shelf tequila. This version for the mornings is a mix of nine to one. At night I do a mix of three to two and call it a C-Fu."

"I am not familiar with C-Fu, but I am familiar with Shifu. I have nephews and have seen kung fu panda. Have you tried it over ice, or with limes?" She may be onto something.

"Sister, I'm not sure you would enjoy the colorful language that the C-Fu is short for." Father Roberts tried to save me from myself.

"I think I can get it now. Thank you, Father. Enough chitchat. Let's get to work."

The rest of the morning was spent working with lumber and rotating between saws. Though many of them were borrowed and a bit older, I was able to get a lot of work done this morning. The only thing that slowed me down was not having enough Santa Fe Fiascos to keep the day rolling. They have a coffeepot here, and a freezer with plenty of ice. Knowing that Sister Sledge is on board, I might purchase a case of tequila and some limes.

As for Maria and Erin, they are stuck in that wait-and-see mode. At the beginning of an investigation, it's a plethora of waiting. There's also plenty of hoping for a lead. You have to look in a ton of different directions before you find anything, and it's brutal in the beginning. It's like starting a thousand-piece puzzle with only half the picture of what you're working with.

"Hey Maria, how's your afternoon going? I'm about to take a break and head into town for a bit."

"What are you running into town for?"

"I'm going to grab some lunch and some tequila. Sister Sledge is a fan of the Santa Fe Fiasco, and we have an idea to step it up a notch. So I'm going to grab some tequila and some burritos while I'm in town. What are you and Erin up to?"

"Nothing. It's simply a game of sit and scout. I think she can do most of this on her own, and I can just help." Maria seemed defeated.

"Well, maybe we can find a different routine. Will that be okay?"

"How about we meet you for a quick lunch? We're just walking around. I'd love to see you all sweaty and dirty from work."

"Okay, I'll text you the address when we get off."

"Thanks, Neil. See you in a bit."

"I'll check in with TJ and Ken, see where they're at with the background information as I'm walking out there."

"Thanks, Neil."

As I walked toward downtown, I called TJ, who got Ken on the line to simplify and make the call more efficient. We went over the paper trail that TJ found from both galleries. He saw large sums of money moving consistently out of their galleries, but no corresponding chatter in the art world. With the amount of cash moving in and out, there should be large shows, and artist showcases grabbing the attention of the media.

As TJ put it, a gallery moving millions of dollars of merchandise according to your tax records has to be in some coinciding art showcases. At the very least there have to be some trending news articles. It would be as if you found a smoking smokestack, with no fire; you would be a bit perplexed. The call with the guys lacked leads, but TJ did have lots of information he was sending over for Maria and Erin to sift through. As I walked up to the small store where I was going to do my shopping I saw Maria and Erin waiting outside.

"Hey Neil, thanks for letting us meet up with you. I needed a break. I saw a bunch of emails come through with a box file link from TJ. Does that mean he's found some stuff for us to work through?" Maria seemed overjoyed for work.

"Yeah, he found a massive paper trail that didn't match the news articles. He said all the other galleries in the area have matching showcases or news publications that mirror significant transactions. Yet Choike and Gaines galleries aren't getting much advertisement but are moving large volumes."

"It's a place to start. Thanks again, Neil. Is there anyone helping you with the work? What's Father Roberts doing?"

"He's helping them with a bunch of accounting and admin work. Helping them clean up their books. For right now it's just me, but I'm doing okay. Know anyone with experience that wants to help?"

"I grew up on a farm with a father that was a contractor as well as a farmer. I know my way around some power tools. If you need help, just let me know." Erin is trying to be helpful.

"You two are really that bored, aren't you?"

"You know what it's like in the beginning; it can be brutal, but we know what we have. I also know it's only a matter of time before Gaines figures out I'm here. The question is whether he's still working with Choike. I'm pretty sure he is."

"I would assume she was his connection to the European pipeline. Without it, he's stuck simply selling domestically."

"Exactly, Neil. Maria and I were talking about that earlier. We just need to map out where everyone stands and gauge the plays."

It's like scouting a team you're about to play. Regardless of the sport, you have to look at previous games, what players worked together, plays they ran, etc. Connecting people in a case like this is no different.

"I can see that you need to set up shop somewhere, get a war room going. That's going to be key for this case. Where are you staying, by the way?"

"I ended up getting a room at the El Dorado. It's downtown and just what I'm looking for." Erin is leaving out, expensive as shit.

"Nice. Glad you were able to find a place." I knew she was just playing us still.

"Erin and I should be getting back at it. Neil, do you mind if we use the kitchen to set up shop for the time being?" Maria was interjecting to the awkwardness of Erin and me.

"Sounds fine to me. There's a garage, but we haven't used it because it's in back and hard to get the car in and out of. That might be a perfect space."

"We'll check it out. Thanks again, honey. I'll see you back at the condo for dinner?"

"Sounds good; probably about six or seven. Going to put in some later days in the beginning to get a head start. If you want me to grab takeout, just let me know."

"Sounds good."

I made my way back to the kitchen to get to work. It was hot, but there is always a cool breeze coming off those mountains. Especially as the day turns into night, you can feel the temperature drop quickly. It's something to be seen or felt. I've never been in an environment quite like this. I can see why people flock here, live here, and enjoy it so much. Though the day was filled with sawdust splinters and raw hands, I felt accomplished and calm. It was just what I needed, what my mind required, but I still couldn't help but drift. I couldn't help but find my way into this case. Working through the connections, the possibilities of what might be, what could be, and where the case is probably headed. I decided to text TJ to check something for me while I finished cleaning.

I had him look into large art purchases by Spanish or Mexican names, then cross-reference those names with the FBI's most-wanted list. The reason I'm focusing on that group versus others, for now, is the likelihood we can make an impact or a play on them if need be. It's more about the angle of how we can get to them than anything else. Sister Irene, I may have forgotten to mention her name; it slipped my mind, my apologies. Anyway, while finishing up, she walked out with a modified C-Fu in hand. Over ice, with a few lime wedges.

"Thank you, Sister. This isn't half bad. You might be onto something."

"You started it. I just stepped it up a notch. Well done, and thank you, Neil, for your help."

"I'm just happy to be here. This town is gorgeous, the mountains, the air, and the sunsets have been amazing. I'm hoping I can give as much as I get out of this experience."

"Gratitude is always a great place to start. Blessings to you tonight, Neil. I will see you tomorrow."

Drink in hand, in a small paper cup, I made my way down the street toward the condo. It's just a short walk back. It was getting late, the sun was beginning to set, and the view was something to take in. I took my backpack off for a moment, pulled out my headphones, and threw on some music. Back to walking at a fast pace, music pumping into my ears, and a smile on my face. I felt my phone go off, looked down, and saw it was TJ calling.

"Hey TJ, what do you have?"

"Well, I have some news for you. Three connections are matching the FBI's most wanted and the art list. The one I think you're looking for is El Jefe, just like you thought. The cartel leader you and the guys had to deal with when pulling Cappelano out of Mexico. You might have an in, not sure what, but that's your play, not mine."

"I'll think of something. There's always an angle. Start digging into his financials. Pull news articles from Mexico concerning him and his most prominent competitors. I'll reach out to a few contacts and see about getting him a message. He owes me for cleaning up the Cappelano mess."

This is something to go on, something to start with. Now it's time to start putting the pieces together. I hope Erin and Maria have something going on. Otherwise I might be doing more than I had planned tonight.

8

THIS IS A BAD CABLE MOVIE WAITING TO HAPPEN.

Back at the condo and I noticed Erin wasn't around. It seemed odd, but I can't say I wasn't happy. They had set up shop in the garage on the backside of the condo, which is the perfect size. There is a stairway from the kitchen to the garage, which is for a single car, with a bit more capacity. Not uncommon for a condo. When I got back, it was a little after seven. Father Roberts had beaten me back by a good thirty or so minutes, and Maria was still in the garage, according to him.

"Hey Maria, how'd your afternoon go? Any leads?"

"We have a lot of connections and could-bes, but we aren't sitting on much. TJ sent over a ton of data to go through, and we started on it, but not quite there yet."

"Well, I'm here now, and you call me the puzzle master. Let's start building the borders. See what we can piece together."

"Did you bring anything to eat? I'm hungry, and I probably should have told you to."

"We have stuff in the fridge upstairs, some leftovers from yesterday. Plus I can always have Father Roberts order a pizza or something simple."

"Let's just get a pizza. It's perfect for a night like tonight."

I yelled upstairs to Father Roberts to have him order a pizza. After we screamed back and forth a few times, he eventually walked downstairs to get the order. He was tired of yelling like two kids not wanting to go to bed. While Maria and I were still working in the garage, I was sitting there nursing water, craving a drink. Trying to get into that vacation, fuck-it-all attitude. It's kind of hard, especially since I'm playing hard to get with Maria right now with the intel TJ gave me.

"Maria, did I tell you TJ found a connection between Gaines's gallery and three people on the FBI's most-wanted list? One name stands out, though, that has a link to El Jefe."

"Jesus Christ, Neil. Way to bury the lead."

Maria is now ranting in Spanish about something. When she gets ultra passed at me, she'll start yelling under her breath in Spanish. I know it seems odd to say, yelling, under your breath, but you'd know it when you hear it. Oh, she just said *"puta."* I know that one. She called me a bitch.

"Sorry, I wanted to see if you had gotten there on your own first. Didn't want to steal your thunder if you had, so I was waiting a bit to see what you had."

"You're trying to tell me that you weren't being an asshole dragging it out, but instead a considerate boyfriend? Trying to be supportive and understanding of the situation at hand?"

"Yes!"

"'Yes' to which one?"

"Yes, I was trying to be supportive, but I was just burying the lead like an asshole."

"Goddamn it, Neil, you're an asshole." She slugged me on the shoulder.

"Do you want my help and my intel? If not, I can just go upstairs and shower, wait for the pizza, and relax with a C-Fu."

"Neil, you know I want your help. You're just an asshole about it. You're just reminding me who is the king in this relationship." Ouch.

"That's not it at all. I just want you to know I have a ton to give in this investigation. It's just that I do it reluctantly. I want to help you push this case, but not at the expense of working with Erin. I'm still having trouble conceding what she did to those agents."

"I know, I haven't forgotten it, I've just weighed it versus the outcome of cutting Gaines off from the world finally."

"It's my trust in you and Mike at the bureau that has me staying around for this."

"Thanks, Neil. With this starting point, we have something to work with. Let's get started."

For the next few hours, Maria and I worked through stacks of files. They had run to FedEx to print everything off that TJ sent them, created a space to review everything. I suggested she run to Office Depot in the morning, grab a printer, and just build a makeshift office out here. If she's going to do it, do it right. We were able to find several other connections to Gaines as well as Choike's gallery with people on the FBI's most-wanted list. Four different names matched each gallery's transactions. We would have to run them down and find some intel on each one of them.

We finally gave up somewhere after midnight, and two pizzas in. We had enough connections that we decided it was a night of work well done. I shot Ken an email to get with Carl and Tony about working some of the contacts we made on the Cappelano case. They were the two guys assigned to staking out and investigating Cappelano's movements in Mexico. They had made a deal with the local cartel to work freely in the city. I'm hoping they still have some contacts we can work with.

The problem with cartels is that they aren't known for having a high retention rate. Too many people get arrested or killed. Not surprising in a place such as Mexico in the middle of the drug era we live in, but it's still worth a shot.

As my head hit the pillow, I kept drifting back into that time frame, the case that brought me to Mexico. Thinking of El Jefe, Mexico, and the fact that I tried to kill Cappelano only to be stopped by a jammed gun. I wonder how my life would have turned out had the gun not jammed. Would I have gone down a darker path? If Frank hadn't shot some of those people in the head, not gone down the path he did in the FBI, would he have been so curious and left? So many questions that led to the worst night of sleep I had in weeks.

"Hey Neil, did you get any sleep last night? You tossed and turned so much I thought you were fighting someone." Maria looked concerned.

"It was a pretty rough night. This case, looking into El Jefe, has me thinking of that night in Mexico with Cappelano, what could have been. What I wanted to do, but what ended up happening."

"Neil, I know you wanted to kill him. Shit, we all did by that point. You had more motive than anyone, but you didn't. It's not like you pulled the trigger or something. Just wanting to do something isn't reason enough to get upset." Maria doesn't know. Then again, I never told her.

"Tell that to my conscience. Tell that to the sleepless nights. They don't seem to care. Time to take a shit shower, grab a Fiasco, and start my day."

"Yeah, I did notice that water pressure is brutal. It took forever to wash my hair. Erin said it was the same at the hotel. Apparently it's a local thing."

"It has to do with water conservation and water pressure. Didn't you notice when your turn on the faucets how slow it comes out?"

"I guess I didn't. That's enough about water pressure for one year. Get ready; I'll make a Santa Fe Fiasco for you and some breakfast."

After a quick shower filled with disdain and a disgruntled participant, I made my way to the kitchen. I grabbed my morning drink, a burrito, then a kiss from my lady. Father Roberts had already started his walk ahead of me. Though I was in jeans, I did have on tennis shoes. I decided to run and play catch-up to him.

"Hey, don't think you're going to get there early and show me up to Sister Irene."

"That wasn't my intent at all. I just thought you might be moving a bit slow from a long night working with Maria."

"Fair point. But I still don't want to hear her shit, even if it is funny, and she's an early drinker like I am."

"You two are kindred spirits, that's for sure."

It was still early, not even seven thirty. We made our way up to the front door, where we were greeted with a smile but attitude. One we are starting to expect from Sister Irene. She was standing there, in jeans, a hooded sweatshirt from South Florida University. She also had a cup in her hand, what I can only hope was a matching Santa Fiasco, such as my own.

"Nice of you to join us, gentlemen. Your friend got here early; she's been working since four in the morning."

"Our friend; I guess I don't know who you're speaking of, Sister."

"The lovely Miss Erin. She came early, started working. She was working quietly when I came out and informed her we are nuns. We always start early. She's been working fast ever since." No shit.

"Well, let's head out back and see how much she's been able to accomplish this morning."

Father Roberts didn't say much, if anything, from the time we waked up to the time we made our way out back. He was merely a bystander, waiting to see if I was going to explode. I don't take surprises well, especially in this case. I'm helping her, putting myself out on a limb to help her. This does show some contrition on her part, but I still don't know her angle. One might think I am paranoid; I'd say I'm measured.

As we walked out back, I couldn't help but notice that her work was impeccable. She hadn't cut corners; precise cuts with framing edges that were perfect. One of the projects I had left for today because it was going to take the longest for me. Erin knocked it out already; to perfection, I might add. It was the framing of the interior walls that I was going to connect into the truss system. I know you're asking yourself, *How big is this shed?* It's more like a large two-car garage.

"Hey guys, how's your morning going?" Erin said with a sheepish smile.

"Great. How's your morning going? Productive, it looks like."

"I'd have to agree with Neil, Miss Erin. According to Sister Irene, you started early. What may we attribute your generosity to?" Father Roberts finally spoke up.

"After watching Neil come around, willing to help, devote his company resources to helping, I felt it was my duty to help. I had asked, though he was reluctant, I couldn't sleep last night. So I just came here to help. I have a lot to make up for and wanted to start the process of rebuilding trust."

"I'm sure Neil appreciates it. I know Sister Irene and I do."

"Father, I'm standing right here. Leave me out of it, I guess."

"That wasn't my intent, you know that." Father Roberts was backpedaling like a professional athlete.

"Erin, I appreciate it. Maria and I made some headway last night. Why don't you stay here and work with me for the day? We'll have her come too. We'll let my team do some work on the leads we have, and we can work on team building among the three of us."

"Hey, don't forget about me." Sister Irene spoke up.

"Sorry, five of us, the band of misfits. A sister who can kick my ass, a father who's seen it, my girlfriend, and a burned CIA agent. This is a bad cable movie waiting to happen."

"I'll drink to that, Neil." Sister Irene raised her glass.

"Sounds good to me. I'm already dirty, sweaty, and covered in sawdust."

We ended up calling Maria, having her finish up work at the condo, grabbing lunch on her way, and spending the rest of the day working on the project for the kitchen. Ken had messaged back that they were working some contacts and leads trying to track down intel on El Jefe. Overall, it became a great way to stay busy while we did the small work.

Cases in the beginning often take a long time to build leads, connections, and follow-up. There is nothing instant about it, not like TV or the movies. However, people are much more intrigued by 24 than they are with 365. The latter is much closer to the truth, though not nearly as sexy. These cases have a way of simmering like a diesel engine; they take a while to get warmed up, but once they do, they operate at high efficiency.

The rest of the week was much of the same: the five of us worked on and ended up completing the project early. It looked great. We even had time to paint everything, something not part of the plan. With Erin's help and working as a big group, we were able to add details to the space that would greatly benefit the soup kitchen and the sisters over the years. From a loading bay door to a receiving window they could use to hand out or receive donations.

This week was definitely needed for me. It may have started rough, and I was pulled into a case I wasn't planning on, but that's life. I rarely choose the things I want to work on. At least this time I was able to make an impact for these ladies and the community.

Earlier in the week, I had sneaked a message to TJ to do a background check on Sister Irene, out of curiosity. Something seemed a bit off. Every time I would ask her about her past, the stories were vague, or she dodged them altogether. With the way the week had gone, I keep forgetting to follow up.

"Hey TJ, how's it going back at the office? Everything still good?"

"Yes, we're still status quo over here. Ken has been working some back channels with Tony to get to El Jefe. Carl struck out; he found out the contacts he had were all deceased."

"Not surprising, especially with drug cartels. It's a risky business. Did you ever have a chance to run background on Sister Irene?"

"Well, sort of. There is no such person on record there. Also, no such history involving the stories you spoke of or anyone matching her description at any of the places you said she might have worked. She's either a ghost, lying, or both."

"Well, this is a fun puzzle to add to the mix. Thanks, TJ."

9

I USED TO TEACH THERE. BEFORE, MY LIFE WENT SIDEWAYS.

After working alongside Sister Irene for a week, I thought it's a perfect time to question her. I would do it lightly, but I still needed to do it just the same. My curiosity wouldn't let me leave it be at this point. I am already working through the issues with Erin, have that bag to unpack, now this. So much for a mental break from everything. Then again, I'm not sure I could ever take a break from anything.

It was a chilly Sunday night with that hint of rain in the air. I had swung by to do some touch-up paint on the project. Maria and Erin were working on the case down in Las Cruces, checking on a lead related to El Jefe. Father Roberts was lucky enough to do some visiting work at St. Francis Cathedral, a favor the sister pulled for him. I caught him in the early Mass, but he was staying all day. While working as usual, the sister and I began to talk. This time I took it down a different path.

"Neil, I know I've said this already. Thank you, especially for the extra work and money you put into helping us. Not to mention introducing me to the Santa Fiasco," she said with a smile.

"Well, thank you for showing me that ice and limes are a better way to drink the C-Fu. As for the project, I'm pretty confident I got more out of this than you ever will."

"That's not uncommon with these kinds of projects. It's why we encourage them. We're not always looking for free labor. We know service can be of great help to many."

"Very true, Sister Irene. That is, if that is your real name?" I said sternly.

"Cute, Neil. Of course it's my name. What else would it be?" Her demeanor changed immediately.

"You tell me. I already know it's not Irene, and I know most of your stories are made up. I just don't know why."

"Neil, I'm not sure what brought this on, or why, but I can assure you—"

"Sister, let me stop you there. I sniff out bullshit for a living. I'm a human lie-detector test, and I know you aren't truthful. I can list the reasons I know, but I'd rather not. I'm just going to give you two choices. The first is you ignore it, walk away, and we act like this never happened and play the game the same way we have been. The second is you tell me the truth, you open up like I know you want to, and we gain trust. I won't judge you either way. I'm not going to judge someone who has devoted their life to the service of others."

Her response caught me off guard. She stood up, put her drink down, walked toward the door, and began to sob. I wasn't sure if she was going to keep walking or turn around; I just let it go on for a few moments. Right then, it began to rain; what had been waiting to happen all night finally unleashed. She turned around and looked at me with a smile, laughing and smiling at the same time.

"Neil, you have to admit, that's a bit over the top. I mean, I'm as religious as anyone, but that's a bit over the top."

"I feel you, Sister. The timing on that was eerie at best." I smiled back.

"I guess this means I'm going to give you the whole story. Consider it payment for a job well done. How much tequila do we have in here?"

"I have a whole bottle and a whole pot of cold coffee. Plus there's a bag of ice in the freezer, so we're set."

"My real name is Margie Wiggs, a pleasure to meet you. The South Florida shirt isn't from Goodwill, its mine from college. I used to teach there. Before, my life went sideways."

She went on to explain to me her life story, how she had grown up in a small town in rural Oklahoma, where she worked on a ranch. It's where she learned to speak Spanish with the ranch hands. Eventually, in college, majoring in English and Spanish literature at the University of Colorado. She grew up rough, was never afraid to get her hands dirty. She was the only daughter with three brothers.

Margie spoke of a home as a place she enjoyed but couldn't wait to get away from. As soon as she could, she went away to college and didn't look back. She was able to get a scholarship to Colorado for track and field and academics. She stayed in Boulder until graduating with her masters and doctorate. She made her way to the University of South Florida in the early nineties, trying to get away from her family even more.

Though she graduated from school and worked her way up the scholastic ranks, she enjoyed the fun parts of life. She wasn't afraid to dabble in drugs of multiple avenues, from weed to cocaine. She said it was easy to rationalize what she was doing, since all the great literary minds she was studying had done just the same.

"Sister, you keep speaking of your past in a way like it's another person. Yet, you have moved on past her. Would you like me to continue to address you as Sister Irene? I'm okay with it, out of respect for the service you have devoted your life to."

"It would mean a lot to me. Thank you for understanding, Neil."

We went back and forth for a few hours, finally finding out the significant issue that she got involved with was with a drug dealer in Tampa, Florida. She ended up getting hooked on heroin, losing her job, and going down a dark path. It was a Church mission that turned her life around. From that day forward, she devoted her life to the service of others. She said she made her way out to Santa Fe to get closer to her family, to work up the courage someday to go home, but has yet to do it.

"We all have different phases of our lives, Sister. I believe yours allows you to have a different level of compassion for people. You didn't judge me one bit, walking in here drinking at eight in the morning."

"We need the help; I can't be picky," she said, laughing.

"You know exactly what I mean. A young blond woman that didn't fit in shows up at four in the morning, and you just let her work with power tools. No questions asked."

"The Lord works in mysterious ways." Now she's fucking with me.

"You're all right by me. I'll keep your secret, Sister."

"Thanks, Neil. I had to know one day someone would come through those doors and figure it out."

Sister Irene and I were talking, drinking, and I was doing the touch-up paint around the place. I noticed my phone buzzing, and it was

Maria. She had texted me, asking me to call her when I had a moment. I hope it's some good news and not another dead end.

"Hey Maria, how's it going down in Las Cruces?"

"The drive sucked. It was pretty sad to see all the dead towns along the way, but I've got some good news and some bad news."

"Start with the bad news, end on a good note."

"The news goes together, so I'll just drop it in your lap."

"Our lead paid off. Tony's connection was able to get us in contact with El Jefe's brother."

"Where is the bad news? If you talked to him, that means he's alive."

"Well, we were also able to Skype El Jefe in Mexico, and when he saw two pretty girls were looking for him, he invited us down to Mexico to talk to him."

"There's the bad news. Does he know you're an FBI agent?"

"It didn't come u; Erin said not to tell him anything. Even Tony said to keep it out of everyone's mouth when I'm down here."

"Not the worst idea. The only problem is when or if they figure it out."

"I know, but this is our best lead, our only real lead to try to get connected to Choike or Gaines and their cash flow. We know we have to make a dent, find a way to prevent them from building a supply of Requiem. Did TJ ever get us an answer on whether the scientist is alive? Has his body turned up? I know Mike said the FBI has nothing."

"As of right now, there is nothing. We also have no way of talking to him, other than Cappelano, and I'm out here. I think I'm going to talk to Ken and see if we can get someone in there to speak to Cappelano.

Maybe I can get Colby to hand him a cell, though Gaines has the warden under control, so it might be harder than I make it sound."

"Good luck, Neil. Tony and Carl are heading down to Mexico as we speak. They fly in tonight. Ken said he knows you're going to want your guys backing us up in case something happens."

"He's a smart man. He also knows I trust them. Not as much as Christian and Nicolette, but they're busy, and those two guys have rapport in the neighborhoods already."

"I hate to cut, but we're leaving now. You know how these things are, no time to waste."

Just like that Maria hung up, the phone went dead, and my girlfriend was gone. She was on her way to a drug cartel's villa, to be wined and dined with a CIA operative, which I'm just now learning to trust a little bit. At least Ken is sending our guys down there to be close in case extraction is needed.

10

I'M GOING TO SEE IF I CAN GET AN AUDIENCE WITH GAINES AS WELL.

I got off the phone with Maria, said good-bye to Sister Irene, and started packing my gear. It was getting late, and the rain was beginning to slow. I packed up my backpack—leather, worn-in backpack. I grabbed my headphones and hoped for the best. The rain was light enough that my hoodie should cover them while I was walking back, plus they double as a link with my phone, so I can call Ken and plan with him. I was a good block or two from the condo when it finally stopped raining altogether and I decided to call Ken.

"Hey Neil, I'm assuming by now you spoke to Maria?"

"Yeah, thank you for always being aware enough to act instead of waiting for permission."

"That's why we're partners. We understand time is always a top priority. What's the next step for you? I know you're not going to sit on your hands and wait for an answer out of Mexico."

"I need to get on a flight to Detroit out of Albuquerque tomorrow, first thing. Then I'll need a return flight before the end of the day back. Can we swing that?"

"Shouldn't be an issue. I'm pretty sure when we booked Maria's trip, there was a five-in-the-morning flight every day. Are you going to need a ride from the airport somewhere? Or do you just want me to have one of the guys drop a car off there for you at the parking lot?"

"Just have someone meet me. I can grab the car from them, they can head out, and then they can get it when I leave."

"You got it. I'll email you the details shortly. How's the project with Father Roberts coming along?"

"We finished early, Erin stepped up and helped, along with Maria and one of the sisters onsite. It ended up being a team effort, but we made it work and got more done than originally planned. I'm going to let you go; I'm almost back to the condo and need to pack for tomorrow."

"Look for your flight info in a few minutes. I'll text you in the morning who's going to meet you at the airport. I'm assuming you're going to FCI Milan to talk to Cappelano?"

"I'm going to see if I can get an audience with Gaines as well."

There wasn't much to pack since I was going to be back the same day. It was more packing my backpack with chargers and backup batteries. Also realizing I will go most of the day without my beloved Fiasco or C-Fu. Then again, I could get tequila at the airport and a coffee there as well. I guess I'll throw my water bottle in the bag, just in case. Father Roberts was buried in his routine, so I just dropped him a text to let him know what was going on.

I've been working on taking into account other people's routines. I know mine is vital to me. Though some people I forget, or honestly don't care. When it comes to the important people in my life, such as Maria and Father Roberts, I try to put forth the effort. Drink in hand, bag ready to go, and I still couldn't sleep. Under normal circumstances I would take a nice long. hot shower or hit the heavy bag, neither of which are doable. Maybe I can try Sheila.

"Hey Neil, everything okay? It's not like you to call this late. Especially not with the way things have been going with Maria lately."

"That's kind of the problem. Maria is deep on a case, on her way to see a drug cartel leader. I'm a little worried and can't sleep. Is this what it was like being with me, or still is?"

"It's hard, but it did get easier over time because you kept coming home. I just started believing you were damn near invincible. There didn't seem to be anything that would stop you from getting home."

"Maria is a capable agent with some backup, and Ken sent some of the guys down there. The same guys we had down there when I went to get Cappelano years ago. It doesn't make it any easier, though; the fear is still there."

"It's going to be. It's the uncertainty that gets you. The not knowing what's going on, that was the hard part."

"Change of subject, how's our girl doing? With it being summer, she has to be enjoying school being out."

"Yes and no. You know that she loves class and her teachers. She always struggles in the summer; I think we should send her to that camp this year we talked about."

"You know I'm on board with anything she needs. Just put it on the blue Visa, and we're good. I know it'll be great for her."

"I'll talk to her in the morning. Are you going to be okay, Neil?"

"Yeah, I just need to get some rest. Long day tomorrow. I'll talk to you later. Thank you for answering. Good night, Sheila."

"Night, Neil."

Off the phone, I quickly fell asleep. Luckily, I set my alarm for three in the morning to check what time the flight was from Ken. It worked out because when I woke up to the alarm I noticed the flight time out of Albuquerque was early. I'm sorry I can't say it without thinking of Bugs Bunny. I just go right back to my childhood. All kidding aside, I hopped in the shower, got ready, ran out the door, threw my stuff in the car, and started the forty-or-so-minute drive to the airport.

The best part of these early-ass flights is a combination of getting through security fast as shit and passing out on the plane. The size of the airport here increases how quickly anyone can get through. I was able to park and get to my gate in less than twenty minutes. This gave me plenty of time to find a place to get some coffee. I decided to save the tequila portion of the day for the trip back. This is no longer vacation time; it's a workday. My girlfriend is hanging out with El Jefe. At the same time, I fly home for the day, pop into a federal prison to talk to my old friend and serial killer Cappelano. Nothing is relaxing or fun about this trip.

I was able to sleep on the plane for the whole trip. I even fell asleep while we were taxiing to the runway, which is always a bonus. By the time we were landing in Detroit, I had emails and messages from Ken and TJ. They were explaining to me intel they had on El Jefe, Maria, and the overall progression of the case. They also said that I needed to call Jordan from the DEA ASAP; he had to talk to me about Requiem. It didn't sound positive; if Jordan is involved, that means it's already on the streets.

As I made my way from the plane, backpack over my shoulder, Tigers hat tucked down over my dirty blond hair mixed with some gray from all the stress and shag over my ears, I caught a glimpse of myself in a glass pane seeing my scruff and hair. Mixed with my distressed shirt and jeans, I looked more like a kid hanging onto his college years than a premier investigator that works with the FBI and has his own company. I took a moment to check in with Ken as I met Christian with the car; he wanted to be the one to drop it off, even if just for a minute.

"Hey Ken, what's up? Do we have any more details about El Jefe? I saw from your email that he is moving more product than usual. Also, the word on the street from the DEA and their CIs is that it's a new drug matching Requiem's description."

"Well, it looks like El Jefe has a bone to pick with Gaines along with other cartels. They are all pissed at him. He is losing his control over them since he has been in prison. He feels he still has it, but it's slipping. The word is that they are going to make a move on him in prison, so be careful when you're in there today. You've already had one run-in while in prison."

"Understood. Do you think I should take Christian with me, have him ride shotgun with me for the trip? I can make some bullshit excuse up for why he's along with me."

"It might be a good idea to minimize risk. We already have one person out there on a limb. We don't need another one." Ken has a great point.

"I'll figure out a reason to bring him along with me. Can we spare him for the day?"

"For this, we'll make it work. It's just a day."

Ken and I finished up, went over a few other items, then I hung up. I made my way through the airport, practicing self-control as I walked past several duty-free shops showing cheap tequila. I did make mental notes of them for the return trip to enjoy a nightcap.

Walking out of the airport, I saw Christian pull up in my Jeep Wrangler. It's old as shit, 1981, but pristine now. I spent a ton of time working on it to make it perfect. New seats, completely redone interior, it has been a fun side gig, but I'm done digressing.

"Hi, Christian. I'm glad you guys brought the Wrangler and not one of the warehouse cars. With all the stress of the day, a little comfort goes a long way."

"We figured. We know what you taught us. The details matter, even if it takes a bit of extra work. I'll get out of your hair; just let me know when you're coming back, and I'll grab it to take home."

"Change of plans, Christian. You're coming with me; think of it like sidekick duty. You might even get to meet Cappelano."

"Your name is on the company; not sure I can tell you no. Not like I would anyway. I'd be afraid you'd drive a truck through my house." Christian always brings that up.

"Very funny. Just drive. Do you know how to get to FCI Milan?"

"Yeah, I know where it is. It's not far from here. Let's get going."

The drive to the prison was simple, as expected. Christian and I spoke of a few different things. I helped him troubleshoot a case he was working on. I just gave him a sounding board and walked him through some ideas. In the early years, I leaned on Sheila and Ken a lot, but Sheila more. She was a neutral person to talk to, someone I trusted. She gave me great advice and would often repeat my thoughts back to me in a more precise version than what I had told her.

We pulled up to FCI Milan and checked in. It took a bit of convincing as well as some schmoozing to get Christian approved. A few people were afraid to let him in, but the warden wasn't around. He probably has tabs on me and saw I was out of town. He thought it would be a good idea to head out of town since I was in Santa Fe. Little did the good old warden, a buddy of Gaines, realize that I was just a flight away from popping in on my favorite inmate.

"Hey Frank, I bet you didn't think you would see me for a bit. How's the last week been in here?"

"You know how it's been. Boring, slow, and shitty, the usual for a federal prison. They don't make it joyful for a reason. I think that has something to do with all the people I killed."

"Good point. Do you know why I'm here? Why I came back on short notice to talk to you?"

"No, but I am a bit concerned about why you brought muscle with you. First of all, you can handle yourself, you know I've got your back, and the guards wouldn't let anything happen this time around. Well, I don't think they would."

"That's just my guy Christian. He's one of our top investigators. Since I'm going to be in and out, we thought it'd be easier if he tagged along."

"Decent excuse. Bullshit, but I'll take it and stop pressing you. Ask me the real question, the one you came here to ask me."

"What do you know about Gaines's involvement in a drug called Requiem?'

"You know that I'm not a fan of drugs. I'm not much a fan of Gaines either. I can tell you that he is deep into it; his company has been stockpiling this shit for a year. What you think you have, you're not even close."

"I figured. It seemed like we didn't have much to go on in the first place. What we did have seemed almost planted to me. It didn't feel real. I didn't think that someone, as measured as he is, would leave important documents like that lying around."

"What is it with deranged killers and me? Why do you guys flock to me?"

"Maybe it's the other way around, Neil. Ever think you're the one with the problem?"

Frank has a point there. Maybe I'm the one who craves the abusive relationship. I could be the one after the chase, not the other way around. I know it's sad that the person who seems to understand my drive the most is a deranged killer. He still struggles with things such as empathy and character. The overall judgment of my motivations, though, and personal relationships, Cappelano is spot on.

"Fair point, Frank. I play a role in who I hang out with and the life I have chosen. I didn't come here to talk about my life choices."

"What did you come here for?"

"I came here for . . . one second."

I stuck my head out and told Christian to reach out to Jordan at the DEA. I told him to call the office, get his number, and get the information they have on Requiem and any details that track back to Gaines and Choike. If he got anything worth noting, to pull me out of the room.

"Sorry about that, I had to remind my friend there to make a call for me. As I was saying, I came here to talk to you as well as a mutual friend of ours. Has he talked to you at all about a new designer street drug that he's been working on?"

"Can't say that he has. Then again, Gaines likes to talk in riddles, walk around the real subject he's talking about. I'm not sure if it's a trust issue or if he's watched one too many superhero movies."

"I know right, don't you get that vibe."

"I kept thinking he is trying to play the role of a slender King Pin. I swear I heard him say 'retired' multiple times when speaking of people that are now dead. It's sad. Actually, he has the wit to be a great villain, but his head is so far up his ass he can't see straight."

"I'm supposed to be sitting down with him after this. I was thinking of doing it as a group. The three of us, see if I can get him to trust you more if the two of us go at it for him. A bit of a show. You up for it?"

"You know I'm not a fan of his after he tried to frame me for your murder. I am always up for a good mind fuck. Especially a long con that will pay off dividends. What's the drug you speak of?"

"It's a new designer drug we've tracked back to his labs that gives you the same high as heroin with a lot less of the addiction, supposedly. It's supposed to wear off faster, allow you to feel better quicker, with less adverse side effects."

"If it's that good, won't it be that much more addictive?"

"Yeah, no shit. That's the point, but no one thinks that shit through. That's why we are trying to stop it from being supplied to the streets at the distributor. Gaines himself, the biggest drug lord of them all."

"Well, you know I'm crazy enough to rationalize killing. However, I can't stand drugs, especially drug dealers. What do you need from me?"

I knew Frank would help as soon as he heard what was at stake. He has always hated drug dealers. It's hard to find anyone that's a fan of dealers, other than users. I haven't been on the same side of a conversation with Cappelano in a long time, with someone on the other side. Then again, we are going to be playing this one a little hard to get Gaines to trust him, so we'll see.

"Right now, we're working some other angles with buyers and cartels, trying to find an in on Gaines and his distribution. We have some of the data about the drug and how they synthesize it. The trick is finding the doctor, and if he's alive. We don't know if Gaines killed him since he computerized the process."

"That's where this little game of show-and-tell is going to come in. We put on a good show, then we hope we can get some actionable intel out of Gaines, and I get it to you?"

"Yes, with Colby still around, he's the only person you can trust, but you'll have to make sure and do it when Gaines isn't around. Since Gaines knows that Colby was part of us breaking up his operation."

"Then let's get him in here and start the show."

"I'll step out and see what I can come up with."

As I walked outside of the room, Christian pulled me aside. He didn't have the best look on his face as he was coming down the hall from the smoking area. I like to call it the cell phone signal spot.

"Christian, judging by your face, the call with Jordan didn't go well."

"I have plenty of info. It's just not what we want to hear in this situation."

'Well, there's no point in keeping it a secret. What gives?"

"Sorry! Jordan said that they have intel from a dependable source that Gaines has been making Requiem and shipping it to different cartels for at least three months. He's been gearing up for a big push on the market. He didn't want to do a small push; he wanted to corner it and take over the drug scene."

"He's using his buying power, ability to mass-produce early and network to stockpile a new drug. That way, he can flood the market and keep it on the streets regardless of the heat he gets from law enforcement."

"That's what it looks like. I think he was hoping if he's in prison, we can't charge him for crimes that occurred while being locked up."

"It's not impossible, but it is uncommon. You have to show explicit control from inside the four walls. FUCK! FUCK! Gaines, you shifty bastard! Guard, can you get me Gaines in here ASAP? It's already been cleared with the commanding officer." The guard didn't even respond; he just nodded and left.

"You're going to put Gaines and Cappelano in a room together?"

"Yup. Let's see what fireworks we can create."

11

CHRISTIAN REVIEWED JORDAN'S FEARS OF THE VAST AMOUNT OF DRUGS THAT GAINES CAN DEVELOP.

The guard was walking Gaines down the hallway as I could see him. It's the view I usually get of Cappelano as he makes his way to our interview sessions. This one seems different, though; I have additional nerves. I need to play it just right, since there is more at stake.

"Is this what it's like when you sit here waiting for me to come in? An eerie silence followed by a bit of anticipation?"

"You could say that I also used to catch you waiting at the door. I knew you made me wait a few minutes longer for you, just for that bit of control."

"How could you see me if I was behind the door?"

"From over here, you can see the security monitor. It catches just enough of the area where I could see you standing there. Making the guard wait a few minutes."

"Isn't that annoying? Here I thought I had some semblance of control. You were merely playing along to make me believe I had some."

"Frank, you're locked up in here for life. I thought I could throw you a bone. It's the least I could do."

"I appreciate the gesture, even if I feel it was out of pity. Want to simply riff and shoot from the hip on Gaines?"

"I don't see how we can do anything else. We're both good at reading people. We'll see where it goes. Worst case, it blows up in our face, and I go back to old-fashioned investigative work. You could always shank him in the yard, to get him to talk."

"Hilarious, Neil."

You laugh, he laughs, but part of me feels if this goes bad, it will work. Stabbing Gaines, even just a small wound, would make him fold like a bitch. The way he went down when I punched him shows a lot about him. He's not used to being challenged. He's the man in charge, the man with the power, but he caves to a real challenge.

With each step, I can feel the air in the room dissipating. Gaines approached, and the room felt smaller. There is pressure looming. I'm used to high-pressure situations. Hell, I tried blowing Cappelano's head off in Mexico; this should be a breeze. There is something about this guy that just drives me up the wall, something that keeps me thinking he's always a step ahead. I think it's because it feels like he's there by accident. With Cappelano, you knew he did the work. With Gaines, it's like he fell into a hole and found a pile of money.

"Mr. Baggio and Mr. Cappelano, what a surprise. I thought I was just getting to talk to Neil today. What is the occasion to get group treatment?"

"Well, Gaines, I'm on a time crunch, and Cappelano and I were running long, so I thought we'd double dip a bit. Is that okay with you? He wasn't forthcoming."

"Fuck you, Neil, you know the only reason I talk to you is to get my story out. I'm not here to talk about anything other than me." Well done, Frank, but tone it down.

"Cappelano, calm your ass down. No need to be rude with our guest here today."

"Don't change your tone toward Neil on my accord. You do you, Frank, don't worry about me. Why am I even in here with you, Neil?" Gaines is already siding with Frank.

"I wanted to question you about Requiem and your missing scientist from Gaines Chemical."

"Neil, I think it's cute that you think I have that much influence in here. Frank is the most influential person in here. Even he couldn't pull off that kind of intel in here."

"Gaines, first of all, prisons are like old-fashioned switchboards. Information gets passed through all the time. It always seems to find its way into and out of here. Don't play me for a fool. I'll tell you what: instead, I'll just do something like plant a kilo of cocaine at the warden's house. Then have my DEA buddies pick him up and throw his ass in jail. Then I'll put one of my friends in here to run the place and fuck with you every day. Then let's see how you'll feel."

"Gaines, I'm not one to give you advice, but Neil is crazy when he wants something. I heard, on a case, he drove a truck through a police station. Not to mention, there's the stunt he pulled to get you in here in the first place," Cappelano softly chimed in.

"I'll tell you what: I'll see what info I can come up with, get you something, and go from there. I don't have the same pull in here as I once did out there." Gaines is trying to play me for a schmuck.

"Okay, then my counter to that is I'll only drop enough drugs in the warden's house to jam him up for a few weeks. That'll still mess with your plans."

We went back and forth like this for a good thirty minutes. I kept changing my counteroffer to throwing his friend the warden in prison for different lengths of time. Thankfully, he wasn't here. Also, fortunately, these rooms are designed to be off-grid unless you bring a camera into them. This means no one will know all the veil threats I'm throwing toward the warden, other than these two jokers.

My favorite part was when Frank started softly instigating Gaines, getting him all riled up. It was hilarious, and it took everything in me not to laugh. Gaines was all puffed up like a rooster, ready to bump chests, when he realized where he was and who had the power in this dynamic. Frank got him to calm down, focused on what was necessary, and we got him to give me a little bit of information. We were able to get the scientist's name and his life status, at least.

"Neil, I don't see why it matters if Jack Cavanagh is alive. He is, but that's a moot point to the information you need. At Gaines Chemical, all the work that every scientist does is recorded digitally so it can be replicated. Even if they do something accidentally, we can repeat it, backtrack, and figure it out."

"You're telling me there's a good chance he made this drug or others by accident, but your system captured the process allowing you to repeat the process?"

"Yes, that's what's made us so successful. My sister is the one that invented the process we use; it's proprietary and why we lead the industry now."

Before I could get any more info out of Gaines, the guard came in to grab him, stating that the warden had caught wind of what I was doing and put a stop to it immediately. It was a good run; I was able to get a good two hours with him and build trust between him and Cappelano. As the two of them were being escorted back to their cells, I walked out with Christian, talking over what went on in the room. Christian reviewed Jordan's fears of the vast amount of drugs that Gaines can develop, mainly if he used his legitimate labs to design them. As we were exiting the building, Christian was telling me to call Jordan ASAP.

"Neil, you need to get on the phone with Jordan and go over what you have from your interrogation today. You two have a shot of putting your heads together. Do you have any other leads? Just one, but I'm not sure if it's going to get me anywhere. Let's start with Jordan."

We had to call Jordan a few times. It went to voice mail the first two times directly. Either his phone was off, or someone else was calling him. We decided to hop in the car and head toward the airport to make sure I had enough time to make my way through airport security. Unlike the flight out here, the Detroit airport isn't as quick. On the fourth or fifth try, we finally got through to Jordan.

"Hey Neil, how'd your talks go with the two jaybirds?"

"It was a pain in the ass, but I got some intel that will probably suck when added to your fears."

"I don't like that sound. What is it?"

"Turns out their system is so high-tech it records all the scientist movements, even accidental ones. This means that if they accidentally create the best drug around, they can re-create it without the knowledge of the scientist who did the work in the first place."

"That means the data you have, according to Christian, helps us, but it doesn't stop shit. Well, that's just a kick to the nuts, isn't it?" Jordan said it perfectly.

"I have a few ideas, but nothing actionable yet. I'll have someone reach out if we get anywhere. You focus on tracking down the current stashes of drugs. I'll work on the creation of the drug and the cartels. We already have some balls in play on that front."

"Sounds good. I'll touch base as soon as I have something to report. Thanks again, Neil."

As Christian pulled up to the airport, I barely let the car slow as I made my way out. We were running a bit later than expected. I still had some calls to make, and Detroit Metro Airport is famous for delays as well as gate changes. I wanted to make sure I had time to get to my gate, sit down, and get things done.

The security line was as expected, a bit hectic mixed with plenty of people who had never flown before. It's those same people who packed a backpack full of water, you know, cases of it. One person literally had a camelback full of something with them as they walked through security. At some point the fact that I don't just start smacking people is a miracle. It's not like these things are new. It has been almost ten years since many of them have been in place. Come on, people, get your shit together for the rest of us.

Rant over, I was through security looking for a coffee. I'm not in the mood for the usual airport national brands. I need some bar coffee, something that's been sitting there for a bit; I know it's a weird habit. I found an empty place, just the bartender sitting there.

"Hey bartender, how's your afternoon going?"

"It's pretty much night now, but it's going good, sir. What can I get for you?"

"I'll take a coffee in a to-go cup, with two shots of tequila in it, some limes, and a bit of ice."

"Wait . . . what? Do you want me to make some fresh coffee? All I have is what was left over from the morning shift. God only knows when that was brewed."

"No, that'll be perfect. I like coffee to be cold and a bit flat."

"Hey man, it's your dollar. You got it. Where are you flying to?"

"I'm heading to New Mexico. Originally for vacation, but it turned into work. I don't want to get into it. Have a great night, bro. Keep the change."

I ended up tipping the guy almost twenty bucks. It was twenty-one and change, I had two twenties and just went on my way. I was so happy to get me a drink on the road after a shit day; I didn't care at that point. The next step was to get TJ on the trail of Gaines's sister and find out where she is. The last detail I got from Gaines on this was that she was doing research in Central or South America somewhere. I feel she may be one of the few people that can help us dismantle this network.

After a quick message to get TJ started on that project, I reached out to Ken to see if we've heard anything back from the guys keeping an eye on Maria. What their ETA is to Mexico, and what type of local support they think they can rally.

"Hey Ken, how's everything going back at the office? Anyone burn anything down yet?"

"Despite our best efforts, this bitch is still standing," Ken said, laughing.

"What time do the guys get into Mexico? The ones giving support to Erin and Maria?"

"They should have already landed by now, set up shop, and established some form of base camp. The two of them are pretty resourceful. They had people working locally for them so that they could hit the ground running when they arrived."

"That kind of answers my next question. Do they have any support down there if this goes sideways?"

"They have a few options. They can bribe the local police with more than what the cartels are, find a rival gang to help you, or do it the old-fashioned way. With a small team, in and out."

"I know they're in good hands. I just want to make sure; you know me. I have a project I sent to TJ if you can help, though I might be staying in the airport when I get to Albuquerque."

"What do you have in mind?"

"If he's able to track her down, book me a flight. Even if I can't get any clothes, I'll just find some crap and a duffel bag at the airport and head down to wherever I need to go. I've always got my passport on me anyway."

"We can do that, make sure you get the Wi-Fi on the plane. If we book a flight I'll email you, so you're aware. Any idea where you're headed?"

"South of the border? Farther south than Maria, that's all I know."

"All right, well, good thing you've got the scruff and long hair going, you'll look like a gringo drug dealer wherever you head."

"Hysterical, Ken. They're calling my flight. Hopefully we can pull this off."

On the plane, I was fighting the urge to sleep, since I had to check if TJ and Ken were able to track down Gaines's sister, Susie. I asked the flight attendant if she could wake me when we were thirty minutes from decent to ensure I had plenty of time to check everything. It's a good thing I did because the mix of the long day, drink in my belly, and soft tunes in my ears put me to sleep.

When she woke me, I flipped open my laptop, hopped on the Wi-Fi. Which merely took me forty dollars, my mother's maiden name, the promise of my second born child, and watching twelve ads for geriatric aspirin. I didn't even realize there was geriatric aspirin. I figured it was the same, maybe a different dosage, good thing for those ads.

All kidding aside, I had lots of emails to sift through, but the most important one was from Ken with my flight information. It looks like I'm heading to Buenos Aires, Argentina. This is going to be a long-ass day. It seems like I have to backtrack to Dallas, then down to Rio, then to Buenos Aires. At least I'll have plenty of airports to shop in along the way. This is going to give me flashbacks to the day I double backed and flew all over to get to Mexico for the Cappelano case.

Oh well, fuck it, flying long trips without luggage is a Baggio specialty!

12

WHEN YOU SPEND AS MUCH MONEY AS I DO FOR MY COMPANY AND TRAVEL FOR BUSINESS, PLATINUM AMEX COMES IN HANDY

I could have spent thirty pages describing what life was like in the air and stuck in airports for the better part of thirty hours. Instead, I will give you an exercise to do that I think might encompass the past thirty hours of my life. I need you to sit down on the floor right now. Go ahead and do it; I'll wait. Then I need you to roll back onto your hips, put your feet over your head, and hold that position until you lose the feeling in your ass. That sums up my trip so far. It has been glorious.

I was able to get a duffel bag for the low price of three hundred dollars. In airport prices, that's a steal, but otherwise a punch to the gut. As for clothes, I was able to get the necessities. Some toiletries and some basics, but I will have to find something local when I get there so I can finish filling the bag with clothes and not look like a tourist.

It feels odd carrying around a duffel bag half full. It almost makes me feel like one of those savages that carry their gallon of milk in a plastic bag. It has a handle already; come on, people. Off the plane, I was able to call Ken and check in finally. They had booked me a hotel close to where they think she is working, so I won't have to rent a car to get around.

"Ken, for the love of all that is holy, I don't think I'm coming home. I've been on the plane for so long I forgot who I am and what the hell we're doing."

"Well, I have some good news for you on a few different fronts. Maria and Erin made contact with Tony. They are hanging with El Jefe still, making plans to run on Gaines's stash if we can't corral it ourselves. Apparently even El Jefe has some standards. He deals with traditional drugs and guns only."

"You mean like weed and cocaine, none of that synthetic stuff? A cartel leader with a heart of gold."

"No, he said it's bad for business if your customers are always dying. He's still coldhearted, just smart."

"Ken, that's messed up. I mean, it's smart as shit, but still messed up. I saw all the info you sent over on Susie. The dossier that TJ put together with Gaines Chemical's offices out here and where I can find her more than likely."

"You mean TJ pulling her credit card purchases so you can bump into her drinking coffee every morning? Yeah, TJ is always good at that."

We continued for a few minutes until I found a cabdriver and gave him my hotel info. It wasn't a long drive from the airport to the hotel, but it was a beautiful one. One thing I learned from the cabdriver is that almost a quarter of the country's population lives in Buenos Aires. It's a gorgeous port city known for being a hub of precious metals. At least that's what the literature says in the back of the cab. This guy who's speaking to me in broken English is saying the same.

Hopefully, I have better help from the hotel concierge when I arrive. I need some things to present myself better down here. I can get away with dressing like a bum when I'm in Santa Fe and Detroit because of where I am or my reputation. Down here, I need to make somewhat of an impression. I need to dress the part. As I made my way into the hotel, the front desk person spoke to me in Spanish. I knew enough from dating Maria to realize I'm lost and get him to speak English.

"Hello, sir. Is this your first time staying with us?"

"Yes it is, thank you for speaking English. I don't speak Spanish very well." If at all.

"Sir, may I ask you to name a place where I can go shopping to grab some clothes? This trip is for business, and it is impromptu a bit."

"Impromptu?"

"Emergency. Didn't pack enough."

"Ah, I see. Yes, I will get you a list of shops close that can help you. Just as soon as we're done here. Only a few are open this late, though." It's ten o'clock here.

"Thank you."

As he finished checking me in, he called a few places, speaking faster in Spanish then I've ever spoken in English. He then told me that he has a friend that will wait for me at his shop past close to take care of me. He did say to tip the man, and he didn't mince words. I'm assuming he noticed the credit card I used for the room and judged from there. When you spend as much money as I do for my company and travel for business, Platinum AMEX comes in handy. Just look at how this moment in my life changed from the perception this guy had from the card. It's crazy, but it works.

The room at the Algodon Mansion was beautiful. Ken knows me too well; after all that travel, he knows I need a place to stay that isn't going to suck. This is a little over the top, but then again, we have so many miles from flying people all over, this room might be free for all I know. The room was more like a condo. It even put the place to shame that I rented in Santa Fe, which isn't saying much. The overall room was detailed in white linens and rich mahogany wood.

Enough about the room, I had to throw my stuff in and head to the shop up the street. I was to meet with a man named Gaston. The shop was just what one might expect on a trip like this. I was in my own version of pretty dude. Insert early '90s movie reference. I am not going to hang out with Richard Geer, though, in a hotel room. I mean, I'll drive a Lotus with him, but not the hotel suite.

Gaston was terrific: he had a flair of the dramatic; great taste, as he should in his job; and he took great care of me. What I expected to be a short stay, in and out, turned into two hours of building a new wardrobe as well as a suitcase. The style we are going for this trip is Spanish J. Crew with a flair of blue Armani suits. It's all custom from this local shop that I can't pronounce. Even the jeans are amazing, the softest things I've ever worn.

Back at the hotel, I had a new wardrobe to last me the week. With dry cleaning, I could make it for two weeks. With a mix of jeans, two suits, and some blazers, I'll be good to go. I even got set up with some shoes and socks; I know I got the full pretty dude treatment. If only

Maria could be down here to help me out, there is no way I'm going to be able to do this cleanly with the language barrier.

Well, I got here, I know where Susie works, I know she speaks English and so does the majority of her company. I just need to get there and figure the rest out as I go. Only the morning will tell how the day will go. For now, I'm going to try to get some sleep. This jet-lagged body and burned eyes are all from flying.

The first thing, though, is a long, hot shower with some real water pressure. As I turned the water on, I turned the knob with anticipation customarily saved for a young man's senior prom. Hearing the water come rushing out with vigor in strength and heat awoke the hair on my neck. This was a shower I had been waiting for. It's been more than a week, and this day's travel has been brutal.

Through the day's flights, I had plenty of time to review files, exchange emails, and sift through as many obscure documents as I should. Judging by the information I had at my fingertips, Gaines was using his current head of security Steve "the Tracer" Hornsby.

The information that the FBI, DEA, and our team was able to piece together pegs this man as Bryan's assistant head of security that worked for Gaines Chemical. He took over for Bryan when he was arrested and later murdered by Erin. Tracer, for short, is ex-military with a connection sheet longer than mine. He's in his late fifties but keeps himself in peak physical condition. He was an army ranger, then worked in private security overseas doing black ops where the government didn't want to get blamed.

Gaines and Bryan hired him to be their connection to the seedy underworld, where he has links. It's a smart play if you need an entrance into a party; just buy an invite. It's through these connections, his skill as an operator that has allowed Gaines to grow his drug trade while behind bars. Tracer doesn't need daily reminders of the goal; he knows what needs to be done, and he executes.

He's been digitally off the grid for nearly a decade. Trying to track him is like trying to digitally track your ninety-year-old grandma who doesn't own a cell phone or have a computer. That shits hard as hell. Other than some grainy security photos from some port deals he did in Toledo and his personnel file. Which is mainly bullshit anyway, we have nothing to go on. It's just old military records, then less and less info as each year passes until it fades to nothing but stories.

Out of the shower and sitting on the bed, in nothing but a towel, I plugged my phone in, set the alarm, and closed my eyes. I gave in to the exhaustion, knowing I might not be able to sleep if I didn't. I guess we'll see what the morning brings.

13

VACATION IS BACK ON!

Ken is going to be the best man at my wedding if I ever get married. He is the ultimate wingman. I wish I could explain to you what this asshole did to me in Buenos Aires. Not only did he get me a gorgeous hotel, but he also got me a masseuse who specialized in hooking. Get your mind out of the gutter, you crazy ass; he didn't do any of that. What he did do is surprise me with a wake-up call in case I forgot, along with a ride to Gaines Chemical. The best part is that my driver speaks Spanish.

"Neil, wake up. Neil, wake up. You're going to be late."

"Holy shit, who's in here? I'm naked . . . Maria, what the fuck!"

"Hey, honey! Surprise! Ken thought it would be a cool surprise to get me down here."

"Heck, yes, this is awesome. Vacation is back on! What happened with El Jefe?"

"I'll tell you about it later. He was a breeze, easygoing dude. He was so thankful you got Cappelano out of the barrio, he said he owes you. Anything we need, just call. I've got his number."

"Where did Erin end up? Did she head back to Santa Fe for the gallery lead, or did she go somewhere else?"

"I'm pretty sure she went back to Santa Fe, but the only way to check up on her is to call Father Roberts at this point. We don't have much else. We're in this case regardless at this point."

"That's a good point, Maria. I just wish it were under a different pretense."

"You should know more than anyone. You can't pick your cases, and you can't pick the way you get drawn into them. All you can do is crush the way you close them. Get off your butt, get dressed, and let's get down to Gaines's offices down here and see what we can get out of Susie."

"Do we even know if she's there?"

"According to TJ and her calendar, she's supposed to be at the office all day. We should be able to get in. Whether she wants to see us, that's another thing."

It took us about forty minutes to get going, since I hadn't seen Maria for a while and we finally   had some alone time. Not to mention, I was already naked, so we took advantage of the situation. Once Maria saw me dressed up for the meeting, she almost jumped me again. She doesn't get to see me dressed up that much, since there's rarely an opportunity for me to do so.

Maria was dressed in a little black business outfit with a skirt and jacket. I was dressed in a blue suit jacket, new jeans with dress shoes, and a white dress shirt. For me, I was damn near a tuxedo. It felt weird walking down the street to grab a ride over to Gaines Chemical dressed to the nines with Maria. Typically, when we're on a case, we are dressed much more functionally.

REQUIEM

On our way over to the offices to try and grab Susie off guard, Maria filled me in on El Jefe. She said he made one attempt with the girls. Throwing an extravagant party the first night going overboard to flirt with and get them to hang with him privately. When they told him that's not why they were there, he dropped it, took some other girls up to his room, and said he'd see them in the morning.

Over breakfast, they talked through everything and figured out how Gaines's new drug was going to be bad for business for him and other cartels. He was going to reach out to other families and see if he can get them on board to see the threat that Requiem is to business.

Pulling up to Gaines Chemical, we were happy we dressed up since we were casual compared to the average person walking around in there. Come to think of it, the way most people were dressed, even on the street, we were a bit underdressed. I feel like we walked into a fashion catalog. Did I miss something when I got off the plane, or in school about Argentina? Is it a fashion capital?

"Maria, is it just me, or are you suddenly feeling underdressed for the day? Shit for life in general right now?"

"Speak for yourself; these are my people. I'm in my element. You are usually dressed causally for even a gym teacher." Maria is harsh but true.

"It's not like I'm rocking gym shorts every day; that was a bit uncalled for. Let's find Susie's office and then talk shit later."

"Sounds good."

Maria is going to have to do the majority of the talking, since I'm going to struggle with the language barrier most of this trip. What I lack understanding Spanish, I can make up for in observing body language and mannerisms. For example, I can already tell the woman behind the desk that Maria is talking to is going to be helpful because she isn't standoffish. Her body language is open, jovial, and she's gesturing to Maria that she can help her with what she needs.

Maria was over there for a good fifteen minutes talking to her; I think they were becoming best friends. After a while, I started messing around on my phone, checking emails and sifting through some of the dossiers that TJ had sent to give me. I used it as some insight into what we were about to get into.

"Hey Maria, were you two becoming best friends over there?"

"A little bit. She said Susie is always helpful to law enforcement. She has kept track of the drama of her brother and told them if anyone from the States ever came down for her, simply interrupt her schedule and give them time. She wants to be as helpful as she can be."

"I know she and her brother Jason aren't best friends by any imagination, but damn, she is really working the other side of this. Trying to save her family's company. I can respect that."

"She's doing it from across countries, though, so we'll see how helpful she can be."

Maria has a point; how helpful can she be while working halfway around the world from the epicenter of the company and from the issues her brother is creating? As a global company, you would think she would have come home by now to help fix the problems.

"Does this mean we are just waiting to be brought upstairs?"

"Yes, Neil, wait a minute. They said it'd be about ten minutes, but she'll make time for us. She's just finishing up a meeting."

After some back and forth, banter, and small talk, a beautiful man who made me question everything I know about fashion walked up to us. He asked us to follow him, which made me feel uncomfortable. I mean someone that pretty should be in a museum or on a runway, not working at a chemical company. I guess I've just been around the dark and dreary Detroit skyline and hardened people too much. Where we wear hooded sweatshirts and hats pulled over our heads. Down here, they are dress to kill and are fit to go with it.

"Ms. Gaines will be with you shortly. Do either of you need something to drink while you wait?" said the pretty man.

"We'll take two glasses of water, thank you very much," Maria said softly.

"This is one hell of a room. It's in the middle of everything, surrounded by glass. I almost feel like an animal in a cage on display."

"Neil, cut it out. It's just your average corporate conference room. Designed for an open feel. They want the space to feel wide open, as opposed to closed off and sheltered spaces. It inspires creativity and teamwork."

"Okay; I still feel out of place here. You may feel in your element, but don't forget one major thing, maybe two."

"What's that, Neil?"

"I don't speak the language or speak fashion. I'm trying, but it's going to be a struggle."

"Okay, fair point. You're out of our element. Good thing Ken sent me down," she said with a smile.

"I'd figure it out, but it would be a struggle, that's for sure."

We were continuing our witty banter back and forth. The assistant came back and dropped off the water. Shortly after that, Ms. Susie Gaines came walking in. She was what one might expect from a powerful woman worth billions who also happens to be brilliant. Just kidding; you couldn't pick her out of a lineup if you tried. She was as normal as you could expect. I felt more comfortable with her, the second she walked in, than anyone else since I stepped off the plane.

"Mr. Baggio and Ms. Garcia. My staff told me that you came down all this way to speak to me about my brother, Jason. I'm a bit worried and confused. Isn't he already behind bars?"

"He is, Ms. Gaines. However, he has been a busy inmate during that time frame. We have some questions to ask you about your company and some of its processes. First, let me ask you a pressing question."

"Sure thing, Mr. Baggio. And call me Susie."

"Call me Neil and her Maria. My question is this: how do you function around so many beautiful people? Its crazy down here. Is it like this everywhere in Buenos Aires and Argentina?"

"Neil! I'm so sorry, Susie. My partner lacks tact sometimes."

"It's perfectly fine. I think it's nuts too. It can be a bit crazy at times, but after a while, they all blend in together. Like a big, beautiful person tapestry. I don't think that's why you flew down here, though."

"No, but I do think you are this far down here to be as far from your brother as possible. That's part of my follow-up; we'll get to it in a bit." I'm fishing as usual.

"Neil, if you're going to keep acting like this, I'll make you wait outside."

"Ms. Garcia . . . Maria. He's fine. Compared to my brother, he's a teddy bear. By any chance, are you the guy who slugged him in his office?"

"I was, but I'm a little reluctant to tell you that. Unless it helps get us information out of you."

"It most definitely does. I can't stand him. Don't get me wrong, he helped build this company to the great state that it is, but he's also going to be the reason it's toppled to the ground." Susie was getting agitated.

"We have questions about the system you designed for recording the researchers and their processes when designing new drugs. Jason found a new drug that's going to be used for illicit purposes. We need to know if there are any fail-safes to remove it from the system."

"You're talking about Requiem, aren't you?" What the fuck?

"How do you know about that?" Maria was shocked too.

"I designed it, took me years, but cracked it. I think it's some of my best work. I just didn't think it would be used for that purpose. That's what brought me down here. I thought I removed it from the system, but Jason found a way to replicate it."

Susie went on for a solid hour, and we followed up with questions like first graders asking our teacher how the sun works. Maria and I were so taken aback when she told us that she designed it, she was the creator, it made a bit more sense why we couldn't connect the dots on the scientist. She was the originator; Jason was just using someone to re-create her process.

Susie explained that she was trying to find a way to create a drug that could be used to wean someone off of traditional heroin and meth. The drug was never intended to be used in the manner her brother proposed. The reason she destroyed her research and moved to the Buenos Aires office to grow it to what we see today is because of that drug.

"You understand, Susie, that running away from the problem didn't solve anything. It just allowed your brother to continue to work in the shadows and grow his holdings in the streets. Now we have Requiem stockpiles all over the United States, and we are trying to track them down before he starts distributing to dealers."

"In hindsight, I should have stepped up more, done more, but right now there isn't much I can do. Jason still has control of the board. I'm just a minority shareholder. A figurehead, essentially."

"You still never answered our question about any fail-safe. Are there any? Is there any way for us to destroy the history of this drug, delete it from the system?" Maria was starting to reach now.

"I wish I could tell you yes, but he was able to replicate my process without my notes. That means he already has it. I don't think he would risk having only one copy for such a valuable drug. I guarantee he already has it in FDA drug trials as well. He's going to sell it legally and illegally. He's a smart businessman. He won't leave any dollar on the table, even if he's in prison."

"Are you willing to help us, willing to come back to the States and work with us to stop your brother?"

"Neil, I'm willing to help you in any way I can, but I'm not leaving here. I'm not leaving the work I'm doing in Argentina. You can call me selfish, you can call me a coward, but I have also seen what Jason can do firsthand. I'll stay on the other side of the globe for now." She's got a point.

"I guess, for now, that's all we have. If you think of any other way to get that process removed from the system, please let us know. Here are our cards. Call us if you have any other info." Maria handed her our cards.

"Thank you for taking out so much time from your day to speak to us. I'm sure you were busy."

"I've been waiting for this day to come for some time now." Susie looked spent.

"We'll see our way out. Thanks again."

We were there for hours, talked to Susie, and I feel like we got nowhere. Yes, we have some insight into Gaines and his plans, but we are no closer to stopping him. No closer to having a solution to stopping Requiem. Where do we go from here? Do we head back to Santa Fe, sit on some art galleries for no reason? Do we sit out here? I guess only time will tell. For now, we head back to the hotel and regroup.

14

HE KEPT CURSING A BIT UNDER HIS BREATH, MAD THAT WE WERE RUINING THE BEANS HE HAD ROASTED TO PERFECTION EARLIER IN THE DAY.

I have to say I'm not sure what I thought we would get out of that meeting with Susie. It's hard getting someone to admit they made the drug, then tell us there's nothing we can do. While simultaneously telling us they aren't doing shit to help. That was not what we expected. Having the door shut on your face, you can handle it. In our line of work, you're used to it. Being told a massive pile of dog shit lies, but this was a curveball of crazy proportions.

Back at the hotel, it was still early in the afternoon, barely lunchtime, and the two of us were just shocked. We just stared at each other in disbelief. It wasn't that we didn't get much out of the meeting; it was how it happened.

"Neil, am I the only one who's at a loss for what happened back there?"

"You mean the willingness to be open, tell us anything but do nothing attitude she had. I think we alluded to it before the meeting. She is hiding halfway around the world for a reason. I guess we shouldn't have been surprised."

"That she developed the drug herself was a bit of a curveball. Holy shit, that was forthright. She does seem too sweet a human being to do anything crazy."

"I feel like we could be setting ourselves up, in the long run, to get burned. It could be my paranoia coming in from Cappelano destroying my mentality over the years."

We didn't make it out of the lobby, just sitting there talking in utter disbelief. It was then that the concierge who had helped me last night noticed us. He made his way over to see if he could help. Unless he has a way to stop an international syndicate from dispersing a drug, I'd say nope.

"Hello, Mr. Baggio, how are you this afternoon? Can I direct you somewhere for lunch?"

"Maria, what do you say?"

Instead of responding to me, Maria and the gentleman spoke in Spanish around me for a few minutes. Laughing and joking, I feel this is going to be a common trend while we're doing here. I'm glad Ken sent her here, I know I keep repeating it. It's true, this is her element. The people, the culture, and fashion. They all fit her personality to perfection.

"Okay, Neil. After speaking to your friend here, I think I know what we can do for the rest of the day. Since neither of us has return flights yet or any idea what the next step is, let's take the day to rest. We're in a beautiful city in Argentina."

"I'm game. What do you have in mind? I can always go for blowing off a little steam. One thing I do ask is that we find a place for a little snack, some coffee, and some—"

"Tequila and limes?"

"You guessed it."

Maria took me to a plaza a short walk from the hotel. We were able to find a café that curiously served me a café over ice, with limes. Once we asked him for a place to find tequila, he smiled and understood. Maria noted that he kept cursing a bit under his breath, mad that we were ruining the beans he had roasted to perfection earlier in the day. Once he had informed her that we needed some tequila for our concoction, he wasn't nearly as mad.

With a drink in hand, we continued to walk down the street through the plaza talking about the case. I started at the top and began to work my way down the row, with Gaines and his sister. Something isn't sitting right with that combination, especially Susie. She is too polished and intelligent to be an innocent bystander in all of this. One view is that she is hiding out on the other side of the world from her brother and the damage he is doing. The different perception is that she has put herself in this position to be insulated from her brother to make it look as if he is doing the biding himself.

His ego is so big it wouldn't be that hard for her simply to mention an idea to him and have him run with it. Though it was her plan all along, he would take credit. Even if she did the majority of the work, since he would want the credit and the status that came with it. Also, if it means prison time, he wants the street credit.

"Maria, I'm still hung up on the relationship with Susie and her brother, Jason. The way she openly admitted to creating the drug herself, then making it sound like Jason was smart enough to reverse engineer the drug without her help. I don't know. It doesn't add up."

"I understand what you're saying. I'm hung up on it too. I just don't know how far I'm willing to go."

"What do you mean?"

"Well, how far did Susie go? What is she willing to do? Is she really the one driving this ship but letting her brother take the credit and the fall? I'm not sure if she's that vindictive."

"I guess I can see that, Maria. We only have a small sample to go off of. I would love another opportunity to try to talk to her. Maybe another run at her might give us some more intel."

"Hey, why don't you check in on Erin, see if she has anything going? In the meantime, I'll take a moment and check in with Susie's office, see if we can touch base with her tonight."

"Sounds good." Maria gave me that old ten-four look.

On the phone, I called Susie's office, though I lacked the Spanish-language connection that Maria had. Susie and I seemed to have a bit more of a normal connection that Maria and most of the fashion-driven workers lacked. I'm hoping that comfort level might help me get through to her. The front desk person spoke English pleasantly, not surprising for a global company. Put me through quickly to Susie's desk, also not surprising with how forthcoming they were earlier.

"Hello, Susie, its Neil Baggio from earlier."

"Yes, Neil, how's your afternoon in Buenos Aires going? Are you calling for some sightseeing ideas?"

"Sort of. I was calling to see if you would like to meet up for drinks. I'd say a fancy dinner, but let's be honest, you and I need a burger and a beer."

"Okay, now you're speaking my language. Leave your angry partner out of it and you've got yourself a date," Susie said playfully.

I know what you might be thinking. Don't forget it wasn't that long ago when Maria went to a drug cartels villa in Mexico with me states away. I believe Maria can survive with me going out for a beer and a burger with the burger-driven Susie Gaines.

"Sounds good. Since you know the area better than I do, just text me an address and a time. I'll make it work. I'm staying at the Algodon if you want to keep it close. Otherwise I can grab a car."

"Sounds good. I'll find a place for us to meet."

That call went as I had hoped. Though I might not get anything out of it, the more intel, the better. It's about gathering pieces of information I can stack on top of the ones we have, to build a better picture. As I got off, though, I noticed Maria was still on the phone. I might as well check in with Ken, see how the office is doing.

"Hey Neil, how's Buenos Aires? Did you enjoy your wake-up call?"

"Yeah, Ken, well done, brother. You know me too well. I wouldn't have survived properly without help."

"You needed a translator of sorts, and with your vacation being ruined, I figured it was the perfect timing." He has a point.

"It was much appreciated. How is everything going on back there? How is the case in Miami going with Terrance and Christian? Are they making any headway for your friend? Aren't they helping track a stalker on tour for a musician or some shit?"

"Yeah, they are. Christian thinks they'll have it tied up soon. They are pretty sure they know who it is. They just need to corner them and get the proper evidence to lock it in."

"They're some of the best guys we have. I wouldn't mind getting them on this case to figure it out."

"I know, Neil. Speaking of which, any new leads? There's nothing up here. TJ has an idea of some crazy shit. He and his team want to try, but he won't talk about it. He doesn't want to jinx it. The only reason I know about it is that he took a quarter of his team off of other projects to work on some private shit. He won't tell anyone, but he swears it's for Requiem. No reason not to trust him or his process. Kind of like you and crashing cars or shooting fish tanks."

"Aren't you the comedian, Ken. As for leads down here so far, all I can tell you is that almost everyone is a supermodel with impeccable fashion sense. Susie is hiding something, and Maria fits in perfectly down here."

"I can see Maria fitting in perfectly down there. She always looks impeccable; she has enough style for the two of you. Especially since you have none."

"Fair enough. Let me know if Terrance and Christian free up. I have an idea I might use them for. It's one of those crazy long shots they are perfect for."

"Will do. I can reach out and put the pedal to the metal on the case. Also, I'll let you know if TJ's crazy voodoo pays off."

"Thanks, Ken. I'll talk to you later."

As usual, we have a team working on different solutions to one big problem and right now nothing to show for it. Hopefully one of them will pan out. It seems to be our MO as of late. We look to do the unthinkable because we have a group of people that believe we can. We keep grinding where others would give up. When an advantageous moment arrives or the piece of missing intel is presented, we are ready for it.

"Hey Maria, did you get anything out of Erin? Ken gave me some hope but no details, and Susie wants to meet up for a beer but without you." Maria rolled her eyes.

"Got it on Susie. As for Erin, she's back in Santa Fe, working on a few leads. The biggest one is Choike's gallery; she has intel that puts Marie in town soon. She is going to work with Father Roberts to have him make an approach on her. I agree it might be the best play to get some intel."

"I can see that. Is Father Roberts on board? He seemed open to it when we were talking about it last week, just wondering overall. Technically he has a parish to get back to soon, as well."

"I know; I told her she needs to make a move ASAP. I guess we will see. We also need to see how long we are going to be in Argentina." Maria has a point.

"By the way, where are we headed? We've been walking most of the afternoon but haven't gotten anywhere."

"That was kind of the point. Just to walk around, get you out of your head a bit, and allow you to think. It got us to a follow-up meeting tonight with Susie, and you even have a few other things working in that head of yours. Plus we made it to the botanical gardens. Somewhere for the two of us to walk around and enjoy some time together. Then we can get you back to wherever you need to be for your beer with Susie."

"Sounds good. For a minute, I wouldn't mind just spending some quiet time with you, Maria."

As we walked around the gardens lost in the beauty, it was the rare moment that the two of us got to share in quiet. The distractions were nonexistent. It was something we both weren't used to. We kept looking to each other, looking for approval that it was okay, that we were sharing this moment together. As we walked around, just starting to settle in, my phone went off with a text from Susie with a time and location of where to meet. With where we were, and where I needed to be and when, we would need to leave shortly, meaning our quiet time was about to end.

"Well, it was fun while it lasted," Maria chimed in.

"It was a great day; let's not act like we don't have the rest of the night."

"Well, let's hope Susie doesn't make a play to steal you from me." Maria was getting a bit defensive.

"Maria, you know I wouldn't do anything to mess us up. Why are you getting worked up?"

"I have no idea. I just am, so let's just deal with it."

That's how we abruptly ended our walk through the gardens. It went from a picturesque late afternoon, where we were finally settling in, enjoying the peace, but life had a way of reminding us it was time to wake up.

15

YOU CAN SEE WHERE I AM STRUGGLING WITH THE WAY SHE KEEPS DESCRIBING HER ROLE IN THIS.

This evening is going to end up with me getting screwed by two women, and it's not going to be enjoyed. I can already tell the night is going to blow up in my face no matter what I do. I just have that feeling, with the way Maria is ignoring me on the cab ride over to the bar that I'm meeting Susie at, to the vibe I got on the phone from Susie. Sometimes you just know you're playing with fire while covered in gasoline, and you know it's only a matter of time before your ass is on fire.

"Neil, it looks like we're here. A place called the Burger Joint is what you said you need to look for. There are small places all over. I'll probably have the cabdriver go around the block and have me grab something, and then I'll head back to the hotel. I'll meet you back there. I don't see any beer, but who knows?" Maria was still gritting her teeth.

"I'll be on my best behavior, Maria. I'll message you as soon as we're done." I gave her a kiss as I exited the cab.

"There's a good chance I pass out quickly, playing catch-up from a long flight. Just be safe. I'm not worried about you, it's her and your lack of Spanish I'm worried about." Good points.

"Good night, Maria. Get some rest. Maybe I'll try and get Susie drunk then and get her to talk. If I bring her back to the hotel, you better be ready to party," I said with a smile.

"Shut up, Neil. Just try not to crash any cars for a change." Fair point.

"Duly noted. I can't make any promises. Did you see how narrow the streets are down here?"

"Good-bye, Neil."

As I closed the door and walked away, I noticed Maria was smiling for a change. It took some doing, but I did get her head out of the gutter. Eventually she was back to some semblance of calm. It's hard doing what we do, but we have to remember it's the only way our lives work. Blind trust, that is. I'm not sure what or how I'm going to get this lady to open up, but it's going to take something unique, that's for sure.

It seemed as though I arrived before her. I guess I'll have to make myself comfortable. Sitting at a table in the plaza looking around, I noticed there were bars all over, plenty of places to choose from. You had the high end, low end, and between. Not bad; we should be able to walk around and find a vibe that fits us quite quickly. I may have failed to mention when I arrived, a detail that caught me off guard as well. Something brought up in geography class as a kid. Seasons south of the equator are the opposite of ours is, north side.

Right now, we are in the middle of their winter. Though the weather is still beautiful in Detroit, it's sixty during the day and a crisp fifty at night. Here she is, Ms. Susie Gaines, and she is dressed to kill. Not the same business, nerd look she had going on earlier.

"Sorry for making you wait a little bit, Neil, but I had to get changed and clean up a bit after working all day."

"It's not surprising. After a long day, wanting to clean up, feel good, and dress up, I can relate to that. This is the most dressed up I've been since a wedding."

"Well, you look great. Thank you for keeping it between just us. Your partner seemed to play it a little rough with me. I wasn't in the mood for good cop, jealous cop." Maria has nothing to be jealous of, missy.

"I can understand. I just wanted to follow up in a more calm environment. There is a lot to uncover in this case. Gaines Chemical is a global company with a huge reach whose leadership is tied to some dark stuff. Local street gangs in Detroit, across the country, stashes of drugs being tied to your labs and your brother. There's a lot to figure out. Then you dropped the knowledge on us that you designed the drug in the first place."

"I realized, in hindsight, I didn't portray myself quite as well as I should have. I left too much open-ended and to your imagination. I was very pleased when you called, so we could talk, get to know each other, and see if I could calm those fears and help you figure this out and get those drugs off the street. The last thing I want is my family's company being dragged through the mud."

Part of me didn't believe what she was selling, for a myriad of reasons. The biggest one was the consistent soft touching of my knee, hand, and shoulder she was doing as we talked. We hadn't even made it inside yet, and she was shamelessly flirting. I think she believes I'm that shallow. She's used to being underestimated and having the ability to control the men around her. Whether it's through being smart or powerful when she needs to be.

When we met here earlier in the day, she had on glasses, her hair pulled back, gray slacks, and a blouse. She was wearing flat shoes, a lab coat, and looked business all the way. Right now she is wearing Louboutin heels, a stunning white dress with her hair done, and what I can only assume are contacts.

"Well, let's start fresh, enjoy a good burger, then walk around and find a place for a drink, maybe some karaoke?"

"Neil Baggio, are you going to serenade me?" Nope, but I am going to con you.

"Depends how well you play your cards. Could be Sinatra, could be Bolton, or it could be Rick Astley," I said, smiling.

"Your reputation precedes you very well," Susie said with a smile.

As we walked up to the restaurant to order, she leaned into me, grabbing hold of my arm. Toward the top, just like Maria likes to do. If I were single, I would be all over the playful nature of what she's doing right now. As we finished ordering out food and sat down, I took a moment to excuse myself to the bathroom, to try and call Maria. Come on, Maria, pick up, come on. The phone kept ringing, but no answer. I guess I'll shoot her a quick text. Okay, I've been in here for a few minutes, no reply from Maria; any longer and it's going to look weird.

Well, the other side is that I stay in here for a while and make it look like I have an upset stomach. Also known as the dookie defense. Maybe I can get Susie to think I took too long in the bathroom, in turn making her flirtatious behavior down a notch or ten.

"Hey, sorry about that. I called back home to talk to my ex-wife and try and catch our daughter before she went to bed." Huge-ass lie.

"Aw, how old is your daughter?"

"She's in middle school now. Before I know it she's going to be in high school, causing me even more trouble."

"It sounds like you and your ex are still on good terms, including your daughter."

"Yes, we just can't live together. It's a really complicated story."

Maybe this can be the way I get her off me. It's the bring up your ex and act hung up on her. Holy shit, instead of just acting like an adult and telling her to stop, I'm throwing every move my thirteen-year-old self can think of. I really should have called my daughter; she'd probably have better advice for me right now.

"As long as you two make it work for her, that's all that matters. My parents put on an excellent show for the world, but it was different behind closed doors. I think that's where Jason gets it from. He and his wife played to the cameras, put on a great show, but he was a demon in the dark. Jason would make you think he is a saint, doing great for the community while poisoning your water supply." Susie has a point.

"He has that kind of vibe to him, doesn't he. Almost like he might be the kind of person to actually piss on your leg and try to tell you it's raining," I said, laughing.

"He would get mad too if you didn't believe him. Hey, can I ask you a serious question before we get too far along into this night?"

"Sure. What's up?"

"What was my brother's face like when you hit him? Hell, during the whole thing? What was he like when you caught him a second time? He's such an ass, I just always wanted to hit him, I can only imagine what it would have been like."

"Well, you can imagine, I wanted to kill him. He kidnapped my friend, my girlfriend, and had her locked in his office, like a prisoner. He thought it was a game like he was untouchable. I coldcocked the shit out of him, and he fell like a sack of bricks."

"What about that second time, when you finally caught up to him?" She seems really interested in this.

"It was odd; he didn't seem to care. It's almost like he wanted to get caught. Like he was planning on being behind bars." I notice she skipped past the girlfriend part.

"That doesn't surprise me. Jason likes to act like he is always in control, even when he's lost. Even as a kid, he wouldn't accept help, wouldn't tell you when he was lost."

"Earlier, you referred your parents being a different pair behind closed doors. That's where Jason learned a lot. Is there anything we can pull from them, do you think? From their background or experience that might direct us to understand what his next play might be."

"Right now, there is nothing that comes to mind. I will keep that thought front of mind. Since we're done eating and have wasted an hour or so, I'm going to freshen up before we head over to a karaoke bar. There's one right around the corner from here."

"Okay, I'll be out here waiting for you."

I checked my phone, called Maria, and texted her a few different times but to no avail. I even tried the room number but no answer. She must be out cold; then again, I passed out hard core from that same flight. Since I brought up my ex, took forever in the bathroom, and dropped the girlfriend nugget in the story, Susie has finally backed off a bit. Hopefully it stays that way.

As Susie walked out and we made our way down the street, a briskness filled the air. I could sense her about to lean into me once more. To minimize the overall closeness, I gave her my jacket as a gentlemanly gesture. Warming her up for the short walk, we went ahead.

"Thank you, Neil, that was genuinely nice of you. Being the boss down here, most men are scared of me."

"I'm rarely scared of anyone, but that comes from my line of work. Being shot at, chased, and almost killed so many times, you almost become desensitized to fear. I'm not sure it's a healthy thing."

"That's probably a good point, but at least you're aware of it. Then again, your awareness seems to be your strength. Everything I've learned about you was that you're one of the best in your field. Not too dissimilar from me. I specialize in research; you track down the truth. I track down a solution."

"I can see what you're getting at."

I didn't want to play this game, at this point it was getting a bit tiresome, but that's because we were sober and hadn't done anything to lighten the mood. I might have to order shots early and often to get her truth-telling machine at an all-time high. The place was already starting to fill up and I was getting impatient, not the right mix for an evening where I'm supposed to be on my best behavior.

"All right, Susie. Since we've already spent most of the night nursing a couple of waters and some burgers, it's time to play catch-up."

"I'm not sure I know where this is headed. I don't get out much, but game on."

"Bartender. I need four shots of chilled tequila with limes. Tequila on the rocks with lime and whatever else the lady is drinking."

"Just give me the same that he's drinking; let's keep it simple." Damn, she came to prove a point.

"Down the hatch."

As we took the shots, she slammed them back like a pro. You could tell being down here as long as she has there is no issue with her knocking back a crap ton of tequila. It was a chilled special reserve Patrón, but still, some people can't hang. We grabbed our drinks and moved to the edge of the bar, where the lighting was a bit darker as Susie tried to grab a karaoke book slyly.

"Don't think I'm not noticing you grab a karaoke book. If you're going to do it, announce it. Don't do it all shy and sheepish. Come on now, you're a leader of industry, a staple in your own company, and you're going to hide a karaoke book?" Trying to build her up, build her trust.

"Flattery will get you everywhere in this life, Neil. As for the book, fair point. Are you going to sing to me as you promised?"

"I didn't promise I would sing to you: details matter here, Susie. I did say I would sing. However, there's a difference between me singing some James Brown or the Righteous Brothers."

"I got it," she said, laughing.

Back to looking through the book and small talk about the town. Susie was giving me the rundown of how she and the company ended up in Argentina. Specifically, Buenos Aires and the other companies that operate out of there. With it being a port city for South America historically for the trade coming out of the Amazon, it's a place where many companies set up as a center for research and distribution to the world. Even Pfizer has an office down here. You know the one that's famous for that little blue pill.

We spent an hour talking, nursing our first and second rounds of drinks. Slowly letting down our guards. I told her what it was like dealing with the stress of Cappelano, an ex-wife, a daughter, and a failed relationship with Sheila. She spoke of her time growing up as a media tool, more than a child. Her parents were great to the community but allowed the help to raise her and Jason. She feels they grew up disconnected from reality a bit because of their upbringing. I'd have to agree; if your maternal and paternal influences are distant to you, it's hard to have them yourself.

I can't help but feel as though she is framing the story the way she wants me to see it. I'm going to have TJ look into the family history and see if any of the help is still alive to speak to. If we can get some background info on how the kids were raised, it will help frame the story a bit. For now I will have to keep playing the game, keep her talking, and pick out the excellent intel from the bullshit she's hiding it in.

For example, she spent a solid twenty minutes talking about the relationship she has with her brother. Jason. In particular, the drug she created, Requiem, and how she ended up in Argentina. She claims she was researching to find a way to help people hooked on heroin. The problem is she is describing a situation where she tried to cure someone of a stab wound but stabbing them with a smaller knife. That does less damage overall and causes less pain.

That doesn't solve the issue at hand. If she had created a drug that helps stop some of the withdrawal symptoms or side effects, I might believe her. She just created a better version of the drug. You can see where I am struggling with the way she keeps describing her role in this. It caught me off guard when she openly admitted that she is the scientist behind it. Then she explains it in a way that doesn't help at all.

I've met Jason, seen him in action. I can see him operate as an evil henchman. I just don't see him as the mad scientist type. It's even possible to imagine him taking her drug and stealing it. My guess is she wanted to sell it legally as a painkiller, knowing it's going to be addictive as shit. Still, Jason saw it as being profitable on the street quicker.

With the night almost over, winding down, I could see I was wearing her out. I figured it was time to have a bonding moment with her. Build some trust, but not in a sexual way. In more of a flirtatious sense, we had a great night; this was our night in a way. I walked up to the stage and grabbed the mic, had them string the tune, and started singing.

"I've got the world on a string . . ."

16

R-1209.

Last night ended cleaner than I was expecting. I thought she was going to push it, but I was able to play all the right cards in the game of euchre us midwestern kids were playing. We weren't playing poker; it was for much higher stakes than that. If you didn't grow up in a midwestern, especially Michigan family like mine or many others, you might not get that reference. Families have been torn apart, holidays ruined, and rifts started for generations because someone didn't play their cards right.

I remember the feeling I got when I was finally able to go from the kids' table, the fun games, to the big table, where they played for keeps, talked shit, and made people cry. It was my grandmother against the world and me. You laugh, but this was my first lesson in learning how to listen and manipulate through talking and giving people only the information you want them to have.

Waking up back at the hotel next to Maria in the beautiful Buenos Aires hotel. The sun glistening in the room, through the big window, had me feeling for just a moment I was on the vacation I needed. That I wasn't chasing a new mystery drug around the world trying to prevent lives from being ruined. Then Maria woke me, reminded me this shit isn't about fun.

"Neil, why do I have so many missed calls and texts from you last night? Did something happen?"

"I'm obviously here, so that's good. It just started off rocky, but I made it work."

"Did you get any good intel out of her last night?" Wow, she skipped past "Are you okay?"

"Not a ton, but I got a place to start looking. I emailed Ken and TJ last night. I even CCd you on it so that you would be in the loop. I'm having them look into the staff that worked for the Gaines family as they grew up."

"You think there's a lead in there somewhere?"

"I think there's context and truth there. We need truth and direction, and right now we aren't getting much from either Susie or Jason. We need to get it from somewhere."

"That's a good point; it's hard to find any context in this case right now. We are going off of only what we get from them. All of it is presented and skewed with what they want us to see."

"Now you're getting it. Let's get some coffee and a shower in, call the offices, and see where we are going from here. See if we are heading back to Santa Fe today or tomorrow, or where we might be headed."

"Sounds good to me. I'll get the coffee brewing; you get the shower going. Would you like me to bring it in there for you?"

"Sure thing, Maria. What's better than a pretty lady bringing a cup of coffee into the shower for you?"

"I'm sure we can think of a few of them once I get in there. Just make sure not to burn either one of us."

I guess we aren't going to talk about the night. She is going to keep it light. Then again, I didn't ask her shit about El Jefe. I simply asked if she was okay. Like I said before all this started, it comes down to blind trust. Not that the other won't do something they might need to for the case, but that we are in this together, and we aren't as petty or thin-skinned as others. That is not to say other people have it wrong. We just live in an alternate reality. Luckily we live in it together.

I think we should head out of here tomorrow; there isn't much we are going to learn from Susie. She is going to lie and control as much as she can. We can get that over the phone; no need to be down here. We need to be where the drugs are, work with the staff to find out how the drug is getting made. It has to be getting supplied somewhere.

In the shower, water rushing over me and the smell of coffee in the air. It was relaxing as can be until I realized a good twenty minutes had passed. I yelled to Maria, but no answer; tried one more time, still nothing. I guess this shower is over. Luckily I shaved already; hair is clean, long, and shaggy, but clean. I threw a towel on, walked out, and looked at Maria, who was on the phone.

I mouthed to her. "What gives?"

"R-1209." Like that helped.

I'm going to grab my phone and hope there is something from TJ or Ken that might shed light on what the fuck Maria was too busy to come into the . . . Oh, shit. I'm reading the email right now that TJ sent back to Maria, Ken, and me. It looks like Susie has been working with multiple countries to get the legal version of Requiem on the market for years, R-1209. He also found on the applications that it is co-signed by none other than Jason Gaines, the head of Gaines Chemical Company. Either his signature has been forged, or the two of them are playing a con on us from either side of the globe.

With this shit intel dropped in our lap—I say "shit" because it smells like a warm pile—I'd almost prefer waking up to my dogs shitting in my shoes right now. The day started off so promising, and now it's shit. I wonder who Maria is talking to. It doesn't sound like Mike, I know that cadence, plus we aren't getting any help from the FBI on this. Right now Maria is on vacation; this is off book for her. I guess I can just call TJ and get more details; I'll call Ken first and have him conference us in to minimize TJ repeating himself.

"Hey Ken, it's Neil. Did you read that shit yet?"

"Yeah, I'll loop in TJ right now. I'm assuming that's why you're calling me."

"You know me well."

"Hey TJ, its Ken. I have Neil on the line. If he sounds like shit its because he's halfway around the world."

"Cute, Ken. But I sound like shit from singing karaoke with Susie trying to get intel out of her."

"Well, guys, joking aside, the info I sent, as I wrote in the email, is just the tip of the iceberg. It looks like the drug is going to roll out in Detroit in two weeks. They have a big event planned, it's on their internal schedules, and the dates match up with the FDA.

"FUCK! FUCK! FUCK!"

"Neil, is everything okay?"

"No, it's not! FUCK ME!"

"Did you stub your toe or something?" Ken has jokes, as usual; he knows I'm just being overly dramatic.

"I'm supposed to be on vacation drinking C-Fu's."

"What's a C . . ." TJ is lost, not surprising.

"I'll fill you in shortly, TJ. Let's leave Neil to get over this shit news. Email us the rest of the details, and we can figure out where to go from here. Neil, just text me if you want tickets back today or tomorrow."

"Will do, thanks, Ken. FUCK!"

The best part of all of this shit is my car is in New Mexico now. That means I need to fly back there to deal with the case. Then drive the twenty-plus hours across the country back to Detroit to find a way to stop these siblings from slowly tearing down the fabric of our communities with their new designer drug. Well, it looks like Maria is finally off the phone, and she looks pissed.

"Neil, what the hell was all that dramatic bullshit over?"

"I'm on vacation," I said sheepishly.

"Get back in that shower, here is your coffee, reset your shit attitude, and come out with your game face on. I won't talk to you until you're ready to fix this shit the right way. Text Ken and tell him to get us on the next flight out of here. I'll explain more when you get done."

"Where to?"

"New Mexico, you dumb ass. Erin has a lead. Not to mention your car is also there." Maria is on my ass.

Back in the shower, coffee in hand, I started working through what I know and what I need to know. Getting ready for the throwdown,

Maria is going to put on me if I don't come prepared. If Susie thinks we don't know what she's doing, and she is used to being able to control the narrative, we need to find a way to use that, hide someone in plain sight, and gather intel. Clear-minded, caffeinated, and clean, I jumped out of the shower. Getting dressed quickly, to ensure I didn't upset Maria any more than I already had.

"Okay, Neil, are we ready now to get through this?"

"Yes. Sorry for earlier." I was a *putz*; it happens.

"No time for apologies, we need to focus. When Erin and I visited with our friend El Jefe, he set us up with Ms. Choike. She doesn't quite know yet that we know you. We're going to keep it that way."

"Probably for the best."

"Apparently Ms. Choike is still overseas and isn't planning on coming over here. She is still helping Susie with something big in Europe, but we are pretty sure it's a legitimate deal. Just being done with some shady pressure. We are thinking at this point it's the R-1209 distribution rights." Maria was fired up.

"Question: I didn't see it in any of TJ's notes. Did any of us follow up with TJ or our science guy to see if the molecular makeups of Requiem and R-1209 match? What are the differences? If the only difference is the way they give it out, then we are fucked. Let's say they sell Requiem as a powder and R-1209 as a pill. Then they can legally distribute that shit all over the world, then sell it illegally."

"Well, I hadn't gotten that far, but now you ruined my vibe. Thanks, Neil, I was holding it together, but you went and ruined it. You selfish prick, bringing me down to your shit level. You couldn't leave me in the positive vibe I was trying to hang in. It's my vacation, too, asshole." Maria is pissed, but I'm not positive at whom.

"We're both pissed at the Gaines kids, right? Not each other?"

"Yeah. Back to Erin and Choike. She set us up with a contact in Santa Fe that is helping Susie do some marketing event that is supposed to coincide with TJ's schedule. They are going to do a multicity marketing event, and we're trying to get the media package to see what their selling point is. TJ and others are still digging through the applications to see what the purpose is. Still, it looks like it's being sold as a painkiller with minimal side effects and addictiveness."

"A painkiller that works great with less addictive qualities is going to be ultra-addictive. How can no one see this but us?"

"I'm pretty sure they do. They just know they're all going to make bank on this shit." Maria has a point.

We went back and forth for more than an hour when we received a text from Ken. He was telling us to get to the airport. With the flight leaving in two hours, we needed to start packing. Luckily we didn't have much and had barely unpacked. That shit took only about ten minutes. We checked out quickly from this gorgeous hotel, hopped in a cab, left the city, and made our way to the airport, trying to catch a glimpse of the fantastic city we barely got to enjoy. It was at this moment that I realized why I learned those math word problems in grade school. Suppose Neil and Maria spent sixty hours in the air round trip and twenty-six hours in Argentina. How many Cluster-Fucks does Neil need to drink on the plane to keep from losing his shit?

"Neil, we're on the plane, you have a drink in hand, it's first class, you just need to calm down. If you keep gritting your teeth, you're going to get a migraine. Not to mention, this isn't the best look on you. Throw on your headphones, get a little drunk, and try to get some rest. We have plenty of time to work through this shit. Plus you do your best thinking when you drift off on other stuff."

"Good point, I'll try my best. Thanks, Maria. What are you going to do?"

"I'll do some grunt work, see what I can come up with."

"I do have one idea I was working on in the shower earlier."

"Shoot."

"Email Ken, see if we have someone we can get into Gaines Chemical for their marketing event. On that team to roll out the product. Someone we can put front and center in Susie's daily life. She won't look there, she'll be too busy looking over her shoulder."

"I'll get on it."

"I'm going to close my eyes and see if the rat pack and master C-Fu can take the pain away."

The flight was brutal, but have you ever heard of anyone saying they enjoyed flying halfway across the world twice in less than thirty hours? Nope, didn't think so. For the record, I gave you a full thirty hours to think through that answer. There was the amount of time it took me to fly from Buenos Aires back to the Albuquerque airport, and where my car was waiting for Maria and me. That was the only part of this shit trip that didn't suck royally. As I started the car up, heard the engine roar, and cranked up some Trombone Shorty, it just drifted away. Maria didn't even raise an eyebrow, which she usually does when I act like an eighteen-year-old kid in his dad's sports car.

"Neil, now that you have that out of the way, we should go over the big decision you have to make."

"I know it's a rough one. I agree with you on that. Nicolette is the best person for the job. Susie doesn't know her; she fits the bill that Choike would love her if this had to be a longtime gig. However, I don't want to pull her off the case she's working."

"Neil, don't get me wrong. The company she's investigating is shady, dirty, and brutal. This is international. This is lives ruined for generations if we don't do something. Maria, I have a daughter, who's getting older. I have an agent in place working to bring down a sexual predator. This isn't a simple decision to pull her off a cheating husband case."

"I need an answer by the time we get to Santa Fe. We have to get this ball in motion."

Maria's right; she's a pain in my ass right now, but she's right." How am I supposed to look my daughter in the eye with this shit on my conscience? I guess sleeping today is out of the question. I hate the way this vacation is turning out. I may never take another one.

17

IS THIS WHAT IT'S COME TO, NEIL? YOU'RE A BROKEN MAN. YOU ARE TAKING A BATH.

Sometimes you have to do what's right, plain and simple. You have to go after the bigger fish, but don't think I haven't stopped thinking about how I'm going to get this piece of shit asshole. Maybe I'm a bit desensitized from my relationship from Cappelano that I can rationalize a killer quicker than someone like this prick of a human Nicolette was investigating. We had to pull her off; this case is too big. We had her try to leave on good terms. She told them it's a medical emergency, leave of absence bullshit. We even have a tremendous medical letter she gave them to make it believable in hopes that we can get her back in there if this case ends quickly.

I'm not a betting man, but I doubt she's getting back to that case. She is going to be tied to this Gaines case for some time. It just has that long-ass kind of shit case written all over it. Even if we get this part of the case over with, more will come up. Just look at how I got Jason off the street, and I'm still dealing with his ass. The hope is, with the right résumé and favors we'll pull, we can get her in a few levels below where we need her. Then she can shine like she always does and gets into the big show of marketing this drug R-1209.

It's so annoying to keep referring to the numbers and letter combo. At least Requiem has a sweet street name. It's a killer, but the name is sweet. I feel like someone designed an amazing energy drink can, great name, and packaging, but the drink tastes like shit. Yet people still buy it because the marketing is so great.

"Neil, we're almost back to the condo in Santa Fe, and you haven't said a single word. You've just been driving more than a hundred and twenty and jamming to some loud-ass music. I've been very patient with you on this." Maria was talking to me calmly.

"I decided like twenty minutes ago we need to pull Nicolette. I even texted Ken about it." Her calm just ended.

"What is your problem? You have been an asshole since you read that email in Argentina earlier—"

"Say it, say it . . . earlier . . . yesterday. We were on a plane so long it changed days."

"I give up. When we get back, please grab your headphones and go hiking. I'm going to track down Erin."

We pulled into the condo, barely talking. Greeted by Father Roberts with a smile. Asking how the trip was, we both walked by him like he was a ghost. Maria tossed her stuff inside, walked back out and toward downtown, in search of Erin. I, on the other hand, took her advice, changed my clothes, and got ready for a hike in the mountains.

"Neil, what was all that about? Did you two get in a fight?"

"Obviously we got into a bit of a fight. Luckily it's not a relationship one. We're both stressing over the case. I'm not taking it as well as she is. I'm going for a run in the mountains to clear my mind and find out what to do."

"I'll say a prayer for you two. It's a terribly stressful life you lead. I don't know how anyone in your field survives the stress."

"That's the kicker, Father. We don't, we usually cave to it in some way. Off-topic, don't you need a flight back since I'm going to be tied up?"

"Ken already reached out and took care of it. I fly out tomorrow. He even has a ride picking me up. He is one thoughtful guy."

"Yes, he is. Ken is always one step ahead, keeping the ball moving. I'm going to head out for a run. Unless you want to go with me."

"I'm good. I'll say some prayers, do my meditation, and hope for the best."

"Suit yourself." Wow, I said that real shitty.

"Go with God, Neil."

I made my way out the door to the Challenger and roared up the hill. Peeling around corners, not even listening to music. I used the roar of the engine and the squeals of the tires to cure my sickness. It wasn't long before I was out at St. John's College. As I walked up to the trail, throwing on my headphones, it was time to disappear for a bit. Listening to music while flying in a metal tube isn't quite the same thing; neither is the music I'll be listening to.

I decided to go a little off-book, throwing on some R & B jams with a beat. Some newer stuff that Maria turned me onto when we dated the first time. A mix of Chris Brown, Trey Songz, and Michael Jackson just to give me that edge. It only took me a good twenty minutes to get to the peak, when I found that same clarity from the last time I was a colossal prick. Still, this time I know, like earlier, that it wasn't unwarranted. I'm still going to make it right and get a plan in place to move forward.

"Hey Maria, you got a minute? We need to talk about what the plan is going to be moving forward."

"I agree, we need to . . . divide and conquer." We said it in unison.

"Exactly. You need to work the angles with Erin, here and alongside Ms. Choike's contacts. I'm going to head back to Detroit and start working our angles out there for when Susie gets back. If we make our way back out here, I'll simply fly."

"Sounds like a plan. When do you think you'll head out?"

"Tonight. My schedule is all thrown off. Meet you back at the condo in an hour?"

"Sounds good."

As I made my way down the peak with a new direction, I felt as if I kept having to leave these beautiful places. I think I'm going to try to drive by the kitchen and see if I can catch Sister Irene before I leave. I guess I will have to find a way to make it out here again. This trip has placed something on my heart, these mountains, working there with Sister Irene, all of it. This case is important, though. Often someone has to deal with demons like this. I am my community's Constantine; they are my devil to send back to hell. I realize it can be a bit over the top, but I need all the motivation I can muster right now.

I have been traveling nonstop for two days, and a week ago I spent more than twenty hours in a car with Father Roberts. Now I'm headed back home in my car solo. As I plopped into my car, my sweaty body hitting the leather seat, I just sat there for a quick moment. Covered in dirt, sweat, and disdain for most of this week. There are some great moments, the work done with Sister and Father. The few moments I was able to share with Maria, the gardens in Buenos Aires, but filled with so much shit along the way. What good is the most magnificent steak dinner if the garnish is a pile of dog shit?

Pulling into the condo, it felt odd realizing that all my plans to stay longer than expected were gone. My hopes of taking a longer vacation had dissipated. I was back to working tirelessly. No rest for the wicked may be a cliché, but fuck, it hits home right now. I hope Maria isn't back yet; I would love the opportunity to take a shower, relax, and . . . oh shit, that's right. The water pressure here blows. I quit, I just quit. You heard it here first. New rule in Santa Fe: I'm taking baths.

I walked in with almost no energy, no skip in my step, just sulking like a kid who just got grounded and lost video game rights for the weekend. Worse than that, like a fourteen-year-old girl losing her cell phone the week before the prom.

"Neil, you okay? You look like shit. Not the usual Neil, the hair of the dog shit, you look down."

"This case just has me worn out. I was already worn down. From the Cappelano chase, then the favor for my high school that had me chasing priests all over the globe, to that mess that had me saving my girlfriend from Gaines's corporate offices. I was really looking forward to a break."

"I know, Neil. However, you are sitting here sulking like a whiny little kid. Think of all the times you did get a break. Think of the mental breaks you did get this week. You had more of a routine change than I've seen you have . . . well . . . ever!"

"I guess I never thought of it that way. You always know just what to say, Father. If you need me, I'll be in the bathroom taking a bath."

"Okay . . . wait. WHAT?!"

As the water filled the bathtub and I began undressing, I could feel the anticipation of relaxation build inside me. It was a similar feeling I get when I need a shower. I feel like a junkie right now, jonesing for a fix, trying to find a new drug to fill it. That's me with my routine. It might be the best thing for me when I get home. I need that hot shower, a session on the heavy bag, and taking down the bad guy's sister.

It was a different sensation than I'm used to as I began to lower myself into the bath. Right then Maria walked in with a drink. You already know which one, she had a big smile on her face. She was shaking her head as she handed me the drink.

"Is this what it's come to, Neil? You're a broken man. You are taking a bath."

"Yup. If it's good enough for the old cowboys, it's good enough for me."

"I don't think showers were invented yet."

"I choose to ignore that fact right now," I said with a calming smile.

"I'm just glad to see you relaxed. I know you wanted to leave tonight, but please stay here. Relax, have a drink, let's grab dinner, get a good night's rest, then get on the road after that."

"I can do those. Plus it's probably better than having to pull off three hours on the side of the road somewhere in the middle of nowhere to sleep."

"That's my biggest fear. I know you're going to do this drive alone. I think you need it. That quiet time to enjoy the road and clear your mind will be good for you and the case."

"I'm going to enjoy my cowboy soak, sip on my drink for a bit, then we can go out to dinner. Any ideas where?"

"Erin and I found a place we wanted to try called the Bull Ring down off the plaza. It's a bit pricey. It's the last dinner you and I are going to have out here together, so I thought it would be nice. Plus you can wear some of those nice clothes you got in Argentina."

"I'm game for that. Give me twenty minutes. I'll be out soon. I'm not sure soaking in a tub of my own filth is going to give me the same satisfaction as a hot shower rolling over me like Niagara."

"I don't think so either. Did you take a quick shower first, to clean off the dirt?"

"Nope, this cowboy didn't."

"Stop calling yourself a cowboy. And make sure you rinse your dirty ass off first. See you in a few."

The rest of the evening was flying by, as the last day of a vacation often does. I'm still referring to it like that, though it doesn't feel that way. I do have to keep it in perspective, as Father Roberts pointed out. I have done many things out of my regular routine that has broken me down, changed my view, and allowed me time to relax. I wonder if the breakdown of my routine is why I've been so on edge. I'm not used to a vacation.

One side would say, never do it again. The analyst in me would say, maybe I need to do it more. Smaller batches, practice, and work up to more significant vacations. I need to learn to unwind, or I might end up burning out and killing myself over it. I have a daughter I need to be there for. I'd throw in that I have a company too, but Ken and TJ run the show. I just shine brightly to point out the work we do, that's it. I'm the spokesman. I know I'm more than that, but without them I'm one guy in a bad private investigator black-and-white noir film from the fifties.

The dinner was nice, getting dressed up with Father Roberts, Maria, and Erin for an evening. A great meal, even better service in a great venue, made the week feel like it was coming to an end. It was something I needed, mentally more than anything. The drive back will give me the transition time required to get back into it, focus on the task at hand. As dinner ended, the four of us walked out of the restaurant into the plaza square, lit up with others walking around enjoying the cool summer night.

"Maria, do you think we will ever get back here?"

"I hope so, Neil. The few times we were able to relax, I enjoyed it."

"Other than the shit water pressure, I really loved it out here. Maybe I can find a way to turbocharge some water pressure. We'd have to buy a house, though."

"Neil, you really have a problem with showers, you know that?"

"It's not a problem for me."

"I hate you right now," Maria said, laughing as she leaned into my shoulder.

"Maria, you really are becoming a better part of me, you know that?"

"Neil, are you getting soft on me?"

"Seriously, Maria. You truly pushed me the past couple of days. You would have just let me go through the motions before. This time you really got on me in a way I've never seen before. I think you're finally comfortable around me."

"I've always been comfortable around you. You don't think so?"

"I think when you date someone, it takes time to reach a level where you can tell someone to eat shit and know they aren't going to take it personally. I think you finally got there."

"I can see that. You've always had that chill attitude where nothing fazes you. At the same time, I'm always a ball of nerves. Always worried about what others are thinking." I'm worried, I just play it calm.

"I'm happy that you're comfortable enough to put me there. There are only a handful of people in that small circle. Thank you for kicking me out of my funk. Also, thank you for choosing a great restaurant. It was just what I needed before I crash and drive back tomorrow."

"I care about you, Neil. I just want you to be happy."

Maria wrapped herself around my arm, slid her fingers ever so gently into my hand. It was one of those moments when time stands still. Like that first date, when your heart is beating a mile a minute, flying into your throat, but you're trying so hard to let her know you aren't falling harder than ever for her. Maria has a way of getting into me, finding my weakest spot, and building me up, or getting my attention with it.

Back at the condo, Maria helped me pack everything up, even put it all in the car. All I left out were my clothes for the drive and my coffee mug. I just was going to sleep in my boxers to make the morning efficient. It's not like I'm going to take a long, hot shower, though it's driving me nuts. It has been good to change routines. Maria and I laid down, and she curled up into my arm, fitting ever so nicely. I'm not sure how many guys will admit it, but it's worth my arm going numb nearly every time. She is so peaceful as she lays there asleep, I'm struggling to fall asleep as I review everything that has happened since we made our way out to Santa Fe.

Up, showered, and dressed in my softest jeans with my Red Wings hat. I didn't forget a shirt. I'm wearing a vintage Daredevil shirt Maria bought me. She thought it was cute since I operate in the dark and blind quite often. You may ask yourself when I say "softest jeans," since I've referenced it in the past. What the hell do I mean? You know when you take jeans out of the wash, they are firm and a bit rough, especially when new? Well, when I say "softest," I'm speaking of my most worn in and sometimes worn since washing jeans. It doesn't always mean dirty if I had done mainly office work all day. They're not going to be as gnarly as a day on the trail of a drug dealer.

I'm not going to spare you the sad details of Maria and me saying good-bye. It was hard, and we said good-bye more times than a high-school senior to her college boyfriend. It was a little pathetic, but we don't know where this case is going to take us.

As for getting on the road, I did head out to the soup kitchen first to catch Sister Irene, or Margie, as I've come to learn. I wanted to talk to her one last time. She made a bit of an impact on me this week, and I wanted to thank her. As I walked up, I heard some commotion out back to find Sister Irene and another sister arguing loudly.

"Hey, sisters. What's going on? Calm down." I had to separate the two of them.

"She wouldn't give a man a second package of food because of our rules. She knows that he always comes with the same guy every day. However, he can't make it 'cause he's sick."

"Rules are rules. If we give it to him, Sister Irene, the next guy will raise hell."

"Because you're afraid of someone complaining, you don't want to do what's right? Sister, you are crazy."

"Ladies, is the gentleman here still?"

"Yes, he's sitting over there while we argue. Why does that matter?"

"If you give me the food, can I drive the man over to where he needs to deliver it to his friend? That way, it appeases both of you?"

"I'm okay with that," said Sister Irene.

"That's okay with me, as well," said the other one.

I guess my trip across the country is going to be slightly delayed and take me on a journey into this guy's world. When you are about to embark on a twenty-four-hour drive that will probably take thirty or so hours because you're the only driver, it's hard to be motivated. I'm in no rush to head out of town, though it's a necessity.

18

I KNEW I WAS TIRED, BUT HOLY SHIT, HOW LONG WAS I OUT?

I walked over, grabbed a package of food from the shelves, and made my way over to the gentleman. I explained to him what we were doing. He looked at me a bit confused for a moment. He was a man with a dark complexion, a mix of Persian descent, a guess, and living life under the sun in the mountains. He stood, a few inches shorter than I am, but you could tell he was once of great physical stature, he still had that gait about him. As we made our way, walking toward my car, he asked where we were going.

"Sir, though, I appreciate your help. I'm not used to the kindness of others, outside of those of the cloth. What are you doing here?"

"I've become close lately with Sister Irene, saw she needed help, and wanted to step up. Also, there is nothing wrong with helping your fellow man. By the way, my name is Neil Baggio. What's yours?"

"Jai Ahmadi, but most people just call me Jai. I know, Jai Ahmadi is a mouthful, I thank my parents every day for it," he said with a chuckle.

"It's a pleasure meeting you, Neil. Thank you for your kindness."

"Jai, I'm just doing what I would hope someone would do for me. Such is how we should live."

"I agree. Where are you from, Neil? Your plates say Michigan."

"I'm from the Detroit area. How about you? You don't look like you're from around here, either."

"Actually, I came through Detroit many years ago when I was a boy. My family immigrated here from India. I was twelve when we came to the States. My father said it took many years and lots of paperwork, but it was worth all of it to get us here."

"How did you end at the soup kitchen?"

"Honestly, a string of bad luck and poor choices. I am lucky enough not to have been involved in drugs or alcohol. I trusted some people, ended up working for a company that took advantage of immigrants. People that didn't know better, and now I'm in New Mexico with nothing to my name."

"If you said you came here legally, what's the hardest part of getting everything back? Just asking, trying to help."

"Honestly, I don't know where to start, not being from this country and still being so young. I'm only twenty. I know I look older, but living on the streets has done that. The house is up here on the right. Thank you for the conversation and help."

As I watched him walk away into an old abandoned house, something came over me. Something that was telling me to do something, help this kid out. Hell, I was about to have thirty hours of driving and time to kill, I could make phone calls, and I could use the help driving. I know Ken and TJ could figure out what we need to do; we can make this work. I yelled from the car,

"Jai, as soon as you're done dropping off the food, come back to the car! I think we can help each other out!"

While I was sitting in the car, I decided to text Maria and let her know I was a bit delayed in leaving the area. Informing her of what was going on. I then sent Ken a text, telling him to loop in TJ to what I was about to send him. I sent them the name and age to start looking for information pertaining to him. If we need more info, let me know. As I finished messaging back and forth with Ken, I caught Jai walking back up, out of the corner of my eye.

"Yes, Mr. Neil. What can I do for you?"

"You said you were stuck out here of sorts, isn't that correct?"

"Yes, sir. Where are you going with this?"

"I'm driving back to Michigan as we speak. I could use the company, and you could use the ride. Care to join me?"

"Sir, I don't think I understand what you are asking."

Jai was taken aback. He has been abused, broken, and taken advantage of so many times he doesn't know what to do. Should he trust again, should he try to figure it out on his own? I need to find a way to build trust quickly. I want to help this kid.

"Jai, I want to help you. Simple as that, and I could use the help. I can understand you've been burned; I have an idea. If you're afraid to go on this trip for me, I have an extra phone in the back of my car in case of emergencies. I can have it turned on and give it to you. That should help get you started."

"You're serious, Mr. Neil? You're about to head back to Detroit right now?"

"I was just stopping to say good-bye to Sister Irene when I ran into that situation."

"I'm in. Let's do it. You have to believe sometimes there is a higher power willing to send you help when you need it."

Jai hopped into the car, and we pulled away. I asked him if he had anything, knowing damn well he had only what he was carrying. I still wanted to offer him that curtesy; he respectfully told me to keep driving. When we stop in Amarillo, I'll wing by a store and grab him a duffel bag, fill it with clothes and other things he will need to start over. You can't be on a road trip without a road bag. Hell, it's just not good karma.

"Jai, if your friend there has been living in an abandoned house, where have you been staying?"

"I was staying at a church mission. Since I'm clean and sober, I was able to work and volunteer there. Which also allowed me clean clothes, access to a shower, and other things that many on the street don't get." He was dressed in jeans and a T-shirt, with some beat-up old shoes.

"See that hat in the back there? It's my lucky Detroit Tigers hat. I think it's going to be your new lucky hat. You got it today, you find a ride home to Detroit."

He reached to the back of the Challenger, found the hat, slicked his jet-black hair back, and pulled the hat down with his million-dollar smile. We continued to speak for thirty minutes about his life in India, what part of it he remembers. Growing up with parents both driven to get to the United States for their children to have a better life. He grew up in the Odisha state of India, one of the poorest regions of that country. They had a family member help work with a mission to get to the States. Once over here, his parents struggled to find work.

When in the States, they settled in Novi, Michigan, where his father was lucky enough to get a job in an auto plant. Where it all went wrong is when the auto industry collapsed and he was one of the first to get cut, which made his parents fight, causing Jai to take riskier and riskier jobs. He ended up on a cross- country gig taking him on a railroad. Where he thought he would make good money for his family, and he didn't make anything. All he got was a one-way ticket to New Mexico, and all of his lively possessions stolen.

"Neil, thank you for all your kindness. I don't know how I can ever repay you."

"When the day comes that you will be in a place to pay it forward, make sure you do it tenfold. That is what I ask, not for me, but for someone else."

"That goes without saying. I'm a big believer in karma, and a good deed must be passed on. How long until we stop?"

"It'll be a few hours; we can stop in Amarillo or Oklahoma City." We'll have to stop for gas along the way, but we might stop there for a longer stay. Grab some food, other items. If you need anything, just ask."

"Sounds good. Not like you would trust me yet, but I do have a US driver's license. If you need to rest, it would be my honor to drive for you."

The drive from the mountains of Santa Fe to the plains of New Mexico and West Texas was an odd one. You felt as if you were leaving Shangri-La as you descended the mountains back to the earthly realm. It also made for a fun drive. Mixed with the radar detector, Jai and I began to have fun seeing how fast we could go, windows down and wind ripping.

You could see by the time we had made our way through Amarillo, and filled up the tank, grabbed a quick burger, on got back on the road, that Jai was ready for some sleep. I kept on trucking, but I'm used to this routine. These crazy schedules are part of my DNA.

"Neil, are you going to be good if I go to sleep for a bit?"

"Jai, you're fine. Get some rest. I'm used to long days like this. I told you these days are part of what I do. Don't feel bad. When you get up, we can switch for a bit, and I'll take a nap."

"Sounds good. Thanks again, Neil."

As Jai fell asleep, I reached out to the office to get ahold of TJ. I knew he would be working; I was hoping to have good news for my co-captain when he woke. This kid has been through a lot in a short period, or he's a great liar, which TJ can confirm, and I can deal with that shortly.

"Hey TJ, how goes the search for our friend in the system? Any luck?"

"At first it was a bit troublesome, but once you gave me some more info on his father and where he grew up, we were able to pinpoint him. When you get here, we can help him get everything squared away. We called Mike at the bureau office; he called some friends to help get all Jai's paperwork in order. His story seems to check out so far. It looks like he was a pretty good student too. It also looks like the kid we have graduated from Dearborn Divine Child. If you can confirm that, we can be certain this is the same kid. The ages line up, et cetera. I'll text you a picture now." I waited for a minute to look.

"The picture looks exactly like him, but I'll ask just the same. He's sleeping right now. Is there any way we can pull a favor just to have this stuff reprinted and waiting for him? Whoever has to stick their neck out, I'll owe big time."

"I'll see what I can do. You still have a long trip, so we have time to figure something out. You know I'm on it." TJ always is.

"Thanks, TJ, I'm going to get back to driving. We're about two hours outside of Oklahoma City, and I want to spoil this kid a bit when we get there."

"Talk to you later, Neil."

The next couple of hours felt like I was in a movie montage. It was sort of an out-of-body experience. When we made it to OKC, Jai woke up as we pulled off the expressway. With a full tank of gas, I made my way to the only store open at this time of night that would have everything we needed.

"Neil, where are we going?"

"You can't be on a road trip without the proper gear. We are swinging by the store to grab you a bag and some stuff."

"Neil, your generosity is too much." Jai fought back tears.

"Jai, one thing I learned on this trip was to continue to serve my fellow man. I can't do life on my own, though I try sometimes. Let me do this for you so that someday you can do it for someone else."

He just sat there and smiled. I mean, what else could he do or say, for that matter? It's a hard place for someone to be in. In such a position of need, it has to be humbling and hard to accept in so many ways. I struggle with help when I know I need it, and I'm never in a place of desperation. I want to tread as lightly as I can to ensure that I respect his ego, his level of pride, but also to ensure he gets the chance at life that was taken from him.

Some of you might ask yourself where I might get this level of service to do this for someone. I'd tell you to send your kid to Orchard

Lake St. Mary's. This might read like an ad, but it's true. It has turned me into this person and taught me the parts of life that are important. If you have success, what good is it if you don't share it? Being given great opportunities is about having the responsibility and wherewithal to make a lasting impression in people's lives when you can. I know it can't be all the time. Life happens. When life drops something like this in your lap, you need to take it.

I had forgotten about the case, almost mentally put myself back on vacation. When I was sucked back in by Maria and Erin, that had a break in the case in Santa Fe. Maria called me as we were walking out of the store. I had texted her earlier, explaining what I had done with Jai. She was happy knowing TJ was checking him out and that I had a companion on such a long trip.

"Hey Neil, you got a minute to chat?"

"What's up? We're just walking to the car. I got done getting some stuff for Jai."

"You're a sweetheart, Neil. Still, I need to get back to the case. It looks like my friendship with our friend at Gaines Chemical in Argentina paid off. I just got a tip that Susie is flying out first thing in the morning on the private jet to the States. She's coming here for a meeting with a few of the cartel leaders. I just confirmed with El Jefe."

"We have a friend at Gaines in Argentina?"

"I used a Neil Baggio trick, tipped one of his assistants a couple of hundred dollars for some new clothes, told her to tip me off if Susie travels. That's why we were talking for so long. I didn't tell you in case it didn't pan out. Didn't want to waste your time."

"Nice! Also, double win on confirming with El Jefe. Is he going to confirm the location and time when he has it?"

"He's going to do one better. He is going to bring Erin along with him, as part of his crew. That way, we can have someone in the meeting."

"Here I am driving across the country in my own little world, while you and Erin are grinding it out. I feel a bit guilty right now."

"Neil, you're making a huge difference in someone's life while you're driving home. You act like you're sitting on the couch. You can't do everything in every case, I know that's still hard for you sometimes. It wasn't that long ago you didn't even want to be part of this."

"That's before I met Susie and got the same creepy vibe from her that Jason gave off. Those two have something cooking together."

"I know you're an impatient man. Don't let a thirty-hour trip across the country drive you insane. You can make calls, get intel, and think through stuff. You do some of your best work away from the field, doing the grunt work. You're the processor for the computer sifting through all the data." Maria has a point.

"Let me know if you ladies get any more info on the meeting and if you need any assistance. We can always fly someone out there on short notice to help. Your vacation is almost up—tomorrow, actually. Have you looped Mike in on any of this yet?"

"That call is tomorrow morning. I'll let you know how it goes. I'm sure he'll just tell me to work it out. You bail us out so much; they don't mind if we have your back on a case like this. They'll probably write it up as a DEA joint case and get Jordan involved."

"Makes sense. We're about to hop back in the car and head out. Jai is going to drive, and I'm going to get a nap. I'll text you when I'm up."

"Good night, Neil."

Back in the car, Jai with a big-ass smile on his face. I showed him how to use the navigation, showed him where the cash was for gas in case I'm out cold, and we got back on the road. I can only assume that I've been sleeping a long-ass time because I can see Illinois license plates, even a few for Michigan. I knew I was tired, but holy shit, how long was I out?

"Jai, where are we? What the hell? The GPS says we're on the other side of Chicago."

"Yeah, you were tired, Neil. I didn't want to wake you, so I just kept driving, filled out outside Illinois somewhere, and got back on the road. This car cruises at ninety-five, just like you said. We're making great time. If you want I can pull off and let you drive," Jai said confidently.

"No, you're good. I'll make some work calls, go through notes, and get situated. Though I might have you pull off soon and get some coffee."

"Whatever you need, just let me know."

The next exit, Jail pulled off, got gas, and I grabbed two cups of coffee. He ended up drinking it, as I did. It was refreshing to see how quickly he settled into the situation. He was no longer embarrassed. I think being able to help me gave him some semblance of pride back. I wanted to let him hang on to that and let him keep driving.

We are making great time back to the warehouse when I realized that I forgot to ask him where he went to high school for TJ. I realized I forgot because TJ had texted me about it. As I was playing catch- up, talking to Maria, Ken, and even Father Roberts a bit before he transferred planes in Dallas.

"Jai, I forgot to ask you. Where did you go to high school?"

"I was one of the lucky kids. My parents were huge on education. They found a way to get me into Divine Child, through one of the scholarship programs."

"That's funny. I went to St. Mary's growing up. We played you guys in all sports. Sorry for still kicking your ass every year."

"Not all of us can recruit the best talent in the state." Ouch! St. Mary's always gets that shit.

"Now Jai is waking and getting that youthful attitude. About time you came to the shit-talking party. It's a road trip with two guys; that should be ninety percent of it."

Jai and I finally started to hit a rhythm. I texted TJ back, informing him that Jai confirmed he went to Divine Child, which means we have his info correct. I hope we can have his stuff for him when we get back. At least within a day or so, I want to get him back on his feet as quickly as possible. It's nearly impossible for anyone to function in life without money, let alone a license or Social Security card. As a society, we should make it much easier to obtain these things. Just saying.

By now we were just outside of Detroit and almost to the warehouse. The trip went much faster than anticipated with the help of Jai. I can't wait to see his face when he walks into the warehouse. I offered him a place to stay; we'll let him use the bunks until he gets situated. Ken thought it would be a good idea. We can pay him to be a janitor and a late-night security guard. Gets him a job and back on his feet, it's a double win.

"Hey Jai, we are almost back to the warehouse, our office. Do you have any plans? Anyone you can call?"

"I don't know who if anyone that is even here anymore. I want to start by getting my life in order. The first step is getting home, and you made that happen for me. I am forever grateful."

"I'm not done yet. My team and I are going to work with you to get your ID. Also, any other info you need to get your life started. My right-hand man has a great idea too. I'm going to call him on the Bluetooth so he can tell you himself."

"Mr. Neil, how can I ever repay you?"

"I told you many times."

"Ken, you're on with Jai and me."

"Hey, kid. We here at BCI have an opening for a janitor. The pay will start at ten dollars an hour. It will also come with room and board in our dorms we have here for the guys until you can get situated. You down with that?"

"Wait, not only did you get me home, but you're offering me a place to stay and a job?" Jai, at this point, couldn't fight it anymore; he had tears running down his face.

"Yup. You on board?"

"Yes, sir. Yes, Mr. Neil." I guess I'll give up on the "Mr. Neil" thing.

"We're almost here. Just pull in, Jai, and give that guy who's walking outside a big hug. The job was his idea."

Finally home. It felt good. Not as good as what we are doing for Jai, but I have a feeling we are going to get back tenfold what we've put into this kid. There is just something about him. Ken was walking him around the place, getting him acquainted with everyone and where he was going to be staying. I was just happy to be home. Happy to get back to it, back to a case, and back to my routine. I yelled across the warehouse to Jai and Ken.

"Are you guys good if I head home?"

"Yes, Mr. Neil! I'll be GREAT!"

"See ya, Neil. Ken will take care of him."

19

THE WONDERFUL, EXTRAVAGANT, AND HEAVILY LUBRICATED MISS AGATHA HANNIGAN.

Well, the team kept the house in one piece. I say "team" because Christian started here, then went on a trip for a case and was gone. Ken made sure the house was in good hands. As the girls heard the roar of the engine hit the driveway, I know they would be sprinting through the house. With the car in park, I grabbed my bag from the trunk. Then I made my way in the door to get pummeled by the girls. They hadn't seen me in almost two weeks, and they were excited. I'm surprised, though: I usually get the cold shoulder from them. That doesn't mean it doesn't have a shot of still coming throughout the week, but for now, I'll take the warm greeting.

I texted Maria to let her know I was back in the house safely. She said that El Jefe was on his way to town the next day for the meeting. The timeline is speeding up. By now, Susie should also be touching down or close to it in Santa Fe. With her corporate jet, she can fly directly to Santa Fe from Argentina. I guess it just depends on fuel tank size more than anything.

Logistics aside, Susie should be in Santa Fe today, planning her meeting with the people she will be leaning on to help her distribute Requiem to the masses. I need to get on the horn with Jordan and follow up with him. Get the intel he has, share with him what Maria found out, and ensure that we have their support. The last thing we want to do is piss off the DEA over a case this big. Shit, I might as well call him right now.

"Jordan, its Neil. You got a minute? I wanted to go over a lead Maria has on the Requiem case."

"For that shit I'll make a minute."

"They have some actionable intel that there's a meeting going down in New Mexico in the next day or two with Susie and a few cartel heads. To plan the distribution rights to Requiem."

"Sounds pretty normal for a new drug push-out. The only difference is it's being pushed out by a legitimate company not normal to this. I wonder how they're so versed in the traditions of the drug game. Do you think she has someone coaching her?" Jordan has a good point.

"Not sure, but that could be what her brother is doing in prison. Then getting word to her outside on what she needs to do through his lawyer. It wouldn't be the first time; hell, it's the company's lawyer. Easy enough to share information."

Jordan and I went back and forth for a few minutes, trying to figure out the best course of action. After explaining to him how we have someone in the meeting, we can trust he was okay with us sitting at the meeting and waiting for the intel we get out of it. We don't have a ton of substantial evidence to make a case. Right now, it's all circumstantial at best. If we keep putting in our time and waiting for leads to pay off, it'll pile on. For example, we still have Nicolette; she has her orientation today at Gaines Chemical. She did a phone interview; they are hiring like crazy for low-level marketing people, and they hired her off of that.

Today and tomorrow have a lot riding on them. To see what intel comes out of Maria and Erin's leads mixed with the first impression of what Nicolette can pull off. It might set the tone for the direction I go now that I'm back in Detroit. I think it'll be time to head to FCI Milan and check in on Cappelano and my buddy Jason Gaines. Speaking of Gaines, I wonder if TJ ever got a lead on Gaines family help, anyone we can follow up with.

"Hey, TJ, did you ever track anyone down willing to give us info on the family?"

"Sort of. I found someone who had been offered a book deal for dirt on raising the Gaines. Then they were silenced by the family with cash. They might talk to you, but not sure they'll go on record. It's still a start. I'll text you the name and address I found."

"Thanks, TJ, I appreciate it. As always, you come up with intel when we need it the most."

"I'm just trying to do my best to support the team. This job is awesome, being a part of the team, being able to give back. I never thought this would be where I would end up. By the way, this Jai kid is awesome. Nice find."

"Yeah, Jai is a pretty good kid. I think he's got great potential."

"I can see what you're talking about. He has a spark about him. It's almost like that star quality. Some people just have it; others don't." TJ is right.

"Back to the part where you sent me the info on the person that worked with the Gaines family. Who was ready to do a tell-all. Do we have confirmation of all this?"

"I have an email from the editor of a book publisher that they advanced this person money for a book deal. Then it was paid back to null and void the contract."

"I'll take that as a yes. Have we tried reaching out to them for comment yet? Just to get some form of baseline."

"I've left a few messages with no luck."

"I guess I'll try a few times. I saw the address isn't too far from here, out in Washington Township. I'll probably just swing by and try and get their attention. I have some time to kill today. Since everyone seems to have shit to do but me, I'll hit you up later. Thanks, TJ."

"Peace, Neil."

I decided to take the girls on a quick run, think of it as a welcome-home run. From there I'll clean up a bit and head over to Lynn McMasters' house. The former head of housekeeping and nanny for the Gaines children. She lives about fifteen miles from here. The drive won't be too bad; I can shoot up Van Dyke, then M-53. Depending on where the house is, it can be a lovely area or something on the low-income level. Knowing that she got a big payout, I can only assume it's the first.

With the run out of the way, a quick cleanup and I was back in the car and on the road heading out to Lynn's place. Using the address that TJ gave me, I found myself on the road again. After being in the car for a day, one would think that I might give up on driving, but it's part of life. Thankfully, I had Jai to finish that trip. It allowed me to regenerate in many ways. I can hit the road in a new way because of his help. Otherwise the rest of today would have been spent sleeping and playing catch-up mentally.

The subdivision is on the nicer side, not quite mansions, but beautiful. I'd say on average the houses are twenty-five hundred square feet to three thousand. Pulling up to her house, the first thing I noticed was the impeccable landscaping. Come to think of it, the whole neighborhood is fantastic. I parked in the street, made my way up to the front door, and knocked, with no answer. I could hear voices out back laughing and some loud music, then heard some faint yelling for someone.

"We're in back!"

I highly doubt I'm the one they want to come back there, but I'll take an open invitation. The driveway, around the back of the house, gives it significant depth. I didn't realize how big the lot was until I began walking around it. This should be interesting. As I began to open the gate, I prepared myself for the worst. Luckily for me, I was greeted with a smile and a group of teens laying out at the pool.

"Hey, you're not Tina. Who the heck are you, dude?"

"My name's Neil, I'm with the FBI. Is Lynn McMasters here? She's not in any trouble. I just need to speak to her about a case I'm investigating." I'm not sure why I led with the FBI.

"That would be my mom over there, passed out with a margarita in her hand. I'll get her up for you." This should be great.

We made our way over to Lynn McMasters. I couldn't help but be reminded of a famous character portrayed by one of the greatest comedic actresses of all time, Carol Burnett. If you have ever seen

Annie, you know where this is headed. The wonderful, extravagant, and heavily lubricated Miss Agatha Hannigan.

"Mom, Mom . . . wake up! There is a cute FBI guy here for you." She jumped, more so, too cute than the FBI from what I can tell.

"Honey, where are my sunglasses and my hat? It's so sunny out here."

"Mom, you're wearing them both. Why don't we go inside and get you some coffee."

I just stood there in a weird version of a TV show surrounded by teens lying around a pool and a drunk mother being led inside by her daughter. Eventually I found a place to sit down in the shade off to the side, waiting for some form of direction from the daughter. Judging by the lack of reaction from the crowd, this is a pretty regular occurrence around here.

"Neil, you said your name was . . . Sorry, my name is Lisa McMasters. My mother is Lynn. Sorry about that, give her about fifteen minutes and a cup of coffee, she'll be good to go. It just takes her a moment. You'll be amazed how quickly she bounces back; it's a talent of hers."

"Nice to meet you, Lisa. If you don't mind me asking, is your mom okay to talk to? The case I'm on is pretty important. I need to make sure the info I get is accurate."

"You can only be here for one of two reasons. She either drove drunk into something, which I'm guessing she didn't since you're a fed. Or something concerning those crazy-ass Gaines kids she raised for years. She won't say much to the police or feds about them anymore; she's over it."

"What about a private investigator? I only consult for the FBI, long story. It sometimes helps when I introduce myself. I don't need her on the record. I just need context."

"That's different on both accounts. She can probably help you then. She's just tired of people coming here thinking she is ready to help them put those two behind bars. We thought this was over when Mr. Gaines was behind bars, but his crazy-ass sister is still out there. She's worse than he is. Here comes my mom; she can give you more than I can. I've just heard the stories."

Her mother came up, changed, freshened up, and looking much better. She still had a bit of a sway in her step. It appears she had changed her sunshining margarita for a bloody Mary. Lynn McMasters stands a mean five nine and is currently rocking some heels. Not sure that's the best shoe choice with her equilibrium, but maybe we can sit down and get to talking.

"Neil, a pleasure to meet you. My daughter said you're with the FBI?"

"Sort of."

"What the hell does that mean?" she said as she swayed a bit and her drink sloshed in her hand.

"I am a consultant for the FBI. I am a former agent who had a falling out with them, wasn't a fan of all the politics over the years."

"Wait a minute. I know that name. Is your last name Baggio? Are you the guy that put Gaines behind bars and punched that piece of shit?"

"How'd you know that? And yes, I am."

"I still keep an eye on those crazy bastards. It's good for my health to know where they are and what they are doing."

"She also thinks they're out to kill her," Lisa chimed in.

"Shut up, Lisa. I used to think they wanted me dead. 'Cause they had me followed while I was working on the book deal. That's all water under the bridge. What can I do for the man that punched that inglorious bastard? I am at your service."

I am sensing a trend of women in Jason Gaines's life, really enjoying the fact that I punched him and dropped his ass. This seems to keep playing in my favor. His sister was just placating me but still gave us enough to work on that we were able to follow the trail of bread crumbs back to Santa Fe for the meeting. Now it's getting me the background info I need from the real-life Miss Hannigan. Oops! There goes the olive. She is struggling to stand and walk in those heels despite her best efforts.

"Well, for starters, can we go inside, or sit in the shade to talk? I'm here looking for context. Background on what it was like for them growing up. I'm building a bit of a psych profile on the two of them. This is less about one case or one lousy deed and more about a history lesson from the person that almost wrote the book on them."

"That I can do. Where do you want to start?" Lynn finally sat down with me in the shade.

"The beginning. How old were they when you started there, and how long did you work for the family?"

Lynn started working for the family before she was an adult. That's why she knows the family so well. Her mother worked for the family as their housekeeper before they had kids, working in the home of Jason and Susie's parents for many years. Lynn grew up as the first daughter or niece in many regards to the Gaines. They lived in the servants' quarters for more than ten years. She explained that Lynn never knew her father and that her real last name was Cela. They were Albanian immigrants, but her mother couldn't find work for the longest time. When she started working for the Gaines family, they helped her mother legally change their names to McMasters.

By the time Jason, the oldest of the siblings, was born, Lynn was already twelve years old. Lynn helped her mother with the kids as well as most of the chores and cooking around the house. It was this relationship from a young age that gave her a bond with the kids that allowed her to play a more extensive role in the kids' life than most nannies ever would. Her role, mixed with the parents' lack of interest in their own kids' lives, pushed Jason and Susie down dark paths at a young age.

Susie was born just fourteen months after Jason, which surprised both Lynn and her mother, since the Gaines played such small roles in raising the baby. To them, it seemed as if they treated the children like accessories. They would spend as little time as possible with them growing up. It was Lynn and her mother raising them, being with them.

"I can only imagine what it would have felt like being a kid growing up in that environment."

"We loved those two; hell, I still do. Even though they are off their rockers nuts, it's like loving a killer. It's a hard place to be in. You have to love them from afar." Lynn was fighting back tears.

"You said that their parents were rarely around, often treating them like accessories. Did that lead to the kids acting out in ways to try to get attention?"

"O my God, yes. It started with the usual small-kids stuff. Acting out, yelling, and fighting, then breaking stuff. Eventually, as they got older, it became grand theft auto and even breaking and entering."

"None of this showed up anywhere. I'm assuming the parents made it all go away."

"They did. Most of that was Susie; Jason was the planner, he was the methodical one. He would do long-game things, such as stealing money from his father in small increments that he wouldn't notice. Or mess with his father's shampoo, vindictive shit like that."

"That's not what I was thinking at all; my initial thought was the complete opposite. Lynn, you're telling me more than likely Jason is doing the planning and Susie is following his lead?"

"More than likely that's what's going on. He's always been the planner between the two of them. She is also the emotional one. If you push her, you can get her to do something rash, Jason isn't so irrational."

Lynn and I spoke for another hour going over the history she had with them and how it hurt her to take the book deal. After the Gaines family fired her, cut ties, and essentially threw them into the gutter, it was the best way for her to provide for her family. She said she tried reaching out to the kids multiple times, trying to tell them she didn't want to do a book deal, but it's too good an opportunity for her family not to. It wasn't until she finally signed the papers and got the money that they finally got involved. She believes it took their lawyer explaining to them how bad it might be for a business to settle with her.

"Thank you for your time, Lynn. Here is my card if you think of anything else. Or if one of the kids reaches out and you think you need help. It's the least I can do. You've given me more help than I ever expected."

"I'm not sure how I helped, but glad I could. Thank you for your kindness and for listening to me without judgment. I'm not used to someone with your approach. It was refreshing, and I hope you find what you're looking for and get closure in this case and with those kids. It's not their fault they were treated that way by their parents. They do need to be held responsible for their actions." Lynn is so conflicted; you can see it.

"We have one behind bars, and we'll see what we can do about the other."

"Don't be so certain that Jason doesn't want to be there. Have a great day, Neil."

"Thanks, Lynn. You too."

That's the second person who has referred to Jason wanting to be in prison. First it was his sister. Now the closest thing to a real mother he ever had. That's too much of a coincidence for it. This is going to stick in my thoughts for a while until I can rectify it. It looks like I'm heading back to FCI Milan. No day like today.

20

THIS SITUATION JUST TURNED INTO A CLUSTER-FUCK, AND THE MARVELOUS KIND WITH TEQUILA, COFFEE, AND LIMES.

The drive over was longer than average since I was coming from Washington Township. The positive was with the extra time I was able to fill in Maria and everyone else with what I had learned from my conversations with Lynn and her daughter. Maria, like myself, was surprised to hear that Jason was the planner between the two siblings. From our interactions, we were caught off guard; this means there is an excellent chance Jason really wanted to be in prison and was pulling all of these strings the whole time.

Maybe all the references to Kingpin weren't as off base as we initially thought. This man put himself behind bars to continue to make moves, line up with drug cartels, and develop the street cred needed to grow his enterprise. He is making chess moves I didn't see coming, putting himself into a position to carry his enterprise into the next decade-plus.

Right now he has all his shares in his company still. We still haven't pegged all the charges against him, not even the one where he broke himself out of custody from the FBI. Since Erin murdered Bryan, he is holding all the cards in what is and isn't true in that story. None of his henchmen are going to throw him under the bus; he controls all the money. Often the person controlling the cash is the person with the most power.

For now I am going to make my way into the prison, sit down with Cappelano, and start with that. Get some intel on what Gaines has been doing inside, see what strategic partnerships he's been making. I'm not sure if I'm going to sit down with Gaines. I might come back twice a day, sit down with Cappelano, and not ask for Gaines, just to mess with his ego. If he is a planner, thinks he's in control, it might be a way to get the wheels turning. For now I'll just sit down, enjoy the room, and wait for Cappelano. This process is getting a bit repetitive, but it's what you must go through when you want to talk to a serial killer locked away for life in a federal prison.

"Neil, nice to see you again. How was your trip? Was it as relaxing as you had hoped?"

"You know damn well I couldn't relax and got involved in some shit. How has your last week gone?"

"It's been okay. I'm getting a bit annoyed dealing with Gaines. He is off his rocker, and this is coming from someone that killed a ton of people," Cappelano said, smiling.

"It's appreciated just the same. I am working on his psych profile, trying to build it. Work through it and see how I can adapt to it. Would you say he is more of a planner or someone that responds quickly to emotional events?"

"I wouldn't say that he is irrational, but I'm not quite sure how much depth he has. Then again, I don't have patience with him or any of these people in here. Other than you, I'm usually fighting my inner dialog to snap someone's neck. Especially Gaines. I have no problem doing that for you, by the way. I've killed in your honor before. Just say the word." Sometimes I'm reminded how nuts he is.

"It won't be necessary. However, I do appreciate the sentiment. I am also aware you would prefer to kill him to end your suffering. More so than to help me."

"You know me too well; I would get much more joy in killing him for myself than I would in knowing I was helping you."

"Speaking of Gaines, has he been making any moves in here? Any partnerships?"

"He hasn't been open about it with me, but Colby and I have noticed that he is making deals with every major gang in here. It looks like he has an agreement with the Aryan Nation and the Puerto Ricans as well as the Black Muslims. I was shocked about the final one, but there is a strategic alliance there I need to dig into. I don't think it's about drugs. I think it's about territory on the outside for distribution from his plants."

"I can see that. Are you having to figure this out from talking to people on the inside? Since Gaines isn't saying much?"

"Neil, you're lucky I'm bored as shit in here. After the first couple of days, I was so bored I started talking to Colby, and he encouraged me to start investigating. He reminded me I used to work for the bureau as an agent. Which I forget sometimes; it feels like a lifetime ago."

"Even for me, Frank. It feels like it's been forever since we were working together. Sometimes it feels like it was a different time or an alternate universe. We have been stuck in this reality for so long it's hard to believe the other one ever existed."

"I know, lucky for you, I can still track down a lead or two. Out of sheer boredom, I started working my way through the prison ranks. Lucky a lot of these guys have wanted to talk to me for some time. Most of them wanted to show off as well. Getting them to give me intel was pretty simple. They had heard of my work with the cartels when I was in Mexico, which gave me some major cred in here."

Frank and I went over the moves that Gaines was making in FCI Milan. It seems he is building strategic partnerships with the leaders of some of the most ruthless gangs across the country. There are leaders in every prison that he has been able to network with, make connections with, and get an audience with whom he may otherwise have to work tirelessly for. Showing people that he's willing to go to a federal prison to get their attention is a shortcut in the process.

Otherwise they look at him like a suburban kid trying to act like a street thug. Frank has explained that he is showing them how it will be financially smart for them to partner with him on Requiem moving forward. I'm starting to see what Lynn was talking about: Jason has more foresight than I ever gave him credit for. I thought he was a kid screaming at the dinner table for more apple juice instead of eating the food in front of him. It's that same mentality that we have when we're three or thirty.

I tell people the same reason people get worked up about their employees making mistakes is the same reason they got mad when someone took their toy when they were four years old. If you think through it, the logic and emotion match. You feel wronged, like someone did it to you on purpose. It was usually them just fulfilling a simple urge, nothing major.

"Frank, do you mind if I step outside for a minute to make a call to the office?"

"It's not like I'm going to be going anywhere. Are you going to talk to Gaines?"

"I'm not sure there's a point to it, so I'll just keep tabs on him through you for now, and when I have all the tools at my disposal, I'll go to work." Frank laughed a bit.

"I've been on the other end of that. I may not like to give you the proper credit. Yet I do respect the approach. It's meticulous and developed."

"Thanks, Frank. I'll be right back."

I walked out of the room, then down the hallway to the exit door. Standing in the small area, standing next to a few guards sneaking a cell and cigarette break, I was reminded of one of my many Cappelano vices. I smoked so much during that run at Frank he drove me down a dark path. I do have more awareness than I ever did before; I'm sure it comes with age. Yet something tells me, the Gaines siblings aren't going down so easily. They will be thorns for some time.

"Hey Ken, I need you to do me a favor. I also wanted to see if we were lucky to get any info back yet from Nicolette. I doubt it; just wondering."

"On Nicolette, we have nothing yet, but she's still there working. As for the favor, always. What do you need?"

"Do you and the guys think you have any way of getting the warden out of here, in cuffs or jammed up? We both know they are tied to Gaines hard; I want them out of the picture. Also, what's the word on the DA and the Gaines prosecution? I keep hearing there's a deal looming."

"I keep hearing the same shit you do. I'll start with Mike, see if he has any new intel. If not, I'll run down to the DA's office, find out what I can."

"Before you run down there, let me know. I might make a run down there myself. I have all this free time and need to be active."

"Neil, you can't sit still for shit. It's one of my favorite qualities," Ken said, laughing.

"I'm heading back in there."

"Back in where?"

"Oh yeah, I'm out at FCI Milan talking to Cappelano, gathering some info. I spoke to Lynn, remember. I need to follow up on all this stuff. Can't wait."

"Neil, take a breath, you just spent thirty hours in the car. I'll get on all of that. Also, make sure you call Maria. I think she has some info on when the meeting is."

"Thanks, Ken."

Off the phone, I sent a text to Maria asking what the info was, also asked a bit why she didn't call me with it. Then again, she probably thought I'd be sleeping at some point, like most people after a trip like this. As I walked back into the room, I saw Frank had this look on his face, like he had been plotting something.

"Frank, I'm not sure I like the look on your face. What are you thinking of right now?"

"I think we can have a little fun with Gaines. We can work together like the good old days."

"You certainly are bored as shit in here, aren't you?"

"It's either this or I start killing people in here and then I'll be in solitary confinement. Which sucks for everyone."

"Frank, you have a good point. Why don't you get to work on some ideas? I have to go see the DA about Gaines; I'll be back tomorrow."

"You better be. Going a week without the interaction of an adult that can think properly was brutal. Don't do that to me again, at least not anytime soon." Frank honestly looked panicked.

"I can't promise that I'll never go a few days without coming again. However, I can promise I will be aware of it. That's the best I can do for you."

"I'll have to take it. It's a start, and it's better than nothing." Frank smiled a bit.

"I'll see you tomorrow."

As I made my way out of FCI Milan and over to the district attorney's office working on Gaines's case, I figured I would call ahead for a change. I usually like the old surprise attack, but I don't feel like wasting time.

"District attorney's office, Angela speaking. How may I help you?

"This is Neil Baggio; I have some new information to go over with the DA about the Gaines case, yet it needs to be done in person. I just need five to ten minutes. Can they squeeze me into their schedule today?"

"We aren't in court today, so we can probably make something work. Are you heading down right now?"

"Yes I am, if that's doable."

"We'll squeeze you in. See you shortly, Mr. Baggio."

Well, that was easier than expected, not a good sign. My guess is that they already knew I was going to be barking up that tree eventually. They told their staff to simply get me in. They'll handle it so they can all go about their day. Not bad advice, and an even better overall plan, but it still makes me worried about the outcome ahead.

Driving downtown toward the DA's office, I figured it was about time I called to check in on Maria and Erin. See where they are with the case. Ken made it sound as if they had confirmation on the meeting as well as some other details.

"Hey Maria, how's Santa Fe treating you? Ken told me to give you a shout."

"Yeah, I had reached out to them for some support. He was able to get a couple of guys on a flight out here earlier in the day to help us out. We have confirmation that the meeting is going to be late tonight, around midnight, at a closed business downtown. I'm going to have myself and two of your guys help me run support on Erin. El Jefe and his guys are covered, but I wanted the extra backup in case it got hairy out here. The bureau wants to keep their hands off it; even the DEA wants to keep it strictly wait and see. With Jason in prison and Susie having nothing on her sheet and no evidence pointing to her, they are handing with care."

"That's fancy for letting us stick our necks out for their benefit. You know that, don't you, Maria?"

"I'm not a green idiot on this case. I'm just doing my best to stop these crazy siblings from flooding our streets with a new drug. Could you imagine finding a way to prevent heroin from ever happening? That's why I'm sticking my neck out." She has a point.

"I get it, you know I do. I'm just making sure you understand the risk."

Maria and I went back and forth at each other's throats for a few minutes. You could feel the tension in our voices. It was less about each other, pushing each other or making each other feel less than. It was more about the stress of the case, the overall situation, and how it's weighing on our shoulders.

"Hey, I'm about to pull into the garage and head in to talk to the DA. I need to ask about the Gaines case and his status at FCI Milan. I'm sorry for snapping earlier; we're both stressed. It wasn't my intention; you know that, don't you, Maria?"

"I know, Neil. It's okay. Have a good meeting. Find out what the hell is going on, shoot me a text about it. Call me curious as to why the DA still hasn't pressed charges on all counts."

"You got it, babe. I'll talk to you later. Be safe out there."

"Talk to you later, Neil."

Walking into the DA's office, his staff was waiting for me; it almost feels like a setup. I feel as if the DA is about to drop a bomb in my lap with some shit. Some dumb as shit like Gaines is an informant, helping build a case while in prison against a drug lord.

"Mr. Baggio, the DA will be with your shortly; he's just finishing up with a call. Can I get you anything while you wait?"

"I'm fine; thank you."

I ended up having to sit in the lobby for a good twenty minutes. Not sure it was a power play or simply a busy day. I did call unannounced, squeeze myself into the schedule, and work my way into their day. It gave me some time to clean up the contacts on my phone. You know, when you're really bored, looking for something to do.

"Neil, come on in. Sorry for making you wait." The DA stuck his head out.

"It's no problem at all. I just popped in, and I knew there was a chance I would have to wait."

"Well, you didn't come all the way down here to high-five me. We're both busy men. What can I do for you, Neil?" He's cutting right to it.

"Matt, I'm working on a case that's still connected to the one with Gaines being put away. I was following up to see why only some charges have been filed. From my calculation, the original plea is set to expire soon, allowing Jason Gaines to walk soon."

"I was hoping you didn't notice. I'm kidding. Calm down, Neil."

"Matt, I'm in no mood to joke. I just drove thirty hours from my vacation to get back on this shit case. Only to hear that this guy is about to walk free 'cause of his contacts. It smells of you guys working with him to get some other fish you've had your eyes on for some time."

"Neil, you know the optics of this job. We got a ton of flack for putting him away. The community still doesn't believe any of the shit we charged him with, and the ones that do, don't care. His family has pumped so much money into the community; they look the other way."

"It's not the only shit he's pumping into the community, Matt, you know this. Is it because you're up for reelection?" I'm being kind of a dick, I know.

"Neil, I'm always running for election. I never get a day off; it's part of this job. As for the Gaines case, I know you'll figure it out and do something stupid. That is why I told my staff if you call and want to talk, to have you walk right in."

"Fuck me, I knew it. What deal did Gaines get, and who is he giving up?"

"He has connections all through the international drug trade now. We are working to bring them down. The deal is predicated on him getting us the intel needed to prosecute a specific case and person. I can't go into details; it's a confidential case."

"The only person he's connected to internationally that he might have even a little intel on is the Choike family. The same one I pissed off when I was in Poland. Unless they put him in contact with a bigger fish, which is what you are hoping for when he gets out. I hate you so much right now." Though it's a standard move.

"Neil, don't look at me like you're not aware of the bigger picture in all of this. If you don't want Gaines out of prison, get me more evidence to keep him in there. Get me evidence on the person we are trying to nail. You're a good enough investigator, and you can figure it out. I don't have to risk my job to get you on the right trail." No, he doesn't.

"I guess I got what I came for. One last question." Then I'm causing a scene when I leave.

"When the original deal is up, is he walking out? Or is he getting out earlier? For the case I'm on, I at least need that timeline information." You tall prick.

"He gets out in five days. You've got your work cut out for you, Neil."

"Side note: wasn't sure I wanted to tell you. Your wife is cheating on you."

"What?"

"Just kidding, but I wanted you to feel the same gut punch I just took."

"You're a prick, Neil."

"Only to a joyous asshole such as yourself. Talk to you alter sunshine."

Walking out, I slammed his office door, making a bit of a scene. I know it was unnecessary as shit, but it was fun and well worth every minute of it. I'm glad I didn't leave this to a call for Ken. We have a shit ton to do in a short period. The clock just picked up on this whole case. What seemed like a stroll in the park with a long game afoot. This situation just turned into a Cluster-Fuck, and the marvelous kind with tequila, coffee, and limes.

Back in the car, I revved the engine, backed out of the lot, and called Ken on Bluetooth. It was time to rally the troops once more. While I was waiting for Ken to pick up, I did a bit of multitasking and sent a text to Maria, giving her a shortened version of what just happened.

"Ken, I just got done talking to the DA about Gaines. I'm on my way back to the office, and it's not pretty."

"That bad, huh? Let me guess: they are doing some dumb shit like letting him walk at the end of that deal to try and catch a bigger fish."

"The only problem is they moved the timeline up to five days from today, and their dumb asses don't realize he's the biggest fish."

"I feel like I'm missing some pieces to the puzzle here. Are you going to explain it all when here? What do you need from me?"

"Have TJ's team all be there. They are going to be on an around-the-clock bender of trying to find out who the DA is going after. Maybe we can keep Gaines in prison if we can lock this shit up first or get them a big enough win to buy us some time."

"On it. See you in a few, Neil."

"'Bye, Ken."

Off the phone, roaring down the freeway, I was doing my best impersonation of hyper speed, hitting more than a hundred most of the drive. I was trying to get to the warehouse almost instantly, which was almost achieved, since it barely took me fifteen minutes to get there. As I pulled in, I saw Mike Ponecelli' s car there. What the hell? Why is he there and why didn't Ken tell me?

21

THE MOUNTAIN AIR, MIXED WITH A NUN THAT GOT DRUNK WITH ME, CHANGED ME.

It looks like Mike just got here, at least judging by the way Ken is talking to him. They look like they are getting acquainted. Something I wouldn't expect to see if the two of them had been talking for some time before I arrived. It's not as if I'm trying to deduce anything. I'm merely that neurotic about shit. Sorry, it's just how I operate. If I could turn it off, I would.

"Ken, how long has Mike been here?" I was acting like Mike wasn't even in the room.

"Neil, I just pulled in a few minutes before you. Maria forwarded your text to me about the case. I drove right over to see if I could help."

"Damn, Mike. I thought *I* drive fast."

"I wasn't too far, already in the car. I was out grabbing coffee after interviewing someone for a different case. I'll just assign it to someone else. I'm at your disposal, you have a short time frame, and you bail our asses out all the time." Mike was fired up.

"I'm sure Neil is appreciative; he was just surprised that you showed up. Since he was unaware."

"Ken, no need to speak for me. Still, I do appreciate it. Mike, let's get started," I said with a smile.

"Let's head to the conference room, TJ has his team in there, and those who can't be here are Skyping in on the video conference."

We made our way down the hall and started to get into it quickly. It was great to see Mike here and supporting Maria and me as we go after the Gaines siblings. With the way they are moving along and the variables in play we are pressed for time and now spread a little thin.

"Ken, can you start going over the basic details of the Gaines case and give everyone a brief history? I need to make a quick call to Jordan."

"You got it."

I stepped into the hallway and called Jordan. He is our reliable connection at the DEA, he's a little off his rocker, but he's trustworthy as shit. I have an idea, but it's only going to work with the support of the DEA.

"Agent Meeks here. What can I do for you?"

"Oh shit, sorry, Jordan, I called your desk phone. Its Neil. I need to ask a favor concerning the Gaines case. You might have to be on a limb for this one."

"You got me a bit of leniency with that huge haul recently. All the drugs, cash, and guns we took off the streets. What do you need?"

"There's a meeting going down in Santa Fe tonight at midnight. We have someone inside, with Maria and a few agents supporting. What are the chances of getting you to round up a few select cartel leaders? But there is a catch."

"What's the catch? I'm assuming you want me to let one of the birdies fly the nest?"

"Exactly. It'll help us frame the story to the others involved. Since we have someone on the inside, we might be able to slow down the distribution rings and hurt the Gaines's reputation on the street."

"Reputation is more important than money to a lot of these gangs. Hit me up when you have the details, I'll hit up our people in the area and see what we can get moving on short notice."

"Thanks, Jordan. I'll get ahold of you one way or another ASAP."

Back in the room, Ken was finishing up giving a detailed breakdown of what the Gaines siblings mean to the community as well as to the pharmaceutical world. He was about to head into all of the illegal dealings they were accused of. As well as the new drug we are working to take off the street. This is the part I need to be in, where my cue is.

"All right, guys and gals. Without further due, here is the one and only Neil to go over what's at stake and where this case is headed."

"Thanks, Ken, and to everyone who made it in or online. We appreciate your time today, even if it's required for your job and to get paid." That got a good laugh.

I went on the next twenty minutes, going over all of the items we have related to Requiem. Susie being tied to this case just as much as Jason, though he is in prison. I expressed to them the timeline we have; it's closer to a three-day window, not five. The reason being that we must get the information to the district attorney if we have a shot at keeping Gaines in prison.

"Okay, so everyone understands we have a seventy-two-hour window to get this shit moving. We need to work around the clock. Unlike the case where I asked for you to donate your time, we will be dropping our bills on the FBI and DEAs desks. If they refuse, I'm sure the press will be happy to know who closed the largest drug case in US history and who paid for it."

"Hey, now, I'm sure we can make it work. No need to get all crazy now, Neil," Mike interjected.

"Can one of you get to the point? Ken will get assignments to you shortly, and we will start rolling this out. TJ's team, get me that name. Who is the DA using Gaines to go after? Also, find me a connection to Susie Gaines, something we can give Jordan and the team he has on standby in New Mexico."

"Got it, Neil. Let's go, guys and gals." Ken wrapped up the meeting and started to get everything organized.

"Hey Mike, can I talk to you for a minute over here?"

"Yeah, Neil, what's up?" Mike and I made our way down to the car bay.

"What do you know about the DA's deal with Gaines? Do we even have a shot at keeping Gaines in prison? I feel like we could try to put out a house fire with a garden hose."

"I know what you mean, Neil. As for what their deal is. I have no idea; they are keeping it under tight wraps. Have you tried taking a run at his lawyer? See if you can get any clues from him?"

"I can send some of our other people that way, or maybe you can go see him, one professional to another. If I do it, he's going to clam up. He knows what my view of Jason is. His guard would be up the whole time; you need a softer touch to caress it out of him."

"I see what you're saying. I can do that for you. Anything else I can do?"

"Find out who the judge is that is signing all the paperwork for the Gaines deal. This will help us a little bit."

"How do you figure?"

"Judges see cases and have logs that become fingerprints. They allow us to look forward and see what a judge might approve or turn down. They are creatures of habit, just like any other human being. It's a long shot, but most of my life has survived on the culmination of three or four Hail Mary plays." Mike laughed.

"I wouldn't call them long shots or Hail Marys. I would say you are detailed in your approach and utilize every piece of data you can to form a crystal-clear picture. Others just don't have as wide a view as you do. I think that's the most significant difference. That and your ability to piece it all together."

"Thanks, Mike. I feel a bit crazy most days, a little off-putting, but then people such as Maria, Ken, and you tend to give me a proper ass-kicking. It's what keeps me on track, or the right encouragement when I'm down."

"That's the best part of being on a team, Neil. We pick each other up when we need it. We also knock each other down a peg when needed."

Mike and I talked for a few more minutes, then did one of those awkward good-byes. We've been on a roll lately for screwing that up. We have no symmetry when we get to the end of a conversation, especially in person. It seems to be okay on the phone, but in person, unless Maria or someone else is nearby, we crash and burn and make it so awkward. It's almost like one guy going in for a handshake and the other a fist bump.

I began to text Maria, who has been hard to get ahold of lately because of the crazy schedule she and Erin are keeping. They are working with El Jefe and his crew, scouting Susie and her team as they arrive in Santa Fe. We have been texting back and forth, which is better than nothing, but the context sometimes gets lost, making it hard to understand. For example, I'm writing her long messages, asking her two different questions, and in response I'm getting a simple "yes."

I tried calling her because I was getting so frustrated, but she sent me to voice mail. If I didn't know any better, she is about to block me, so I'm going to stop messaging and calling. I'll just have to wait for her to respond. It's the hardest part of what we do. Sometimes you just want to talk to your significant other; with us, you can't sometimes.

Mike pulled out, headed to get the information we needed, and I made my way back inside. I was trying to rally the guys. I was working with them on individual tasks; Ken had assigned them. It was more about context and support. Making sure that each team of two we put on a task had everything they needed to accomplish their goals. Aside from putting away bad guys, building a team is tops. Ken and I love that part; we are in the people business. Without great people, we can't help others. I know it seems a bit sappy, but we wouldn't have figured out the case of Andrew Malinowski, found Cappelano, or tracked down Gaines. It's the team that we have, working tirelessly, growing, and maturing that allows us the success we enjoy. Speaking of growth, leading to our success, TJ is really growing his section of our company. I couldn't be prouder to see what he does for our team and the community.

"Hey, TJ, how's it going, man?"

"Neil, can I be brutally honest with you about something?"

"You usually are. Not as rough as Ken, but you're a straight shooter."

"You seem a bit off today, I know you were on vacation, I know you were supposed to be relaxing and grabbed this case. Still, you seem a bit off. Something just seems different in you all of a sudden. Did Santa Fe make that big of an impact on you?"

"The mountain air, mixed with a nun that got drunk with me, changed me. I hope it sticks, but only time will tell."

"You'll have to go into more depth on that someday, but for now I have some news for you. I think through good old science. We can narrow down the possibilities of who your local DA is targeting. There can be only so many people a DA can go after. It's not like they have free reign to do whatever they want. We're going to comb the database along with Christian's roommate, Ashley. She is studying for her bar exam, figured she might be a good person to help with this."

"When did he have time to find a roommate? I thought he lived alone."

"They don't call it dating, so we call her a roommate. I don't argue; I just live in the crazy reality you people bring me into." It's not like I can say anything, with Sheila and now Maria.

"Good point. It's easier that way if you just go with the flow. Let me know what's going on. Can you do me a favor? Try to tap into Maria's phone. I haven't gotten a response from her in a while. I'm starting to get concerned." Inside I'm losing my shit trying to stay cool.

"I'll do it really quick. Are you going to hang around the office for a few? I'll come find you."

"Yeah, I'll be here, one way or another. I'm trying to help the teams as they work on their projects and get ready to head out. It's getting late; it's almost seven here, which means it's five there and Maria should be getting ready for the meeting tonight. I know she might be with El Jefe, but she can text back. Especially with the way she made it sound."

"We'll figure it out, good or bad. I'll come get you."

"Thanks, TJ."

I spent the next hour working around the office, helping people out. We were going over case files, sifting through cases that Gaines was attached to. As well as the drug trafficking the street gang had been arrested for. We even went over all of the related drug trafficking schemes Gaines had been associated with. Using the gang affiliated with Gaines and who they had worked with allow us to create a possible network he is going to tap into. I ran into Ken while working with some of the new hires we have brought on. They were working on the bullshit case, building and sifting jobs that big cases are built on.

"Hey Neil, just who I was looking for. I have some good news."

"You heard from Maria?" Still freaking out inside.

"No, I didn't know there was an issue. Terrance and Christian are freed up now. They were able to close that case for us. They are packing up and getting in the car now."

"Ken, they drove there. What is it with Christian and repeating my bad ideas?"

"Like driving across the country?"

"They were touring with that band, to find the stalker who had attacked the stagehands and threatened the lead singer. It's not like they got in the car and drove down to Miami. However, they do have a long- ass drive up here. It's not as bad, they have two of them, and it should be a twenty-or-so-hour drive. They didn't take the truck. They are driving in Terrance's Camaro."

"They're about to leave, drive through the night, and get here tomorrow. To help us out on this case. What's this about Maria, though?"

"I haven't heard from her in a while. She usually checks in, at least text messages. If she is going dark for some reason, she always gives me a heads up. Since it's so rare for her, that's why I'm a little worried."

Ken tried his best to console me like a good buddy should but without the proper ammunition. I was missing the bathtub and a C-Fu drink with my girl Maria by my side. I really am starting to fall for her just as hard as, if not harder than, any other woman in my life. I might even say that I love her; that's why it's so hard for me right now. I haven't said it to her, but that's because I'm so worried, always guarded. As Ken put his arm around me, gave me that "we'll get through it" speech, TJ came busting in.

"Neil, I have some bad news. You're going to want to sit down, then perhaps slug something."

"What is it? Don't just stand there, TJ." Ken looked pissed.

"I was able to ping her phone. She's in Santa Fe still, but it looks like she's at the airport out there. That's the last known location before it was turned off. I was able to access the microphone with the help of one of the other guys. If we heard it correctly, sorry, Neil, we didn't act quickly enough to record it."

"Sorry for what?"

"It sounded like she was getting on a plane; we could make out what sounded like someone yelling "Gaines." Then we heard a female voice, not Maria's, say something about heading to Argentina."

"I guess I'm heading back there. They have Maria. Is that what you're saying, TJ?"

"We heard some fighting, some yelling, then a couple of shots, and the phone went dead."

22

AS OF RIGHT NOW, THEY HAVEN'T COME BACK TO THE AIRPORT ACCORDING TO RECORD.

Did TJ just tell me that my girlfriend is dead, the woman that I finally admitted to myself I love? The woman that has pushed me to finally get over some of the most significant neurotic parts of my character, she's gone. I dropped to the floor. As my back hit the wall I slid down just as the tears began to run down my face. I couldn't fight it back anymore. I had been hiding the fear inside all night. I knew something was wrong, felt it, this was the fear. The worst of it, the biggest and scariest issue of them all, I didn't know what to do.

I sat there, lost in my own sorrow, for what felt like hours but turned out to be merely a few minutes. As I worked through all the possible things I would do to the Gaines siblings, the fear and pain turned to anger and drive almost instantly. It felt like a switch was flipped on.

"TJ, get me a flight itinerary for Gaines's private jet. We know for a fact that they still have to register their flight plans. Let's see where they are headed. They don't know we have this head start on whatever happened on that plane. Also, someone track down that sneaky, slimy Erin. Why isn't she anywhere to be found in this mess?"

"I'm on it, Neil." TJ headed back to his office.

"Ken, I need a big-ass cup of coffee. I'm about to call Mike and tell him he has an agent missing and perhaps down."

I can only assume Mike is going to instigate some crazy shit within me, as he normally does in situations like this. He played it safe last time. Now it's getting too close, too personal. I don't think he can keep playing the PC part of this case.

"Hey Neil, I know you're eager, but I haven't had time to dig around and get the info you need."

"Mike, there's no easy way to say this. I had TJ access Maria's cell 'cause I was worried. From what we can tell she is on Susie Gaines's plane, and there was gunfire right before her phone was turned off."

"Do we know where they are headed?"

"We're pretty sure they are headed back to Argentina, but we're checking on their flight plan. Do you have any major favor you can pull to get you and me to Santa Fe, then down to Buenos Aires if needed?"

"I'll make some calls. I know for a fact I can get us to Santa Fe in a hurry. Get your shit together and meet me at your warehouse. I'll pick you up. How much time do you need?"

"I'm already done. I keep a go bag at the office. I have issues, remember, Mike."

"I have one in my car too. Do you have your passport?'

"I just got back from a long trip, yup."

"Me too. I'll swing by and grab you. I'll make some calls and we can get organized. I think I can get us to Mexico City. You might have to get us to Buenos Aires if you don't want to fly commercial."

"See you in a bit."

I got off the phone with Mike, headed into Ken's office, and gave him the lowdown of what's going on. I asked him to track down a ride from Santa Fe to Buenos Aires, if possible, call in all favors if we need them. Then I told him to make sure we have some guys to housesit for me still. As I walked out of Ken's office, I decided to make a beeline for the heavy bag in my office. Well, my version of an office. No wraps, just bare knuckles, I started slamming my fists into the bag, reeling with anger and pain.

This is what Lynn was talking about. Susie is impulsive, and I can see Jason now losing his shit. Yelling at her for doing something rash. She'd probably say something reminding him of his kidnapping of Maria. He would point out it was for a purpose; she would try to make one up on the spot. I'm playing with this shit in my mind, still can't find Erin, can't find my girlfriend, and have all these loose ends. What is Susie's play if she is going to leave before their meeting? Did El Jefe set up Maria and them?

As I grabbed my phone to call Jordan, I noticed I was getting a call from a 505 area code. No idea who that is; ignored. Damn it, they keep calling in. Finally they texted me. "It's Erin. Answer, you asshole." So I did, and I was kind of an asshole.

"Hey Neil, do you know what's going on? Did Maria get ahold of you?"

"No. What the hell is going on?" I'm not going to give her anything to work with.

"El Jefe sold us out. My guess is that he thought he could make more money working with Susie than he could working against her."

"What does that mean for you, for Maria, and for the meeting?"

"The meeting already happened. They did it this morning, Susie is on her way back home to Argentina; I barely got out of there alive. I got shot trying to chase down the plane with Maria on it. As they were carrying her on the plane, she fought back, grabbed a gun, and shot one of Susie's men. Then I got caught in some crossfire. There were bullets all over; I'm not sure if she's even alive anymore. What I do know is that bitch Susie has her and is heading to Buenos Aires."

"What is your play? Where are you headed?"

"I'm heading to Buenos Aires to find Maria and get her back. She stuck her neck out for me; I'm not going to leave her hanging."

"Hey Erin, I need you to get your stuff organized and give me twenty minutes. I have Mike, Maria's boss, calling me back. We're working on the way to get down there. Maybe we can pick you up or get you a ride."

"Okay. If I don't hear from you in a few, I'll assume I need to find my own ride. I'm sorry, Neil, I didn't plan on any of this happening."

Mike called me, telling me that he had a ride for us to Santa Fe. He said his team checked the flight record, and it didn't look like the flight was leaving Santa Fe. This means Erin is lying, or Susie had to change her plans on the fly. Mike and I figured for now the best idea is to head to Santa Fe and send Erin ahead to Buenos Aires in case we need her there. Also to get her out of the way; I don't trust her.

TJ came rushing into my office as I was leaning against the heavy bag on the phone with Mike confirming what Mike had told me with a different piece of information.

"Neil, I confirmed that Susie's plane did leave the runway, but according to the flight record, they were supposed to land back in

Santa Fe. As if they were flying around, then coming right back. It doesn't make sense. As of right now, they haven't come back to the airport according to record." TJ was a bit frantic.

"Thanks, TJ. I need to get on this."

I shot Erin a text to let her know what was going on. I told her to sit on the airport, see if she can get boots on the ground. I was communicating the updated info to the team when I saw Jai was sticking his head in. He asked me if everything was okay. I gave him the nod that it was okay to enter.

"Hey, Mr. Neil, are you going to be okay? I have been able to piece together what's going on from everyone. Is there anything I can do? You have done so much for me, I don't know what I can do, but I would relish the opportunity."

"Unless you have an idea on how to spot a random plane landing in the middle of nowhere outside of the city. That's the big hurdle we have right now."

"Have you tried asking Sister Irene?" Jai said sheepishly.

"How can a nun who likes to drink help me right now?"

"Do you know the whole story behind that mission and what Sister Irene does for us? For Santa Fe and all the surrounding areas?" At this point we can assume no.

"Nope, we don't have all day, so short version."

"She delivers food and medical supplies to people like me, covering a hundred-mile radius around the city. Easily, if not farther. That's one of the biggest issues with the homeless problem in Santa Fe. We are spread out, in the mountains, some in groups, some on our own."

"I guess I'm still not following, I know she's an amazing woman. All of them are over there." I'm also in a rage, so my vision is a bit fucked.

"There are a few of the key people in her network that have cellphones. She lets them charge them from time to time when they come in. This way, if there's an emergency out somewhere and they need help, they can call her. She is a saint, more so than you might have imagined. If anyone can help you find that plane in Santa Fe or the surrounding area, outside of the authorities, I'd ask for her help. Plus it can't hurt to have God on your side right now."

"You have a point. Great idea, too. I'll give her a call in a few minutes. Thanks, Jai."

Just like that, Jai gave us a crazy idea, but those are the best ones. Those are the ideas that BCI was built on. The ones involving me driving through a police precinct in Warsaw or shooting up a fish tank in Gaines's office. I'll throw up a prayer in more ways than one; it can't hurt. I had still been hanging out near the heavy bag, hitting it in between phone calls, waiting on Mike to arrive, when Ken caught me.

"You going to be okay, Neil? We will find her. We did it once before, and we'll do it again."

"I'll get through it; I just need to get moving. Right now we are standing still, and that's what's eating me alive."

"I know. As soon as Mike gets here, we'll get you two moving out to an airfield and on a plane. What were you and Jai talking about?"

"He gave me some great advice. He is a smart kid; he has that street-smart savviness to him. We need to get him working with the

teams on small projects ASAP. Especially the grunt shit; he'll do well."
I think he could be up there with Christian.

"I know what you mean. I'll make sure it happens. Side note, with
Christian and Terrance on their way up here. Do you think we can get
Christian on a flight to Buenos Aires just in case Susie tries to make a
run for it? I want a backup plan."

"What are you going to have him do? Kidnap her?"

"No, detain her with restraints so she can't move. Were not going
to test an international scandal again." Yes, I mean kidnap.

"Neil, that sounds a lot like an international crime spree. First, the
shit in Poland; now, Argentina?" It's Ken's job to keep me in check.

"I'll take it all under advisement. Get Christian to Argentina. I'm
sending Erin out there if we don't have confirmation on Ms. Gaines's
plane."

"Will do, but only to observe and report."

"Understood."

Off the phone I saw Mike pull in; I didn't even wait for him to slow
down. I grabbed my go bag that was waiting for me up front. Once
Mike was on his way back, I threw it by the door to make sure I was
ready to go. I've been waiting around. Time to get a move on.

"Mike, how's it going?"

"Shit, Neil, I barely stopped. I get the urgency, however. Let's get
out of here. I have a ride to Santa Fe. I also have eyes on the airport
and a few news choppers searching. Next round, we'll send up search-
and-rescue choppers to look for the plane."

"Do you think they'll be able to see the plane at night if it already
landed? Or if it's in a hangar?"

"That part will be hard, damn near impossible, but I'm not going to give up. I called a CIA buddy who owes me a favor. I also tried to clear the air for your girl Erin. He said if we bring this case home, he'll look at helping her out."

"I'm not the world's biggest fan of hers, but she's a great asset. The CIA knows that they also know they had to disavow her after that stunt causing the death of a civilian."

"The drive over to the airport we're flying out of is about twenty minutes. We're taking a G6 out of the old Detroit airport downtown straight into Santa Fe."

"Nice; it'll give me time to catch a nap. I need to make a few calls before we hit the plane."

"No worries; I'll turn down the music for you."

I called Erin; no answer. Instead I left her a text, telling her we need her in Buenos Aires, that I'm sending someone down there to meet her. I also informed her of the news that Mike will be working to help her when we close this case. I was digging through my notes to find Sister Irene's number. I don't know why I didn't save it. I got a text back from Erin, and it was a thumbs up and a plane emoji. Followed by the words "I'm off to Argentina" and ending with "Thanks." There it is, I found Sister Irene's phone number, dialed it, and got a dial tone; nothing. Oh shit, my fours and nines are brutal; even I can't read them.

"Sister Irene. May I ask who's calling?"

"Hey, it's Neil. I'm calling because of an urgent matter involving Maria."

"Your lovely agent girlfriend? Other than say a prayer, what can I do for you, Neil?"

"You know our friend Jai? I ended up bringing him back to Detroit, giving him a job and a place to stay. That's a different story for a different day. He told me of a network you have access to, of people that might be able to help us find a huge needle hidden in a haystack."

"Well, tell me what you have going on and we'll see what we can come up with."

The rest of the drive to the airport I spent walking Sister Irene through everything, giving her details, texting her intel, and getting on the horn to get TJ to text her as well. We needed to get as much information as we could into the hands of these people so they can spot what we're looking for.

"So do you think you can help us?"

"I've used this network to track down people before, so I don't see why we can't try it for this purpose. This is much easier; one would think to see a plane rather than a person. Getting confirmation of the right plane is another thing."

"Just have them tell you the tail numbers for confirmation; it's like the license plate of a car."

"Sounds good. Be safe, Neil, and bring that lovely girl home."

"That's the plan, Sister Irene."

Off the phone and on the plane, Mike and I buckled up, with the pilot telling us we were about to take off shortly. By now it was almost ten at night, the flight was going to take just short of six hours to get there, and we would gain two hours heading back. We should land at about one in the morning, according to the pilot.

REQUIEM

This is going to be a long flight for me mentally if I don't fall asleep. That being said, there is no way for me to lubricate to try and sleep. Drinking at a time like this is irrational on so many levels. Not to mention there isn't a flight attendant on the CIA middle-of-the-night last-second express to Santa Fe. I guess I will just have to sit back, start a deep meditation, and find a way to slow down my thinking.

Maybe if I think about the past week, the positive moments, working with the sisters, the mountain hikes, and the sunrises, I can trick myself into thinking it's all good. I don't think I can get my head out of the gutter, but I am slowing down my breathing and thinking. Starting to work through the case, putting people in their spots, and starting to associate their plays. Susie is irrational, acts on her gut. Trying to show her brother she has what it takes to be the big shot, but it doesn't look like it's working.

This is all conjecture, since I'm not in her head. I'm trying to use the time I spent talking to her, the moments with her brother, and the detailed conversations I had with Lynn. There is a story there, a path that leads those two here to this crazy path of destruction and crime. Had they been broke, I think they would have been two thugs in an inner city somewhere, but due to their parents and trust funds, they had access to great wealth for their dumb and illegal ideas.

Here I am calling them dumb, but somewhere down the line they have created a new drug. Aligned with some of the biggest cartels in the country to disperse the new drug and found a way to get to me multiple times and kidnap my girlfriend. I guess they are either incredibly lucky or pretty good at being bad guys and gals.

As I began to finally fade away into sleep, I couldn't help but think about the way Susie kept trying to tell us that she created the drug but wanted to stop it. Then her brother tried to release it to the world without her will. She claimed there were no fail-safes, no way to re-create it. Obviously there was a way for all of this to happen, but it doesn't make sense. Before I fell asleep I shot an email to TJ and Ken, asking them to look for former employees of Gaines Chemical, higher-up scientists that can speak about their processes. Track them down, and we'll contact them in the morning.

23

DO YOU FEEL LIKE GETTING IN A GUN BATTLE, OUTMANNED WITH A NUN AS A BACKUP?

We were on the ground, and the landing abruptly woke us. The best part was as we landed, Mike and I woke at the same time, as if someone threw us off a bed. We looked at each other, smiled a bit, and chuckled.

"Hey pilot, was that our wake-up call?!" Mike yelled up front.

"Sorry about that, guys. I've never landed here, and these mountains at night through me for a loop. Especially with most of the airport shut down. We are kind of flying blind out here. Is there anything else I can do for you two gentlemen?"

"I think we're good. Thanks for the ride on such short notice. I've flown Erin before, take good care of her. Let's get her back into the fold; she deserves it. I'm not sure what she did, but I'm sure she felt it was the best thing to save the most lives." The pilot was concerned.

"We're working on it." Along with a myriad of other shit.

"Neil, our ride is waiting for us. Let's get going."

"Who is picking us up this late, Mike?"

"No one. I got a local contact to grab a rental for us and leave it down the street. He texted me a picture of where it's parked. We have to get to walking; we have about a good mile to go."

"Then let's get to stepping. Good thing I didn't pack an arsenal. Just a few guns, knives, and cameras." Mike checked my bag weight.

"Dude, what is in here, dumbbells?"

"Hey man, I'm not going to let anything go to chance."

I tossed the bag over my shoulder, and we began to walk toward the end of the airport. It was an odd feeling to walk out of the runway in the middle of the night at a closed airport. I watched the plane taxi to a hangar, was a bit surprised that he wasn't taking back off or getting fuel.

"Mike, is the plane hanging around for us?"

"They'll wait around thirty-six hours to see if we need a quick jump back. He'll need to fuel up, clear his flight plans, et cetera, tomorrow."

"Well, then let's make this shit quick and try and get out of here."

"I'm with you, Neil. Let's find our girl and get her home."

The walk took us a solid thirty minutes to get to the car. By this point, we had both checked in on our phones, looking through emails, text messages, and even made a few phone calls. Mike checked in with his office, about a local DEA contact he can work with that we set up through Jordan earlier in the week. I spoke to TJ about the little project I emailed about and got the information needed.

For now, Mike and I were about to start searching around for anything and everything, but the first thing we have to do is stop at the kitchen and talk to Sister Irene. I already have a message from her saying that she'll be awake when we land. That's where we are heading; it seems to be a decent drive from over here.

"Mike, nice job on the rental. You love your SUVs, don't you? An Explorer, it's pretty nice, leather interior."

"Neil, I feel like you are patronizing me a little bit. I called in favor from the local field office. They brought me a car and left it. It's not a rental but an FBI car out of Albuquerque."

"This is too nice to be purchased; my guess is someone obtained it through search and seizure?"

"Probably. According to the GPS, we are getting close to that address you gave me. Is this the place you were at all week working?"

"Yeah, it's where Sister Irene is. She's the one with the network of people that we are going to use as our eyes and ears to aid in tracking down Susie Gaines, that plane, and Maria."

As we pulled up, the lights were on out back, and I could hear what sounded like Sister Irene talking to someone. With it as quiet as it is in Santa Fe at almost two in the morning, it wasn't hard to hear her loud voice carry around the kitchen to the front. As Mike and I made our way around the back, we found Sister Irene talking to Erin and another man.

"Erin, what are you still doing here? I thought we told you to head down to Argentina."

"I will be; I couldn't get out until tomorrow early afternoon. So I made my way to the only contact I can trust in the area, Sister Irene here."

"She has been a great help most of the night working the network with me, tracking down leads. We didn't want to say anything to you guys because we hadn't quite narrowed it down."

"Narrowed what down? The plane search?"

"We have two different leads on where the plane is, but both guys that spotted it can't check the tail numbers. I guess we split up and see where it takes us?" Sister Irene said, concerned.

"Sister, you've already done more than you need to. You can leave it up to the three of us. We'll be fine." Mike chimed in, "Here we go."

"Mr., I don't know who you are. I'll have you know I've dealt with drug dealers in the barrio all over Florida while messed up on meth. I can handle whatever this is."

"Fair enough. Neil, what say you?"

"How about you and Erin go check out one. Then Sister Irene and I can check out the other one."

"I guess that'll work, but I don't see another car. How is everyone getting around?"

"We can use the truck. It's old as shit, but reliable and runs great. As long as we don't have to go above sixty-five, we're good to go." Sister Irene smiled.

"This should be great for old speed demon Neil. I would love to see him in that car. Just point us in the right direction and we'll head out. You ready, Erin?"

"I'm good, Mike. You two be safe."

"We'll be fine. I have my shotgun and softball bat in the car. Neil, did you pack anything?"

"Sister, he has a small arsenal in his bag. You'll be good."

"I didn't pack an arsenal, but I have what I need. I'll grab my bag and throw it in the back of the truck. Let's head out. Erin, do you have the place where you're going?"

"I do. They're actually in similar areas only about two miles apart from each other. They're at the edge of the city, and yours will be farther east and ours west. Good luck, be safe, and holler as soon as you know one way or another."

"Sounds good, Erin. Right back at you."

As we got in our cars and parted ways, I couldn't help but laugh a bit because we were driving to scout a plane, try to do it in secret, and the truck almost sounds like a jet engine. From the hole in the muffler, I can only guess, and the rattling body. We aren't going to sneak up on anyone in this thing. It took about twenty minutes for us to get to our spot, but Mike and Erin texted a few minutes earlier, saying they were pulling into their spot. Not surprising since they could go twenty miles an hour faster than we could.

"All right, Sister, I'm going to have you stay in the car while I scope out the place and see what's around here."

"Okay, but I'm not going to sit here all night while you have all the fun."

I went around the back of the truck, grabbed my gun, and put a scope on it, mainly to give me a range of sight to look around. It's not as if I have some video game–like range with my handgun. It's a standard Glock with a long barrel, which allows for a few more accessories when needed. I think it's more about comfort than anything else.

I had Sister Irene park on the street as I made my way up an embankment and through some brush where I could look over to the property where the plane was suspected to be. It took me a few minutes to get up there, quietly to ensure I wasn't detected when I felt my phone going off. It was a text from Erin and Mike, saying their plane doesn't match Gaines's. How many planes are landing in Santa Fe? Then again, it is a large international art city, as well as a vacation home for many of the rich and famous.

I messaged them back saying I could see the front end of the plane, which matches the description, but I need to get a better vantage point. I told them to head this way and find Sister Irene; might as well get backup if needed. No point in having them leave and head somewhere else at this point. I realized the sun is going to be coming in soon, an hour or so. Which means I'm going to lose my cover; I need to get moving.

I swung around the property, moving at a much faster pace, especially since I noticed there weren't a large number of armed guards surveying the property. If anything, it looked more like a few security guys stationed at the door or two surrounding a vacation home. For all I could tell, the scene TJ heard and what Erin described aren't matching what I see here. Maybe it's just a coincidence and another dead end.

I finally got a better look at the plane but could barely make out the tail numbers from my angle. Even with the scope, I could only get half of them, but they do line up. I called Mike and told him and Erin to make their over to my location so I could have her try to confirm the plane or guards that we can make out.

The house is the standard adobe-style mini mansion you see in Santa Fe. It's less about size out here and more about location. I'd say it's barely two thousand square feet. It sits on a gorgeous piece of land at the base of a mountain. With a small runway to land a G6 on, that's where the price tag comes in.

"Hey Neil, we're here. Let me see the scope. Mike is over to our side, flanking us for now."

"Okay, I see him over there. Here you go, Erin."

"That looks like the plane. It even has a bullet hole in the door, probably from when I was shooting back at them. Also, that's definitely one of the guards from earlier. The only problem is that I don't see Maria or Susie anywhere. Did you catch either one of them when you were looking?"

"Nope. Let me see that scope again; something doesn't look right. Over in the corner, what is that?"

"It looks like a body rolled up. Before you get worked up, it could be the body that Maria shot. Remember, I told you she grabbed someone's gun and shot them. At least that's what it looked like."

I became fixated on the body, rolled up in canvas. It was off in the distance, hard to make out, but if you've seen one, you recognize it. It's hard to tell if that's Maria, but I can't help but feel the pit in my stomach curling up to the size of a small basketball. I could barely handle the news back at the warehouse. If I see her dead here, it's not going to end well.

"Hey Mike, do you see that canvas over there? Can you and Erin go check it out? I'm going to get a closer look at the plane and see what's going on over there. Try to get confirmation of it's Gaines's plane."

"Sounds good. I have Jordan's local DEA crew on high alert. They are a good hour out, though. Trying to get to town," Mike said with a long pause.

"We'll go check on that body for you, be safe checking on the plane. We can't take everyone on by ourselves." Erin has a point.

"Hey, if we see Maria, her safety is the top priority, even if that means we have to hightail it out of here. No cowboy shit. I know I'm talking to myself mostly."

"I was about to look at you crazy for a moment there, Neil." Mike gave me a death stare.

As they took off to the right and I went around to the left of the property, I could see movement, but not enough to slow down. We were losing darkness and had to get around before the sun gave away our position. As I approached the mini hangar, more of a large barn, I could make out the tail of the plane. It was Gaines's plane, that's for sure. There was also a noticeable pool of blood at the base of the steps. Someone either died or was wounded poorly on that plane. My heart sank to my gut; I couldn't function for a second. I just stopped moving, my legs frozen in place.

I noticed someone moving around the building, doing a general sweep of the area, but making their way toward Mike and Erin's location. I called over there since we aren't doing this very professionally. We don't have the proper gear; we aren't using walkie-talkies even from a sporting goods store.

"Hey Mike, get down, someone is heading your way. I'll text you when it's clear."

"Got it. Erin, get down."

They tucked behind some brush, laid low, and let the guard finish his half-ass sweep of the area. This isn't a movie, and these guys are probably thinking, no one is coming after them in Santa Fe. Not the worst assumption ever, though if you exchanged gunfire with someone, you would think you might be a little more vigilant. I sent a message to Mike and Erin to let them know they're well to go. As they started making it over to the area where the body was, I realized we had taken a lot longer than expected. I noticed that the sun was coming up.

I didn't want to scream over there, but they have to realize we are in a hurry. I decided to cause a bit of a distraction, nothing major, just a little disturbance. I made my way up to the top of the hill by the side of the barn/hangar. Tossed a rock into the barn and started pushing rock down the side of the hill to make it look like something had just run by. With all the wildlife out here, they'll assume something merely ran through the woods, but it should give Mike and Erin enough time to run down and check on the body.

I couldn't make out what they were doing from my vantage point, so I ran back around the barn to our original location to get a better view of everything. As the sun started to come up, I looked over to the area where the body was, but it was gone. This can't be good. I doubled back to the truck and hoped that it was Mike grabbing a body to ID them later for investigative purposes and not my worst fear.

I was about halfway back down the side of the mountain when I started to hear gunfire from the house. I think I spooked them pretty badly. It sounded as if they were firing in the general direction of the area I had just come from. As I made my way back up to catch a glimpse of what was going on, I noticed Susie walking out front to find the body missing, and yelling for the guards to investigate. This is my cue to hightail it out of here, get down the barn, and hop in the car. Sprinting down the side of the hill, I noticed that Mike and Erin were at the back of the truck with Sister Irene and the body.

"Guys, they are searching for the body and whatever took it. We need to get out of here."

"Neil, we need to talk about what we found."

"We can talk back at the house. Do you feel like getting in a gun battle, outmanned with a nun as a backup?"

"Fair point." Mike caught on.

"Sisters, get in the car. Let's go."

24

AWAKE ON A SLAB IN THE CORONER'S OFFICE IS NOT THE WAY ANYONE WANTS TO WAKE UP.

I'm torn up with emotion right now. The fear of getting caught in the middle of something and not being prepared is eating at me. The fear of knowing I might be driving away, slowly in this shit truck with the body of my girlfriend, and not knowing if I'll be able to handle it. I keep looking back to check on the body, see if I can catch a glimpse of anything as the sun comes up. I'm worried that if we get noticed on the road with a dead body in the trunk, someone will question us and what we are doing. My phone was buzzing in my pants, probably Mike or Erin calling me, since they are also flashing their lights.

"Yeah, Mike, what's up?"

"Hey Neil, follow me. We need to go somewhere with the body. We can't just take it back to the soup kitchen. I'll call ahead to the morgue, explain to them what's going on. It's not perfect, but it's better than getting arrested."

"We can deal with the rest once we get there. I'll drive slow enough that you can keep up."

I'm not sure how Mike plans on handling this one. I know there is a field office in Santa Fe, even if it is a small one. It's a capital, and there is going to be an office there. Mike is probably calling them, finding out where to go, then driving us out there if he hasn't called already. There was a ten-minute lag time from when we pulled out until he called me.

The drive to the coroner was a long one. I still kept looking over my shoulder, with an eerie silence coming from Sister Irene. She just kept praying under her breath. Not sure where she got the rosary, but not surprised she had one on her either.

"Sister, did you see who it is?"

"No, I did not, Neil." I feel like she's lying, but I'm not about to accuse her.

"Did Mike and Erin get a look? What are we doing driving with a body around Santa Fe?"

"Mike said we need to get the body back to a coroner. He said some evidence is better than no evidence. Even if it might not be admissible in court, he was shaken. Then again, you guys were running, and there were gunshots."

"Good points all around. It looks like we're here." Mike called me again.

"Neil, they said for us to pull around back and have you pull into the loading bay. It'll be open so you can back it in."

"Understood."

As we made our way around the back, I realized we are at the FBI field office. In Santa Fe, Mike is worried the evidence isn't going to be admissible, but he didn't want to leave the body behind. This has to be Maria; there is no way it isn't. As we were about to get out of the truck, Sister Irene put her hand in mine and said a little prayer. Now I'm really shaking. I can barely breathe.

We stepped out of the truck, almost in unison. She rushed her way around the front of the truck to meet me on the driver's side. She came up to me and slowed me down, noticed I was worked up and tense. She could see my breathing change dramatically as I tried to walk to the end of the truck. Even though it was merely a short distance, Mike looked to be a block away.

I felt my hands get sweaty, and my heart pound harder and harder until my head started to spin. As I walked to the edge of the truck, my legs gave way, and I passed out back into Sister Irene. The last thing I heard was Sister screaming for help as I passed out.

Awake on a slab in the coroner's office is not the way anyone wants to wake up. Then again, it beats being there dead and unable to move. The room was cold as shit, and when I woke up, all I saw was Sister Irene and an empty room.

"Where is everyone, Sister?"

"Mike and Erin are in the other room visiting with a few agents getting things squared away with the shit you guys pulled tonight."

"Don't forget you were part of this heist."

"I was just the getaway driver. Before you even ask, I don't know who the body is. I was too busy tending to you." The more she denies knowing, the more anxiety it gives me.

"Okay, I guess I can just get up and head out there. I'll see what's going on."

"Hey Mike, he's up!" Or she can yell from in here.

Right then, Mike, Erin, and two other agents I have never met walked in. Slowly behind them came a doctor, more like the coroner. I'm sitting here trying to psychoanalyze them, look at their body language. If it was Maria, their eyes should be red, puffy, and a bit distressed. I don't see any of that. Maybe it was a guard and she's okay.

"Hey, Neil. Nice of you to join the land of the living." Real funny Mike.

"Nice joke. Do we have any intel on who the body was?" I'm tired of waiting.

"We'll get there. First thing, let the doctor check you out. You hit your head pretty hard and have been out for almost a good hour. We want to make sure you're okay."

"It's not like you took me to the hospital. You left me on a cadaver slab."

"Fair point."

While Mike and I were jawing back and forth a bit, the doctor checked my vitals. Gave me a quick once-over and then the old "you're good" sign. He didn't want to get between Mike and me sparring at the moment. I noticed while we were verbally sparring, Erin and Sister Irene sneaked out of the room, along with the other agents. Leaving only Mike and myself alone in the metal room, reeking of death.

"Neil, we should probably sit down." Mike's eyes started to well up.

"Don't say it, Mike, don't you fucking say it!" She's dead, I knew it.

"It was Maria. The coroner said she died of a gunshot wound to the head."

"From all the gunfire?"

"No, they are pretty sure, judging by the residue at point of entry, it was execution-style."

I dropped to my knees, lost all air in my lungs, and began to sob. Though I fought as much of it as I could, there wasn't much I could do. Mike dropped down next to me and began crying with me. We just sat there, two grown men, not that long ago fighting for her attention. Now grieving over her death. Eventually Sister Irene and Erin came in, and the four of us began to fight back tears, talk of Maria, and console each other.

"I barely knew her, but she was a beautiful soul. I will make sure we keep a candle lit for many years to come in her honor."

"Thanks, Sister. That means a lot. Erin, I know the easy thing would be for me to blame you. I do a little bit, but the adult in me is fighting that urge. I know you cared about her."

"I'm so sorry, Neil. I know that you two were close. She cared about you so much. She was one of the few people that believed in me, tried to help me." Erin was gasping.

"I know, Erin. We will get through it. Figure it out and get the Gaines kids. Mike, did you arrange transport back to Detroit for her parents and a proper burial?" I know it's quick, but it's how I cope.

"Yeah, I put the calls in already. I haven't spoken to her parents yet because I wasn't sure if you wanted to call me or how you wanted to do it. Seeing as you two had such a great relationship."

"Thanks, Mike. It's going to be rough, but I do think we should tell them together. Is there any way to make sure an agent is there for them when we call?"

"That's a good idea. I can get someone to drive there now. I'll shoot a text to Jen; I'll have her coordinate it."

We sat there, fighting back the tears, crying, and talking of Maria. The memories we had, things we were supposed to do, and how shitty it was to be in this situation. It's the hardest part of this job, dealing with death. We can feel indestructible at times because we're around so much shit for so long. To have to deal with this; it just takes you to the honest moment none of us like to deal with. We walk the fine line of life and death.

It took some courage, some coaxing and lying to ourselves, but Mike and I were able to muster the strength to call Maria's parents. Hearing them sob on the phone crushed me, made me feel responsible. I brought her on this vacation, where Erin brought her into this case, where she lost her life. I know rationally this isn't my fault, it's Susie Gaines's and her people. Still, my heart doesn't care right now. My heart wants to blame me for everything right now.

"Okay, guys, we've been moping around here for more than an hour. It's time to focus and use this energy to find and get the bitch that's responsible for taking this angle from us." Sister was pissed.

"Damn, Sister Irene. You've got a great point, though. We need to get focused and push through this. It's not going to be easy, and we're not going to get over it anytime soon. What better medication to overcome this pain than to serve that bitch the justice she deserves."

"I think we can all get behind that. Sister, do you think you can work with your network to keep an ear to the street? Erin, we need to find out how we got blindsided by El Jefe, what his play was by Susie. Also, where is she headed, what's her next move/ We've already got

Jordan's team heading there now to the house. As soon as we pulled in, they were a few moments out to the house."

"Mike, we have them already on their way out there. She's going to be gone. I guarantee that they took off as soon as we spooked them and took Maria's body. Which reminds me, was there a slug that could be pulled for evidence?"

"I'm still waiting on the coroner's report. Let's get out of here. Head back to the kitchen, drop off Sister Irene. Then we can head over to the house and see what the DEA has found."

"I'm fine to drive back myself. Why don't the three of you just head over to see what they have found." Sister Irene makes a great point.

"I guess we're not thinking straight. Not surprising; it's been a rough night."

As the three of us made our way over to the scene we had just left hours earlier. It looked different with the light of day on it, covered in crime scene tape, DEA, and FBI agents. The three of us made our way through the checkpoint keeping people out. The plane was there still, but not in any shape to fly. It looks as though someone set the plane ablaze to hide what had happened here earlier. It's a little brutish, but it is effective at destroying evidence.

"Mike, are you seeing this shit?"

"Yeah, but I'm not sure I believe it. Susie lit her own sixty-million-dollar plane on fire."

"I bet they think they can make an insurance claim on that shit. These crazy rich fucks always believe they can get away with murder.

I wish I could see Jason in his cell losing his shit right now. Knowing his sister is ruining his plan left and right."

"I still can't believe all this is happening right now. I get that Susie thinks she can do no wrong. I understand this is a billion-dollar venture and that she isn't going to let anything get in her way. Yet, how did they get out of here?"

"I think I know how. Keep looking around. I'm going to have TJ look something up."

Mike and Erin went inside to find out if the DEA or FBI teams had found anything useful. I took a moment to message TJ. To look at flight records from Detroit to Santa Fe, and any other city that Gaines Chemical has a headquarters where they might have another plane. I remember reading somewhere in our stacks on these kids that between them and their parents, they had some absurd net worth, and it involved a fleet of planes. This plane looked like an older model, almost like she wouldn't mind missing it.

As I continued around the property, I remembered that there were no shoes on the body. Maria's heels were in the corner of the hangar, off to the side, discarded like trash. I know I can't touch them; I need to leave them there to be processed, but it's just another reminder that she's no longer going to be there at the other end of the phone. Speaking of Maria, I haven't told Ken or the office, Sheila, so many of them. This is going to be brutal, having to relive this hell over and over as I speak to people about it.

This scene is going to be useless. I decided to walk away and message the condo owner to see if we can get the place again if needed. He messaged back, reminding me I have it paid through the end of next week. Its mine, not to worry; then I called Ken for what was going to be one more reminder of this shit.

"Ken, it's bad. It's horrible."

"Neil, you sound brutal, bro. What happened? I haven't heard from you or anyone. I even tried Maria, figured she would know where you are. Please tell me it's not the worst."

"Maria is gone, they killed her. From what we can tell, it was execution-style. I'll tell you more when I get back to Detroit, and I'll have Mike and the FBI keep you in the loop with the coroner. For now, I need to figure out our next move."

"What can I do? What can we do? She was one of ours. You know our motto."

"Protect ours, fuck the rest. We couldn't protect this one. I'm hurting bad, Ken. This one is harder than anything else."

"I know, Neil. Do you want me to call the important people for you and fill them in so you can do it on your own time?"

"Yes, Ken, thank you. I need to focus on this case and figure out the next move. Can you transfer me to TJ?"

"No problem. I'm here for you, Neil, always." Ken was fighting back tears.

"I know, Ken."

While waiting for TJ to pick up, I thought of what moves Susie had and who I could use to punish her for this shit. I don't feel that prison is enough or killing her. It needs to hurt; I need to take from her, take from Jason, make them hurt. I need to find a way to put a wedge between them. There needs to be some doubt, some dishonesty that pushes them apart, makes them feel on an island. This is how I'm going to get back at them. I'm going to alienate them from each other.

They have always had each other, always been able to push to extremes and fall back to their sibling. I have one in prison on the way out, and it's time for one to head in. If I can't have them both in prison, I will keep one in jail at all times, continually rotating them, pushing them farther and farther apart. They have enough illicit behavior to keep them locked up forever, and it's my job to prove it.

"Hey Neil, sorry for keeping you waiting, but I was just confirming something I thought you'd want to hear."

"What's that, TJ? Give me some good news."

"Well, I can give you some good intel, not sure if it's good news. It turns out that Gaines sent a plane out from Houston to Santa Fe with a flight plan returning it to Detroit. It looks like you need to come home."

"Well, we have a plane waiting for us. I'll let Mike know, and I guess I'll see you in a few hours."

"See you soon, Neil."

As I got off the phone with TJ, I let Mike know what was going on and told him and Erin we should get going. Erin asked if she should still head down to Buenos Aires to sit at the airport with Christian. What do you think I said? Fuck yeah, get your ass down there, help him out, cause there will be a good chance she runs down there. If that happens, I want them waiting for her.

25

I ABRUPTLY HUNG UP AND BEGAN TO LET THE TEARS FALL.

We dropped Erin off at her hotel; then we took off toward the airport. This case had me feeling empty from the way it ended up with the Gaines siblings, not merely the death of Maria. I'm so over the way we were pulled into the case. I had Jason behind bars, Susie was in Argentina, leaving everyone alone, and Maria was alive. I guess the Maria part is bothering me a lot. Not surprising that I'm thinking about the time we spent walking around Buenos Aires, handing me a drink in Santa Fe. It's as if I'm having the last several days playing over in my head.

As Mike and I sit on the plane, knowing Erin and Christian will be there as a backup plan seems to calm me a bit. Now I need to think through the process by which I'm going to mess with Susie and Jason. Come to think of it, I have Susie's cell phone number. I need to get ahold of her and figure out the best scenario to getting her to act irrationally. Knowing what I do now with the information Lynn gave me, things are beginning to add up with how they are operating. Jason is the meticulous one, thinking it through. Though it looks crazy, he has a plan.

Susie just shoots from the hip, acts out of emotion, then leaves it for Jason to clean up. He's due out in two days. I think I'm going to focus on getting her in prison for Maria's death instead of preventing Jason from getting out. I don't think there is enough time or energy to do both. The first half of the flight was just quiet, Mike and I in our thoughts, working on our laptops, working through our own stuff. I finally broke the silence.

"Mike, we've only got a few hours left on the flight. I think I have an idea for the way we need to play this. I wanted to run it by you." I want to talk about Maria, but I need to build up to it.

"Sure, thing Neil. What do you have?"

"I don't think we have enough resources or energy to try to link things back to Jason and go after Susie at the same time. We need to focus on getting her behind bars. Especially pinning Maria's murder on her, getting her on a capital crime."

"I agree that if we spread too thin, we might blow both opportunities. We owe it to Maria to put Susie in prison for a long time." Mike was getting worked up.

"Do we think Susie is on the way back to Detroit for the new drug unveiling for her company? And to pick her brother up?"

"It's beginning to look like it. You said after speaking to the nanny they had, you had more context in how the two operate. Does it sound like something she would do? To operate as if she hadn't just killed an FBI agent and burned down her plane?"

"I do. I think she would do it over and over. So would Jason. The difference is he would do a better job of hiding it. Have we gotten any info back from the DEA that was investigating the crime scene with your FBI counterparts at the scene of the plane burning?"

"They did say they found trace evidence on the plane, bullet fragments as well as some other items, but it will take time to process. There is a rush on it, but we won't know until later today or tomorrow at the earliest. The hope is that they find trace evidence that puts Maria on that plane, along with the evidence of her murder."

Mike and I went back and forth, working through the case and fighting back the tears. Every time Maria would come up, you could see the two of us struggling to keep it together. With her death still so fresh in our minds, it was nearly impossible to focus. That's what gave me an idea on how to utilize Susie's number, how to get at her.

I took out my laptop to email TJ and had him program a cell phone for me with a New Mexico area code. I told him just to throw it in my car, since I probably won't sit around when we get there. I am going to use it to text Susie and act like an anonymous person who knows what she did. It's just one layer of messing with Susie, but it's a start. The next will be using Nicolette on the inside to sabotage as much shit as possible. That will get inside Susie's head and have her increase security, making her even more paranoid.

The remainder of the trip was quiet again, quick, and productive. Mike spent the time emailing and following up with his agents to inform them of what happened, while I reached out to Ken and other team members to lay the groundwork for the plan. I sent Nicolette an email explaining to her what my goal was. I need her to start looking around for weaknesses in their security that she can exploit, making them feel unsafe.

Jason was going to be out soon, and Susie was going to be on edge. The more pressure we can put on them, the better. Ken emailed back with the idea that just might work. If we make a play on some of their street gangs, like a rival gang, it might make Susie think she's being challenged from all sides. In the car, Mike was driving fast, back to the warehouse to drop me off before he made his way to his office. It was nearly six in the evening now, back in Detroit, and we had lost multiple days of investigating because of this shit with Susie in Santa Fe.

"Mike, thanks for the lift. More importantly, thank you for your friendship."

"Neil, just because some things have changed, don't think for a minute that I'm not here to support you and work with you. You're a friend and one hell of an investigator."

"Thanks, Mike. We'll get Susie one way or another. Worst case, we can always make Jason think he's next, make him move on his sister through paranoia."

"Do you think that will work? I have Frank in my back pocket. If I have him go to work on Jason, anything is possible."

"Remind me never to piss you off, Neil. You can be one vindictive bastard. Also, it beats us going to prison for murdering one of them ourselves."

"See, those are my thoughts exactly. See you, Mike."

Mike pulled in, dropped me off, and pulled away. I didn't hang around for the pity party I know would happen. I just took off in my car and headed toward FCI Milan to give Frank the heads up and work on Jason a bit. I have a few calls to make and tears to shed. Talking to Sheila is going to be tough, but I'm lucky I have her to talk to.

"Neil, are you all right? Ken, let me know what happened. Are you home?" I just let it hang there in silence.

"I'm okay, Sheila. As okay as I can be. I finally admitted to myself and was ready to tell her."

"Tell her what? Neil. It's okay; you need to get it out."

"I loved her; she's the first person since you that I truly fell for. I don't know how I'm going to get over this one." I was fighting hard not to lose it.

"Neil, you never will get over it. You'll just get used to dealing with it. Used to the pain, become numb to it. Where are you headed?" Sheila was concerned.

"I'm heading out to FCI Milan to talk to Frank. I need his help on the case. With Susie's brother about to get out tomorrow, Frank has one last shot at getting in his head."

"Neil, can you make me one promise?"

"I can try. What is it?"

"Can you promise you won't go off and kill one of them? These emotions are raw, and you're not thinking rationally."

"I'll try, but I can't promise anything right now."

I abruptly hung up and began to let the tears fall, even pulled off the road to compose myself. I sent Sheila a text to let her know I'll be safe, and she had Carol Lynn send me a quick video telling me she loved me. It made me cry even more but reminded me that I am not without love and will get through this. I need to keep my head on straight so I can put Maria's killer behind bars.

Pulling into FCI Milan, I was composed and found focus. This is going to be hard because there is no privacy in federal prison. I can't hide my emotions. I must walk a fine line and hold them inside. The process from outside to inside felt longer than usual, and each detail passed with that much more scrutiny. Then again, I had daydreams of me killing Gaines or watching Cappelano do it. I had to get those dark thoughts out of my mind before I sit down with him. Though it's late, it's part of the deal we have with Cappelano.

"Hey, Frank, how are you doing?"

"Neil, you promised you wouldn't take too long between visits. You better have a good excuse. Don't get me wrong. I kept myself busy looking after and messing with Gaines's network."

"I have a pretty good excuse. We can get into it shortly, but what did you find out?"

"It's what you thought. Gaines tried to get arrested, was open about it. He wanted to meet me, get in a room with some of the biggest names and contacts in the underworld. The quickest and easiest way to build street credit, contact the underbelly, and communicate is to thrust yourself into Hades. He just happened to know he would be able to get out sooner than later." Frank's calm tone was soothing.

"One thing I've learned recently is that Susie is off her rocker. His sister is irrational, runs on emotion, and makes rash decisions. If her brother knew what she has been doing leading up to their big day this week, he would be livid. He is trying to pull off an international drug trade, legal and illicit. This kind of move would put him in the books of criminal legends. Shit, even I'm a bit impressed. I want to slug him again, perhaps kill him, but that doesn't take away from respecting the level of balls that guy has to think big."

"You've always been able to understand and respect a level of genius. Even if it was dark, such as me. It's what makes you a great investigator. You don't get caught up in the shortsighted good versus evil. You allow yourself to understand the effort it takes to accomplish those goals, good or bad. Then you work to understand it, find the drive, and exploit it."

"Is that another compliment from Frank, without a backhanded mention of your tutorship?"

"Sarcasm aside, being here has allowed me to reflect on the past. Realize how far you've come on your own. I used you as a way to rationalize my own poor choices. Watching Gaines in here, seeing him consumed with the goal and his reasons for it are giving me a bit of perspective."

"Too bad you didn't get this before you killed close to if not more than a hundred people. Then there might be a little less damage in the world."

"True, but to think there isn't pain without me is laughable. You know there will always be evil. That's why you fight so hard to extinguish the biggest ones." Frank is building me up.

"You're unusually forthcoming and positive with me. I feel like you know something but don't want to say it."

"Neil, earlier today, Jason received communication from his sister about what he did. He lost his shit in here. Threatened to kill her. A few of us in the library with him heard it."

"Frank, who was the guard in there with you guys?"

"There was some guy that Jason always has with him, who gets him his outside line to the world. B. Adams, but not sure what the B is for. Then Colby was at the door, but I'm sure he heard it. Gaines wasn't composed as usual. He went a bit crazy."

"I'll have to follow up with Colby and have our guys figure out Gaines's angle with B. Adams. Whoever that is. Thanks, Frank."

"Did you hear what she did, the details, did he tell anyone?"

"That's what I'm trying to tell you. Gaines essentially threw his sister under the bus without realizing it. This place is under constant surveillance. He can hide the call, but his rant, that shits on tape somewhere. And yes, I heard it was Agent Garcia that his sister murdered. I'm sorry for you, Neil. I know you don't want to hear any more condolences, so I'll leave it at that."

"Thank you, Frank. You understand; sometimes you don't want the constant reminder of the wound."

Frank and I went back and forth for a few minutes, then settled into talking about old colleagues we had worked with that we had lost over the years. His were before my time, since he started killing when I was around, but the sentiment was the same. Though it's brutally hard now, we know it's part of the job we signed up for. Especially when you are in a relationship with someone who is in the same field, it's scary. Some might say that excitement is what can drive the relationship in the first place, and they aren't wrong. At least in the beginning, you understand each other, the risks, and all they come with. Then you forget about that and fall into a healthy routine. Still, suddenly a day like yesterday happens, and your reality is thrust upon you.

You're reminded that you chase killers and criminals for a living that might want to see you and others around you harmed or killed.

It's not that we aren't trying our hardest to stay alive. Following the greatest precautions, even if to some we may look careless at times. We can't be held responsible for every other person's behavior. I said my good-byes to Frank, thanked him for the info, and headed out.

Not even a few steps outside of the door, I called Mike, told him we need to get a warrant out to the prison immediately. We need to ensure that the warden doesn't have time to delete the tapes. I then sent TJ a text to dig into the digital files and see if he can protect them in case they try to delete them. I hope they do; it will implicate them even more. Finally a turn in the case, something that will make this a bit easier to manage, but at what cost?

26

THOSE ARE THE THINGS MY EMOTIONS HAVE BEEN BLOCKING.

I'm dead exhausted; drained mentally; and physically, I just need to sleep. I messaged Sheila, telling her I was on my way home, asking if she could swing by with Carol Lynn. I'm in major need of some family time, even if we're dysfunctional. My daughter is growing up so fast, and it seems like yesterday she was in grade school. Where did she go? The girl getting on and off the bus was a feat with her pigtails. Now she's almost in high school, has a bit of an attitude like me, and is a knockout like her mother.

Just thinking of them has me calming down a bit. Knowing I have that support system is going to be a saving grace to get me through this. Otherwise I would have sunk deep into my poor routine of self-pity, drinking, and rash behavior. Which can sometimes lead to great case closures but at the expense of friendships and my body. As I pulled into the driveway, I saw Sheila's car parked in the street. Just knowing I wasn't walking into an empty house certainly lifted my spirits.

Slowly, almost sloth-like, I made my way into the house lacking energy and the usual Baggio vigor. Today was a gut punch unlike any other. Today drove me to a place that will be hard to recover from. Sheila and Carol Lynn gave me a huge hug as I walked in, just quietly embracing me. I stood there, with the two them around me, fighting back tears; it was gut-wrenching. Picturing the time Maria had been at my house waiting for me to come home, the cases we worked on. Hell, catching Cappelano was with her. So many of my memories over the past couple of years have her in them, one way or another. Knowing it will merely be a memory is killing me.

"Dad, are you going to be okay?" Carol Lynn was the first to speak.

"I will now. I have two amazing women in my life that support me and show up in the darkest of hours."

"Dad, I love you. I wish I could say something or do something that could make it all better."

"Actually, there is something you two could do for me. I don't think I have it in me."

"Neil, I think I know what you want, and we already did it. We put all of Maria's stuff in a box. I don't think we missed anything. But I thought it might be too hard for you. So we set it aside to give you time to cope and deal with it when you're ready."

"Sheila . . . thank you. Can we just watch a movie or some TV? I just need to relax and let my mind wander for a bit."

"Sounds good. Why don't we watch your favorite movie of all time?" Sheila chimed in.

"I know you two hate that movie. It's okay."

"We can watch it for you." Carol Lynn smiled.

"Instead, how about we compromise and watch a favorite of mine you two can stomach?"

"You mean instead of the usual *Tin Cup*, we get to watch *Bull Durham*? I'm okay with that. Do you want a drink? I can go pour you one, just sit here with Carol Lynn."

"No, I think I'm just going to sit down, relax with you two, and hopefully fall asleep."

The next twenty minutes went by quickly as we spoke about the school and what Carol Lynn was excited about next year in high school. As the movie started, Sheila got up and turned down the lights, knowing I would fall asleep shortly. She could see the exhaustion in my face, the lack of spirit in my body. I didn't even make it to the middle of the movie, and I was out like a light. I can only assume that they tucked me in on the couch.

I woke up at about two in the morning, with a text from Sheila telling me they had left me there, tucked me in, and even unpacked my bags, did some laundry, and did some grocery shopping. They really took care of me, knowing I would be focusing on limited mental capacity for a few days.

I realized it was two in the morning, but I forgot to tell Father Roberts. I can only assume Ken would have reached out to him, but I'll shoot him a text telling him to call me first thing in the morning when he starts his routine. That's usually about four in the morning for him, which means I have two hours to kill. I know just what to do: for starters, I'm going to take the girls for a quick walk, nothing fancy, just some fresh air, then come back and hit the heavy bag.

After a good thirty minutes outside, we made it back to the house, where I quickly changed into some workout clothes. I went downstairs and threw on some music, something to hit the bag hard and with everything I had. I put together a quick internet radio station with a mix of rock, Frank Sinatra, and DMX. I know this early morning/late night session is about to get a bit weird. The girls were good and tired upstairs, music blaring with me downstairs, wraps on, and ready to go.

Combinations started flying, working through my usual set. Clearing my mind, I began talking to myself as each combination landed.

Simple 1-2: Breathe. Think through the case, Neil. What are Jason and Susie's next moves?

Combo 1-1-2: If Susie is acting fast and irrational, we need to use it. What's the move?

Combo 1-2-3-2: Longer combo, means less thought, more anger. Why Maria? Why kill her?

Simple 1-2: Even if you're acting on emotion, there's no reason to shoot Maria. It doesn't add up.

Combo 2-3-3: Did Maria find something? Where is Ms. Choike in all of this? Where is Erin in all of this?

Those are the things my emotions have been blocking. By now, Erin might be in Argentina, but I can email her first, then try calling her. I know I should have done that in reverse, but it's three in the morning. Damn it; the phone went to voice mail. I'll message TJ, have him look up Erin's flight info, see when she lands so I can plan on when to hear from her. Back to the bag for a few more minutes, I started to lose my footwork and my combinations and just started throwing hook after hook. Launching my left hand into the bag over and over until my hand went numb.

That's it, that's got to be what I'm missing. I have to get past Maria being gone. I know it'll take time emotionally, but I have to focus on the case. Why would Susie react the way she did? How the hell did Maria even end up on that plane? How did Erin get free, and Maria get kidnapped? Too many people are dying around Erin; something isn't adding up. I need to make a call.

"Christian, its Neil. I know its early as shit over there."

"No problem, Neil, it's been a vacation pretty much. I heard the news about Maria. If you need anything, maybe a misplaced bullet, you let me know." Okay, that made me smile.

"Well said. I need you to keep an eye out. I think Erin killed Maria and is hiding it. I have some intel that claims Susie did, but I believe its people misunderstood that she put a hit out on Maria. There is no reason for Susie to get her hands dirty, it's not in her MO. On the other hand, Erin keeps piling up bodies."

"That makes sense. I'll keep my guard up. You should probably have TJ look into Erin's financials and see if any money made its way to her somewhere. We haven't done a TJ deep dive on Erin, though we are trusting her."

"I had him start a background on her a while back but never followed up. I'll see what he has. Great idea, Christian, thanks for everything. Please be safe. I can't lose another person right now."

"You got it, boss. Want me to hire someone to watch my six, at least for a few days?"

"Also not a bad idea. Not sure what you'll find, but go for it. Just expense it, I've got you covered."

"Thanks for making sure I stay alive. We'll get these crazy bastards, I promise."

"Thanks, Christian. Get some sleep, I'll have me or Ken follow up if we find anything."

"Night, Neil."

Off the phone, I called the office and got TJ, 'cause he never sleeps. We joke, but he operates on night hours. He'll sleep from eight or nine until five. It's been his schedule as long as we can remember, and it works. We have created a schedule that allows us to count on getting intel first thing in the morning from him and his team. A few of them work through the usual nine-to-five hours, but most are working in reverse of that.

It's a little after four in the morning, and I saw my phone had started to ring. It was Father Roberts. A phone call I have needed but have been dreading all day. He has a way of forcing me to deal with my personal shit. At least by now, I've openly admitted to a few people, maybe, that I loved her. That's what is going to make this even more difficult.

"Hey Neil, I saw your message. I didn't call you right away, but you are getting a call early enough. How are you holding up with everything?"

"I'm doing better than I had expected. Had you spoken to me earlier yesterday, it would have been a different conversation altogether. I'm not over it by any means, just accepted that the pain is going to be there for a while. I have to deal with it, knowing some days are going to be brutal compared to others."

"That's called growth, Neil. Had this been a year or two ago, I'm not sure your drinking or irrational behavior would have survived it. You would have gone down that path that Cappelano led you down when you've got blinders on and let your emotions control you."

"I know, Father, it's been a running dialog in my head all day. Focusing on staying clear of those triggers that might get me back down that path."

"Are you drinking? Or going to drink?"

"No. I'm pretty sure for a while I'm going to keep my mind lucid and sharp. I don't want to let go of any of our memories. I want to embrace them, embrace the pain, and know they're there because of what we shared. I don't want to hide from them."

"That means the world to me, Neil. As your friend, as a pastor, and as a man, I am worried about you on so many levels. Hearing that come from you, so quickly after a tragedy like this. I know it won't be easy, but you have never shied away from the tough days."

We went on talking for a solid hour, talking about how great Santa Fe was with Maria. Going over the places we went to dinner, the different things we were going to do. She was a force in my life and that of the FBI. She will be missed, but now it's time to get angry and focused and get these two stuck-up kids that need a good spanking. A time-out isn't going to be enough.

Off the phone with Father Roberts, it's almost five thirty, and I'm dripping sweat. It's time to go upstairs and hit the shower. Walking up the stairs, I noticed a call from TJ; that was quick. Then again, he had been working on searching Erin's background for a while now.

"Neil, I know we just spoke a little bit ago. I took your hunch and pulled a few guys to revisit Erin's financials. We hadn't looked at everything the way we would if she were a criminal. We dug deeper into her financials. There we found large sums of money being transferred from an Argentinian bank, and it's from a shell company. However, it's not hard to connect the dots."

"Fuck! From day one, I knew not to trust her. I should have listened to my gut. I was so focused on relaxing and enjoying Santa Fe. Helping Sister Irene and the others with their project, I let a snake into the henhouse to take out Maria. This shits on me . . . FUCK!"

"Neil, first of all, remember what you tell us all the time. You can't hold yourself responsible for crazy assholes. We just work our asses off to make as big a difference as we can, but we will go down a dark hole if we start taking responsibility for everything we can't prevent." I needed that.

"Thanks, TJ. Sometimes I need to be reminded of my own advice."

"No problem, boss man. I'll let you go; we'll keep trying to connect the dots to make a case."

"Thanks, TJ. You know that shit bugs me. Still, between you and Terrance, it's growing on me."

"We know; that's why we do it. We're wearing you down, Neil." TJ started laughing.

"Thanks, TJ. Talk to you later."

Off the phone, with some news that doesn't make me feel better, but I do know I'm on the right path. Today is going to be an interesting one. Jason gets released today, even though he has other charges pending. The DA doesn't think he can make them stick. That means he'll get out on time served, Susie is back in Detroit, thinking she got away with killing an FBI agent. She probably assumes that Erin is going to be scot-free in Argentina. Little does she know that Christian is in town waiting for her.

I'm never making it to the shower. I decided to call Christian back and give him a bit more direction. I had an idea, and I think we need to make a play on Erin now. We need to get her pinned down now. If we can get her in cuffs and under wraps, we can call her old handler and see what they have in store for her. I'm pretty sure the name he uses is Mr. Johnson. We know its fake, but it's the CIA life.

"Christian, I know we just got off the phone, but TJ confirmed that Erin got paid from a bank in Argentina. A large sum of money just days ago. That means Erin probably did the hit on Maria. We need you to grab her and keep her on lockdown until you hear from us."

"Got it. I won't let you down. I'll call TJ and get her flight info and any other info I need to get her ass under wraps."

"Thanks, Christian. I need to get going."

Okay, now I'm going to get in the shower. I smell brutal. You know it's terrible when you can smell yourself. Part of it might be that I forgot to take off my wraps. These things are nasty; I need to wash them ASAP. With my wraps off, in the wash waiting to be saved, I made my way back to the shower, only to hear my phone ring. Son of a bitch, who is this now?

"Hey Ken, can't a brother get a shower?"

"I just got off with TJ. Did you follow up with Christian already?"

"I just got off with him. We should probably talk to Nicolette and make sure she understands what's at play here. If we make it look like Erin is going after her, it'll change the whole perception. Hey, that phone TJ made for me, can he make a sim card that mirrors Erin's cell that we have on file?"

"I don't see why not. It's not like you're trying to clone the phone. We could also have Christian turn the phone off when he gets her. It'll take some coordinating, but we can pull it off. What's your idea?"

"I use the phone to make Susie think Erin never left. Then we'll have Nicolette set traps around the office to mess with her. That should get her on the brink, and then it would just be a little bit more to push her. Or Jason to realize his sister is a liability he might have to sacrifice to us."

"According to TJ, Erin's plane lands in about an hour. Get clean and get over here. We'll figure it out from there. I'll let you go."

Like that, Ken hung up, and I finally got in the shower. With a night that started off brutal, it has turned and given me a bit of life. I have a direction and a lead in the case. We have a course to close this shit, to get some closure. I can't wait to mess with them. It wasn't that long ago I was able to get Jason, put him behind bars. This time it's going to be Susie, then I'll set my sights on him. First thing, I need to get Maria's killer off the street. As far as I'm concerned, the one who paid for everything is worse than the gun hired, who has no skin in the game.

That water hit me, sent me into a trance, and gave me a moment of peace. A moment to hide in my thoughts, think of Maria in a positive note. I need to practice doing this. I can't keep being brought to tears, I can't keep thinking of what was and the pain, I need to remember the great moments that brought me joy. Hang on to those and keep my sanity.

27

I WAS SO FOCUSED ON THE VIDEO OF MARIA I DIDN'T EVEN NOTICE.

I was a few minutes out from the warehouse when I called Nicolette to fill her in on what was coming up and what I needed from her. She was on board and wanted to get them just as badly as anyone else. Being a young investigator, Maria was a goal for many. She was brilliant, at the peak of her profession and driven; losing her is like losing an icon. Nicolette knew what was at stake and was ready to hop on board with everything. She knew she might have to push past her normal limits but was willing to try. I'm so proud of the team member she has become, along with so many.

Off the phone, pulling into the warehouse, and I saw TJ was in Ken's office. They were arguing about something, not loudly, but you could tell it was a disagreement about something. As I walked up, I could see them stop almost instantly. This has to get corralled right now.

"Hey you two, don't think you can't act out when I'm around. This isn't walk on eggshells when Neil is around. That shit will drive me nuts. I can only assume then you two were arguing over something stupid."

"TJ was just trying to remind me that the Buckeyes were going to kick the Wolverines' ass this year all over again."

"Ken, I love you, man. Still, your team is just so bad. You and your other Wolverines talk so highly, but you just don't win."

"TJ, we can't all recruit criminals and people on parole for homicide."

"Hey Ken, even for you that's fucked up."

"Good point, I got carried away. I should have said, "dumb-ass great athletes." The second you put that linebacker Kat, something on the field, you lose the argument."

"TJ, he has you there. That guy was talented, but no way he could even read."

"Neil, I thought you didn't care about this argument. Why are you giving me shit too?"

"Sorry, that guy was dumb as a brick. There's nothing wrong with it. I'm just pointing it out."

This shit went back and forth for a good twenty minutes until someone pointed out that Erin's flight had probably landed and we needed to be ready for Christian's call. We eventually got back to reality and focused on everything at hand. If Christian can get Erin, then we can use her cell number freely to mess with Susie.

"Like I was saying earlier, Neil. If Erin isn't using her phone and we don't have to worry about that feedback, then we can easily assign or clone that number to a different phone for you. The problem lies in someone else using the phone. If Christian can keep it from being used, then we will be golden."

"Thanks, TJ. I guess now we just sit and wait for a bit and see what Christian can come up with?"

"It shouldn't be too long, her flight already landed, and Christian works quickly. I can only assume what he'll do, but you know he's not going to wait around. He knows time is of the essence," Ken said, clearing his throat.

"Ken, you know one of these days your late-night cigars are going to catch up with you."

"Neil, I already have my wife and my doctor on my ass. Not you too?"

"I'm just saying: it's something to be aware of, we like having you around."

"I'll keep that under advisement."

With a plan in place, the three of us went on bantering for a bit. TJ disappeared back to his office to work on the cell phone. While Ken and I waited to hear from Christian, I began milling around the warehouse, cleaning up, talking to staff, and doing whatever I could to kill time. It was going on for three hours, and I was beginning to lose my mind. We didn't want to keep bugging Christian in case he was working, so it was a waiting game. Let me be honest: I wanted to bug the shit out of him, but Ken stopped me.

Finally, at about the five-hour mark or noon, just when my stomach started growling, I saw Ken walking down the hall toward me. I was working with a few guys on a case about some stolen watches from a jewelry shop. We were contracted by an insurance company to verify the claim after the police barely put forth any effort. I hope this is good news from Ken.

"Hey, I just got off the phone with Mike, he said he tried calling you." Not Christian, shit.

"Yeah, I'm charging it in the bunks right now. What's up with him?"

"They got back the trace evidence from the plane that they pulled in Maria's murder. They think with the information you have, statements from the guards about Jason running his mouth, they can peg at least conspiracy to commit murder on Susie. But he wants your feedback if you think you can get more."

"I hope we can, and we need to hear from Christian. It's been five hours. What's going on down there?"

"Neil, you get cranky when you get hungry. Why not order something delivered?"

"I'm not in the mood for a pizza or something like that."

"Dude, just order Jimmy Johns; you know that's what keeps us alive on the midnight shifts. We load up before they close."

"Okay, I'll order a sandwich. Calm down, guys. Someone at least text Christian."

"Neil, give it until one before you bug him. Give him time to operate."

"Fine. I'm getting some food."

It took only twenty minutes to order and get my food, which was sweet, and it wasn't expensive. The best part of the whole meal was by the third bite Christian had messaged Ken, telling him he had Erin and they were in a secure place.

"Neil, I just heard from Christian. It was quick, but he said he has Erin. They are in a safe place with her phone in his possession. You can get to work with TJ on the next part of your plan."

"Finally we're on a roll. We've had a few different things fall our way."

"Before I head back and support Terrance on his op and a few others, is there anything else you need from me?" Ken hit a hop in his step.

"No, I'm just ready to put an end to this. Push Susie over the edge. I'll call Mike and let him know how we're going to proceed."

I know what I want to do. I know what I should do, and what I will do is somewhere in the middle. Tormenting Susie and Jason for years to come, trying to break them and cause havoc on their psyches mentally is my first choice. Death, killing them is an easy way out for the pain they caused Maria's parents and me. All the death and destruction they are trying to bring to our communities with R-1209 and Requiem deserve the proper punishment.

I feel if they are going to deal with mind-altering drugs, then let's mess with their minds a bit. As I made my way down the hall toward TJ's wing of the warehouse, I called Mike to follow up on the next steps.

"Hey Mike, Ken said you think you have enough for conspiracy to commit murder on Susie."

"I think we can make it stick, especially with the witness statements of the guards. That guy B. Adams—by the way, his name is Brian—threw Jason under the bus pretty quickly when we gave him the complete details of what his sister did."

"Well, let me ask you something then. Do you think I'm crazy to want to push for more? To push to get her on drug charges, get her connected to El Jefe and other drug cartels?"

"No, I think we can use what we have for wiretaps for a few days. Especially leading up to the drug announcement party. I do have one big question, though; I remember Maria speaking about a Ms. Choike. Do you think that has anything to do with this?"

"I did, but became fixated on Erin, and we had found the connection back to Argentina so quickly I didn't have TJ continue looking. Have your forensic accountant work with TJ's team on what they've already found. Maybe we can find a connection among Choike, Gaines, and Erin that leads to those payments."

"Will do, Neil. I'll text you when the wiretaps are in place. Ken told me what you were planning. Not sure how admissible that will be, so get the hairy stuff out before the wiretaps kick in. I'd say you have a few hours," Mike said with a chuckle.

"Understood. I'll make sure and hit the ground running and get her all riled up. I'll see if we can get any intel out of Erin through Christian on El Jefe and his role. Suppose he was even aware of what they did to Maria, or they just blamed him. We need to get ahold of him; he might simply roll over on Susie if he knows what she's trying to pin on him."

"I see what you're doing, lining up all the people back at her and Jason. Burning down one bridge at a time. Neil, remind me never to piss you off. You can be one vindictive bastard, but I love you for it."

"Thanks, Mike. Let's get these assholes."

On the phone with Mike, I spent the next two hours working like a machine. Talking to Ken, TJ, and communicating to Christian about what we needed to get out of him. We really needed to try to find Maria's phone. That is one significant open variable that we never saw. It wasn't at the scene, and it wasn't on her body. Is that what this is about? Did she find something and get it with her phone? I had an idea for TJ, but I'm not nearly the tech wizard he is, so we'll have to see.

"TJ, we never found Maria's phone; it hasn't turned up still. Is there any way to try and ping it? At least find its last known location. I was so concerned with her safety and we knew where she was I forgot about her phone."

"Yeah, she had an iPhone, newest model, so it always has on GPS tracking, should be easy enough to see her movements too. I'll put together a timeline of everything. Give me an hour to get it all together."

"Thanks, TJ. I'll get to work on Susie and some other items in the meantime."

"Have fun hunting."

The next forty-five minutes were spent in Ken's office, working through different ways to reach out to Susie. I started with something simple. "I just texted her, hit a snag, can't talk, text me back." Just waiting for a reply. There are so many variables up in the air over the next couple of days with Jason getting out, Gaines Chemical's big announcement tomorrow, and these connections among Choike, Gaines, and Erin.

"Ken, do we really think this was Choike or Susie acting on Maria through Erin? I just don't see Erin doing it on her own. She looks like an old-fashioned burned agent turned rogue assassin/spy for hire. She just needs a check, wants to keep surviving."

"I'm with you on the Erin angle. I don't see her doing this on her own. The motive is lacking. As for Susie or Choike, both of them have reason to hate you. Do you think we can get her to roll over on them if she thinks she has a chance to come back to the CIA?"

"It's worth a shot, but they pretty much disavowed her. Maybe reach out to her handler again, see if he'll help string her along for us."

"Yeah, I'll do that while you mess with Susie, and check in on TJ."

As I was walking up to TJ's work space, there were a few other guys around his computer; it looks like they're all watching something. Looking at his screen intently, but I can't see shit because there are five people between me and TJ's computer.

"Ah-hem," as I cleared my throat loudly.

"Sorry, Neil, we found the smoking gun. I was about to come get you. But I wanted to run through it a few times, so I knew what I was showing you first." TJ looked shaken, since I caught him.

"You're fine, TJ, as usual. What's there to look at? Is this from Maria's phone?"

"It is, it's from her cloud server, it's a video she uploaded. I'm pretty sure this is what she was killed over. I'm going to let you have some privacy; there's something at the end for you."

"For me?"

"You'll see."

TJ cued up the video. It was shot from around a corner. It looked like Maria was hiding in the back of one of the art galleries. Judging by the surroundings and the info TJ had written on his notepad, the geo-location has her in Santa Fe, downtown at Choike's gallery. Back to the video, Maria is shooting the meeting. Yet I don't think Erin knows that Maria decided to crash the party since she is talking openly to everyone about our investigation to R-1209 and Requiem.

The video goes on for a few minutes, and it shows Erin double-crossing us. Then it shows Susie working with El Jefe and the overall scheme of what they planned on doing. There weren't any details, just alluding to the scheme on how they are going to connect R-1209 to Requiem and distribute it. It's enough for Mike and me to continue down our path, but not enough for a jury or a judge without concrete evidence. Susie having a meeting with two highly questionable individuals may not look great, but it's not against the law.

The video went on for about two minutes. Then Maria hightailed it out of there, turned the camera around, and sent me a message. She knew something was up, knew that it was going to be bad. I watched it over and over, listening to her speak to me one final time.

"Neil, if you are watching this, I hope it's with me. In case it isn't, know I love you very much, and I'm genuinely sorry that I didn't make it out of this. I'm going to upload this video to my account and stash my phone. TJ can track it later. Erin has been working with Susie all along, from what I can gather. I'm not sure how Ms. Choike ties into this, but I'm pretty sure she's just a business asset for Gaines Chemical and their drug distribution in Europe. I love you. If I don't see you again, please don't let this stop you from getting these assholes. 'Bye, Neil. I love you."

I watched it over and over, for a solid fifteen minutes, until TJ came back in. He said he has the address of where the phone should be. He asked if he should get it to Mike so they can have the local field office look for it. That video, that phone are evidence in Maria's homicide. I was so focused on the video of Maria I didn't even notice the Susie had texted back on Erin's phone number. Asking what the issue was, and if she needs to do anything on her end. I feel the longer I make Susie wait between texts, the more anticipation and impatience it will create. Causing her to focus less on the words and more on the emotion attached to the messages. I'll set a timer for one hour to make sure I don't send it too soon.

As for the rest of the day, I need a distraction to keep me busy with the wait on Gaines getting out of prison and his sister getting away with murder, so far. I guess I could always go to the bunks and take a nap or a shower. I could go to the workout area and hit the heavy bag for a while, or I could head back to FCI Milan and talk to Frank. So many choices for the day, tomorrow, and tonight are going to be filled, but this afternoon is open. I don't do well with free time, as we've all learned. I walked back to Ken's office and stuck my head in.

"Hey Ken, do we have a time when Jason is supposed to be walking out a free man?"

"I'm pretty sure it was earlier today. I can check for you."

"That won't be necessary; I'm right here, guys." What the hell is Gaines doing at the warehouse?

28

WE LIT SOME TRASH CANS ON FIRE, LEFT A FEW MESSAGES . . . WROTE "YOU'RE NEXT."

Gaines just walked in with his lawyer with what looks like a lawsuit of sorts. I'm not sure what he has in mind since I didn't harass him when he was in prison, nor did I do anything crazy. Other than sucker-punching him and shooting up his fish tank, I guess I did do those things.

"I could have had my lawyer or a processing agent deliver these. But I wanted to do them myself." He handed Ken an envelope.

"What's in here?"

"Look for yourself."

"You're billing us for the fish tank and damage to your office?" Ken looked stunned.

"You need to pay for the damage."

"Sounds great. We'll send you an invoice for the damage caused to Maria. We'll see who's is bigger." Ken is standing up for me to keep me from killing Jason in front of his lawyer.

I took a deep breath and walked away, just sat down in Ken's office. I didn't say anything, just sat there with my hands over my mouth. Breathing, trying not to stay something to tip our hands. I can't believe the nuts on this guy, to walk into my place of business fresh out of prison days after his sister had my girlfriend killed. He makes Cappelano look sane on many levels.

"Neil, what are you doing in there? Why did you walk away? Don't you want to talk about this?" Gaines kept on it.

"Sir, I think it's time you leave." By now, the whole office was standing in the bay among me, Ken, and Jason Gaines.

"I get the picture. I'm not wanted here. I expect full payment for the fish tank, Neil."

"Get out of here before you regret it!" one of the guys screamed from the back.

Gaines and his lawyer made their way out of the warehouse. I was moved in a way I have yet to feel. Seeing all those employees rally around me, support me, and stand up for me. They knew I couldn't, and they did what needed to be done. I was still sitting in Ken's office as he dispersed the crowd.

"Neil, are you going to be okay after that shit show? I know you're not a fan of the, you okay shit. But it keeps piling up. I just want to check in on you."

"I'm okay, Ken. I just didn't want to say something I might regret. Something that might jeopardize the case. I'm sure that's why he came over here. To placate me, rile me up, and see if he could antagonize me into doing something stupid."

"At least you were aware of what he was doing, and you wanted to walk away. You were smart. You used to fall into that stuff before; you'd go rushing in. You'd save it, clean it up, but it would take so much more energy. I'm proud of you, buddy."

"Thanks, Ken. I'm trying to grow. This trip, the past couple of days have really turned my routine, my habits on their head. Actually, since the Poland trip, I've been working on those."

"It shows. It's getting late, though, and we need to get ready for tomorrow. Do you have any ideas for Nicolette before she leaves for the day?"

"I do. I'll shoot her a text, should give her enough info to run with it. You need to get ahold of Erin's CIA handler and get that moving ASAP. Also, we need to coordinate with Mike about the whole thing. Line up all the evidence we have. I'll shoot him a call after I message Nico."

"I forget you've been calling her that sometimes. She is growing into a great team member. I'm very proud of the coaching Christian did with her in Poland. I'll get with the CIA handler; you circle back with Mike. Talk to you in a few."

"Sounds good."

Ken and I went over the video for a bit, and he said TJ shot him a message about the video with a link to it already. He was waiting for me to come to him. He knows when I'm ready I'll talk to him. Ken and I have had that kind of relationship for some time now. He is patient when he needs to be. Ready to pounce when needed.

Out of Ken's office, I quickly messaged Nicolette. With my phone in hand, I want to mess with Susie a bit. I shot Susie a text that simply said, your next. I waited over an hour to respond to draw it out. That's all she gets. She is going to lose her shit, which is what we want. We need to play right into her ego and lack of control.

I messaged Nicolette to try and do something small but effective as a threat to get Susie's attention. She has proven herself resourceful enough, and with me not there, I have to leave it open-ended like that for her to follow through with it on her own. If I'm honest, curiosity has my mind wandering to the different things that she can do. Tonight and tomorrow are going to be a mix of emotions that I will have to work to control. I'm still trying to figure out how I'm going to wind down and sleep if I'm giving up alcohol for a while, and tonight is filled with stressors. I'll deal with that later; it's time to talk to Mike about the video and the steps for tonight. We also have to get organized for tomorrow. Susie will be arrested tomorrow; no matter what, it's just a matter of how many charges we can get her on.

"Mike, it's Neil. I've got some good news. Tomorrow we are going to arrest Susie Gaines at her big- ass party in front of all her friends. It's just a matter of how many charges we can get to stick between tonight and tomorrow."

"I like where this is headed. I am not a fan of letting a killer walk any longer than we have to. Has any new info or evidence come to light?"

"Maria uploaded a video to her cloud account from her phone. TJ was able to pull it. She caught Susie talking to Erin, El Jefe, and Ms. Choike. There is enough information on it, along with the evidence that we have, to implicate her on a few charges. I want to try and get the drug charges to stick, though, because it will hold up the release of R-1209 legally. That's going to slow everything else for them."

"Neil, that sounds good to me. What do you need from the FBI? We are at your disposal."

"TJ has already sent you over all of the info from her cell. As well as the last known location for the local FBI office to go searching for it in case there is more on there that didn't get uploaded. I need you to get an arrest warrant ready and wiretaps on Jason and his lawyer. With the video, it shows they are colluding to use legitimate means for distributing illegal drugs."

"Consider it all done. Just get ahold of me in the morning and give me a timeline of when you want us there. We'll throw a couple of plainclothes agents in the crowd and media members to blend in. It'll also give us a backup if something goes wrong."

"Sounds good as usual, Mike. We got this. Thanks for your support. We will get these bastards one way or another."

"Damn straight, Neil. Talk to you in the morning. Unless something else comes up."

Let's see running through my list of to-dos from Ken. I have contacted Nicolette, communicated with Mike about tomorrow, and even had time to send a cryptic but threatening text to Susie from Erin. I wonder how his call is going with Erin's handler from the CIA. Come to think of it I might just text Ken, tell him to come to find me in my office. Also known as the heavy bag and small table in the gym. I could use a good sweat and decompression from the day's activities.

I do feel a bit bad that I didn't get out to see Frank today, but I can make an early run out there tomorrow morning and talk to him before the day gets carried away. The events at Gaines Chemical won't kick off until two in the afternoon, leaving me plenty of morning time to get things done. After a quick stop in the bunks to change and grab my headphones, I made my way to the heavy bag to get a workout in.

As I worked, my wraps in, following my pattern that has become therapy in and of itself, I noticed that Terrance hasn't been around the warehouse all day. Then again, he did drive up most of the trip by himself after we made him drop Christian off at an airport to head to Argentina. He is probably playing catch-up on sleep, something I will be doing once I'm done with this case. I might fly out to Santa Fe, find a quiet place to sit, and just remember Maria.

Fifteen minutes into working the bag over, I felt a tap on my shoulder. It was Ken with an update on the handler and Erin's willingness to cooperate. He didn't look sad, he didn't look pissed, which means we have a shot at getting some more good news.

"All right, so what's the news? Good, bad, or who really knows anymore?"

"It's closer to the last one. After talking to the handler, I'm a bit scared at what they might tell Erin. They could tell her to eat shit, for all I know."

"If she isn't talking, it doesn't hurt us to make an effort. Worst case, we can say we tried for her. It gives us some leverage in the equation, still helping the killer of our best friend. In her brain, it could build a bit of trust."

"If you think it's worth a shot, I'll follow your lead. They'll only deal with her over the phone. They aren't willing to fly down there to talk to her. Also, not a great sign." Ken has a point.

"It's true. If they were on board at bringing her in, they would fly down. Have the conversation and bring her up, bring her home."

After ten or so minutes of Ken holding the bag and me working combinations into it, we decided the best thing is to go for it. Allow the handler to make their play into Erin. Then we will know where everyone stands, and we can go from there. If they alienate her, it puts her on an island. We can isolate her from Susie, show her what we're doing. This gives her limited to zero options on who to turn to.

The best option we have is to make a play on Erin, try to get her to turn state's evidence for some form of leniency on sentencing. She killed a federal agent, after all; she's kind of screwed. I don't have any doubt that Christian won't be able to get her back to the States. I guess there is only one way to see how it goes. Send Ken into the office to get the handler on the phone with Christian for a conversation with his CIA operative Erin.

"I guess you get the handler on a call with Christian ASAP; tomorrow is a big day. I'd like to know what cards we're holding. I have an idea; it just depends on how the CIA handler goes about everything, that could mess with Susie. First things first; let's get through this and move on it."

"The handler was waiting for my call. I just wanted to see what you wanted to do. I'll conference them in together, and we'll see how it goes. Do you want to be in the room for the call?"

"I'll head over there in a few minutes after I get done touching base with Nicolette and trying to track down Terrance. I just want to make sure he's all good."

"He got back safely. I'm pretty sure he's just recharging. See you in the office shortly."

Off the phone, I cleaned up, took off my wraps, began to unwind a bit, and made my way into the bunks where I could get some quiet to call Nicolette and see how her night went. By now she should have been done working and home; I wonder why she hasn't touched base yet. I called; the phone rang and went to voice mail. I tried once more. After the same result two different times, I decided to try Terrance. Even though his phone was the same result, ringing to voice mail, I guess I'll take a quick shower and go from there. Not like them to go silent for a bit unless she's in the middle of messing with Susie.

Thanks to being ruined in Santa Fe and breaking from long showers, I may be able to take short ones without crushing my psyche like once before. In and out, changed back into my clothes from earlier, and I noticed I had a text from Nicolette, I decided to head into Ken's office and check in. The message read, "Call you in a few."

"Hey Ken, where—" He shushed me.

He was on the line with Erin and her handler. He was giving her the business, saying that there isn't much they can do for her after two deaths at her hand, especially one being an FBI agent. The best thing to do is to turn herself in at the embassy and let the long governmental process work itself out.

We may never know what comes of her if we do that. They could just as easily throw her back out in the wind in some European country, knowing she has nowhere else to go. I'm all for second chances, but damn, that would hurt. I think if we find a way to get the press involved, we can use it to our advantage. It can put some pressure on Susie and Jason Gaines. It just depends on how we time it.

The handler got off the phone, and you could hear a deafening silence come over Erin. She knew the run was over, but there was some completion to it. I couldn't take the quiet anymore, so I chimed in.

"Hey, Christian. You two hunker down for the night and get some rest. We'll get the ball rolling at the embassy. I think it's the best bet with the least amount of damage. Sometimes we need just to play ball, and this is one of those times."

"You sure, boss? I know I can get her up there. It'll take some work, but I think she'd rather come up than deal with the embassy out here and all the bureaucratic bullshit."

"If I may, Neil, I am truly sorry for everything and all the pain that I—"

Click.

"Neil, did you just hang up the phone on them?" Ken looked befuddled.

"Yes, Ken. Are you truly that surprised? I wasn't going to give her that satisfaction. I wasn't going to let her take her grief and give it to me. That's for a priest, not me, and I don't give absolution. I'll shoot Christian a quick text to finish what I was going to say. We're all set."

"Fair point. Are you finally going to go home and get some rest? I'll call Mike and have him start the process with the embassy for tomorrow morning."

"Yeah. I hope I catch Nicolette in the car; one less thing to do at home. Thanks for taking care of things like that, Ken."

"Get some sleep. I'll see you in the morning."

Little does Ken know I have something brewing in my Neil Baggio skeptical brain of mine. I like to keep Ken out of some of these ideas to give him and the company a bit of plausible deniability. I need to call my old buddy Larry; he has since been promoted to a desk at CNN in DC. That interview with me and the get with Cappelano got him some national attention. I'm going to get the local office in Argentina to pick up the story on the murderer of the local Detroit FBI agent. Then find a way to make sure Susie sees it.

"Hey Neil, as usual, you're in the thick of shit, and I get a phone call. I heard what happened, and I know you don't want to get into it. I'll just say we're all here for you. You know I have contacts in the bureau; that's how I heard already." Larry was always keeping tabs on me; it's good for business.

"Well then, this conversation will go quicker. We have Agent Garcia's killer in Argentina, and one of my guys is going to escort her to the US embassy tomorrow morning. Think you can have a camera there to cover the story? I need it run, though. specifically at 2:45 p.m. local time in Detroit, but the footage will be from earlier in the day."

"You know I always oblige for a story like this. Just email me the particulars tonight so I can get it organized and have them waiting there tomorrow morning. Take care of yourself, Neil."

"Thanks, Larry."

Finally, in the car and on the way home, after sitting in the parking bay, sending an email to Larry, Christian, and Ken with the particulars of the embassy drop-off. I may have blind CCd Larry, I don't want Christian worrying about it, plus I want him and Erin looking surprised; it'll sell it better. Almost home. While jamming to some Bob Seger playing on WRIF, I was rudely interrupted by Nicolette calling me through my Bluetooth.

"Hey Nico, I'm assuming you were busy. Hope you didn't get caught or in trouble."

"All went well; we might have gone overboard, but you gave me a blank slate to work with. Don't forget I was in Poland when you drove that truck into Duda's car."

"We? Is that where Terrance has been?"

"He's sitting next to me in the car. We're on our way out of here. We kind of attacked her building in a bunch of little ways to mess with her. I'm not sure you want me to go into too much detail over the phone, but know that we lit a few things on fire, and I made sure we weren't on the security footage," she said, laughing.

"No one got hurt, did they?"

"No. We lit some trash cans on fire, left a few messages as you said, wrote 'You're next' all over. Then when she was outside from the fire alarms going off, we may have lit her car windows on fire with gasoline. No explosions, just a great effect. Some other things may keep her up tonight."

"That's the point. I want her tweaking and exhausted tomorrow when we arrest her. It gives us the best shot of a confession. Think of it like pregaming before drinking at a big event. This is prestressing before a big interrogation the FBI is going to give her. She's the weak link between the siblings. I want to exploit that."

"We should be good to go then, Neil. She looked beyond freaked out. Her brother kept trying to calm her down and yell at her."

"At the same time?"

"Yeah, even he's starting to see their plans unraveling."

"Let's hope we can continue to hurt this new venture of theirs and save some lives along the way."

"You got it, boss." I don't mind it when she calls me "boss."

Done driving and in the house, I was finally off the phone with Nicolette. It was time to give my girls some attention. They were pouty, though; not surprising, I have been very neglecting lately. I'll take them for a quick walk around the block, get some fresh air, and check in with Sheila. She's left me a few messages today, making sure I'm okay. Other than small responses, I haven't given her much to work with.

"Hey Sheila, how's your night going?"

"It's better now that I'm talking to you. I'm worried about you. I mean, someone has to."

"I know, it's going to be a rough one for a while, but I'll get through it. I've got people like you and Ken checking up on me and heavy bags all over the place to hit," I said, chuckling.

"Hey, I know it's late, and you already have a ton on your plate. But you haven't told me or anyone, for that matter, the details for Maria's funeral. I know there are protocols with the FBI and her death, but what about her parents? Are they going to do anything? I want to make sure we are prepared to be there for you; that's going to be a rough day."

"Under normal circumstances, it could be open-ended, but we're hoping tomorrow. 'We' meaning Mike and I. To give his parents some good news, about Maria being released for burial by the end of the week. My guess is next week sometime. I'll get the info to Ken, and he can spread the word. You know I don't have it in me to do that."

"I know, Neil. Please take care of yourself. How's the not drinking going?"

"I'm still holding true to it; I think it'll stick for a bit. Remember the last time I gave up smoking and drinking. I made it a year; it's just habit and stress for me."

"You have lots of stress right now. That's why some of us are worried."

"I know; something happened out in Santa Fe. Not just losing Maria but also finding something in me. I think I'll be okay. I know it's still fresh, so we'll see. It could just be similar to a New Year's resolution."

"You never do anything normal like that. I'll make sure Ken and I stay on your ass. Have a good night, Neil. I just wanted to check in. I need some rest, and so do you."

"Night, Sheila."

This day has been lived on the phone. From the moment I woke until now. I have been managing my day and moving parts all over through my phone. Finishing the walk back to the house, I started going through the checklist of items I wanted to get done and needed to get done to make sure we are set for tomorrow.

We got under Susie's skin, which may seem a little overkill, it may even seem petty. I certainly am doing it for a purpose. I want her ready to break when she gets to the FBI offices for interrogation and processing. Gaines Chemical's network is vast with so many moving parts. Even if we shut down half of it, Jason is worth millions and is smart enough to turn it back into billions. That's a lot of weight to carry, knowing that. We need to ensure we have every advantage covered going in. Having the stronger sibling in prison didn't make a dent in their operations. The hope is getting the weaker one to roll over on a few items to save her own hide can help us.

As I changed into something to sleep in, I merely grabbed a pair of Chelsea FC shorts I have. I love that color blue and that emblem on the bottom. I threw on my Pistons hat with my hair tucked back and walked to the kitchen. I began to grab a glass, put some ice in it, and walked over to the liquor cabinet. When I grabbed a bottle of whiskey, instead of pouring it into the glass, I poured it down the drain. As I watched the liquid pour out, I began to fight some tears.

I realized this was going to be a recurring part of my routine for a while. If I'm going to get over this, get through it, I have to deal with it head-on. I can't try and run from it; I have to learn to accept what is in front of me. How do you do that? How do you accept the fact that a woman you finally admitted to yourself you loved was taken from you? Taken from this world, violently, abruptly, and cold? I guess I just have to figure out a new way to function. I decided to do something that Maria had asked me to do for some time.

I sat down at the kitchen table with a notepad and a pen. I began to write a letter to Maria, one I would never be able to send, but I had to get it out. I had to tell someone to tell her in some way that I love her. I never did, I held it in too long, and I have to live with that forever. There are times your parents, friends, or pastors will tell you don't keep things inside. You need to tell people how you feel. You need to express joy and sadness with others. I have struggled with that in the past, and I regret it mightily right now. For her, for my daughter, and me, I need to work tirelessly to improve it.

REQUIEM

29

YOU MAY BE LOCKED UP, BUT YOU SEEM AT PEACE FOR THE FIRST TIME.

Waking in the morning when you haven't had a drink in a few days makes life easier. I used to love the old Frank Sinatra quote about people waking up early who don't drink. He would say, it's the best they'll feel all day, versus fighting a hangover all morning. I guess that's one way to look at it, or you can look at the fact that he and the other members of the Rat Pack were characters of themselves. That's the part I didn't get until I got older. I thought that was a lifestyle they led, not an act.

With a renewed energy on the day, lacking a hangover or my body working through a crazy long night, I threw on my running shoes, grabbed the girls' leashes, and went for a run. We got a good two miles in before I realized I didn't even have my phone on me. Could this be a new routine, waking up, not checking my phone, just going out into the day, and starting to see what's in front of me?

Its nearly seven in the morning, which means Christian and Erin are getting ready to head down to the embassy. I told them and Larry to be there at eight in the morning. I wish I could be there to see what they are going to cover live, but I'll settle for seeing it on TV. We have until later this afternoon to get organized, since the Gaines Chemical event doesn't start until three. I have an idea I want to run by TJ, but I'm not sure it's even doable; I guess we'll see. It'll have to wait a little bit longer as I finish my run with the girls.

I guess it might be a bit ironic as I keep this sobriety thing up and have two dogs named after a whiskey. A reminder of a previous life, and I'm okay with that. The cool morning air on this summer day in Detroit has me ready to go. We made it back to the house, me sweating and the girls with their tongues dragging on the floor. I went to the bedroom to text TJ. I wanted to get him before he went to sleep. With today being a big day, though, he might just grab a nap in the bunks. I should also check in with Ken, make sure we're all set, so many calls for this morning. Let's start with Christian, since he has the most at stake.

"Hey bud, you ready for this morning?"

"It's just a simple drop-off, isn't it?"

"Sort of. The embassy is going to want to interview you and go over all the details of what you know. Mike and Ken have cleared the way, but they will also get you a ride back here, as a thank you."

"I'll make sure and grab a breakfast burrito from the cart outside then, to make sure I don't get hungry. We'll be good. Erin and I spoke last night, and she's ready for whatever comes her way. She's more afraid of being let loose in some Third World country to keep operating than to go to prison."

"I could see that prison may suck, but at least you have shelter. Life on the lam as a spy is a constant state of fear, especially knowing

Gaines will be gunning for her. She has a ton of intel on them, though, so we'll see how they play it."

"It almost sounds like you're preparing yourself for her to walk on this."

"I have to; that way I won't get caught off guard if it happens. From a state-run side I understand the play; I might even do the same thing if I wasn't me."

"Neil, you always have a crazy way of keeping shit in perspective. We'll be good to go. If anything changes, I'll make sure you or Ken knows what's up."

"Thanks, Christian."

He has a point about asking me if I'm preparing to find out Erin walked. I don't think I'll ever find out unless I run into her somewhere. That's how these things get handled when you're dealing with international shit. You have to weigh the benefits and rewards; throwing her in prison doesn't help you stop an international drug ring. Throwing her back out in Eastern Europe gives you a fighting chance. I can't remember who, but I remember a coach once saying that you can't treat every player the same. If you do, then you're horrible at understanding differences. The same goes for this situation: it may suck, but it would make sense.

The call to Ken was a usual one, making sure we are set up for the day, that we are going to be good to go over at Gaines Chemical. I asked him how we were going to get in, and he told me not to worry about it. I guess I'll just trust him. Worst case I'll walk in and push it, not my first rodeo with these clowns. Plus Jason wants to show off; that's why he came to the warehouse yesterday. He wants to rub it in and gloat a bit. He'd probably roll out the red carpet for me. I think that's why Ken isn't worried.

I have to make sure I have time to run to the store. I need to pick something up. Maybe a little gift for Jason on his big day. Hey, I may be trying to arrest him and his sister again, but I can still be gracious. My grandmother said never to go to a party empty-handed. For her, it usually meant a plate of homemade cannoli's, but that's not what I'm going to grab, you'll see. Midway through my grandma's cannoli memory TJ called me back.

"Hey Neil, what's up? I saw you messaged. If you're asking if I will be around, the answer is yes. I'm just going to get a nap in the bunks shortly, then back at it to support all day. Under the circumstances, I figured it would be all hands on deck."

"If one of your other guys can handle what I'm asking, pass it off and get some rest. You have a great tea. I just wanted to know if there is any way to get into Gaines's TVs and tune them all to CNN at the same time when a news story breaks."

"If I remember correctly, they were more concerned with their pharma software and overall camera security. Most companies leave gaping holes in their multimedia systems, especially with Nicolette inside. I can get her a flash drive to plug in, and we can dial in. But I'll do some checks. What time?"

"I need the TVs all tuned at two forty-five when CNN runs the story of Erin being turned in for Maria's murder at the US embassy in Argentina."

"Oooh, that's quality. Do we need to have a photographer there to capture the moment for you?" TJ said, joking.

"Very funny. I think we'll be okay. There's going to be plenty of media there. I'm sure CNN will find a way to pick up their reactions."

"Give me an hour or two and my team can get it all set up. If there are any issues, I'll let you know. Otherwise we should be good; don't worry about a thing. This is one of the easier things you've asked me to do recently."

"Then I will leave you to it. Thanks as always. Also, how's Jai?" I heard you're taking him under your wing, even gave him a place to stay. I haven't seen him around the warehouse a ton."

"Yeah, I got him doing some coding practice and signed him up for some online classes. He has a real knack for it. Just trying to pay for the generosity you and Ken gave me."

"That's awesome, TJ. Give Jai a high five for me."

"You go to it. Good luck today. If you need anything, just holler."

Things are lining up, it's still early, and I have some time to kill. I think I might talk to Frank and try to get some more info out of him and see if there any new points I can push on Jason. In and out of the shower in five minutes, a quick shave, and a cup of coffee in my hand, I caught myself smiling a bit. I wasn't over anything, but I was feeling good that we were going to get some quick closure for a change. Knowing I could bring some peace to Maria's family, to my heart, and perhaps the tormenting going on inside right now.

The drive to FCI Milan is usually filled with me speeding, jamming to loud music, and getting worked up. Taking a moment to reflect, I realized that's not the smartest way to prepare myself for Cappelano; a federal prison; or any case, for that matter. Taking the moments Father Roberts and I shared on the road to Santa Fe, I enjoyed the morning drive, let the road be my music, and pulled in with a sense of calm I rarely have when I walk in. Usually I'm amped, antsy, and filled with a bit of anxiety. To me, though, fear and anxiety are bad only if you let them stop you. Otherwise they help you notice things, make you aware that something is going on. They heighten your sense of awareness; it's how you respond to them that matters.

Inside, I was waiting for Frank, as usual, I wish I could call ahead and have him waiting for me, almost like a reservation. Then again, he's not a pet I can keep on a leash. I'm sure he feels that way sometimes as he is stuck in a cage, with limited free time.

"Hey Neil, you look a little better than the last time I saw you. Some rest did you some good, perhaps something else? It can't be joy that Gaines is out there walking free right now?"

"Frank, never one to beat around the bush, are you. That's why we get along. That and we're both a bit crazy. We have some things in the works that should make today a good one. Especially for Maria and a bit of closure."

"Will I get my buddy back in here?"

"No, but we have found the person responsible for Maria's death. That's a start for me. A big one too, so I'll take it. Did you learn anything else, find a piece of leverage we can use to disrupt the underground system Gaines Chemical plans on using to disperse Requiem?"

"The simple answer is money talks, and right now that drug and those siblings have a lot of both. It's a matter of making it a financial problem for them; that's the way you stop it."

"It's not the magic bullet I was hoping for. It sounds like they aren't aligned with Gaines in any way but his money. Which means we hit his money and his power dwindles."

"That's the play, I think. Otherwise he has too much control. No one is going to listen to or do what is right. It's going to simply be a matter of what is the best business decision for the cartels and other gangs he has affiliated with. They are only loyal to their own kind and the almighty dollar." Frank has a point.

"Enough about that, since we don't have a ton to go over. We have been sidetracked with Gaines now that he's out of here. We need to get back to your list and all the different bodies that have piled up. Did you ever get around to counting how many lives you took?"

"I haven't given it much thought. Then again, I was having a decent amount of fun investigating and talking to all the leaders here. It was a great distraction that got me out of my comfort zone. It even helped me gain a bit of perspective, talking to some of the lifers in here that are going on ten or even twenty years."

"In a good way or a bad way?"

"Neither. I won't know until I reach that point. But they all had something in common to say. They said people in here without a hobby, a group to associate with, or something to distract them don't last long. I have you, but that can't be the only thing I rely on."

"Does this mean Frank Cappelano is doing interviews for prison buddies? Or perhaps thinking of picking up a new hobby? Maybe go back to school and get a degree?"

"Don't laugh. I thought about the school thing, I might do a degree in philosophy, spend time on introspection and deep thought. Maybe work on some other items. I have a lifetime, and maybe I can gain enough knowledge and accountability to make the impact I claimed I wanted to."

"Working with Gaines flipped you on your head, didn't it?"

"It made me realize how misguided I was, not just the killing. Let's be honest. I enjoyed that, but the reason I created was shallow. I have all the time in the world now. It's time to put this knowledge to use with you and share it properly. It's going to take deep thought into what I've been doing and how I did it." Frank looked different.

"Frank, I don't think I've ever seen you like this. Could the two of us be going through a midlife crisis together? I think it's more we were stuck in the hamster wheel of the chase. Now that we've had time to settle into it being gone, being different, we're finally growing up a bit. It's as if we were stuck in that frame of mind. When this all started when we were in our twenties. What do you expect?"

"I think it's that without the driving force to distract, it forces us to think through shit. Neil, you and I have been great at two things."

"What are those, Frank?"

"We both overanalyze, especially ourselves. And we have an uncanny ability to rationalize our poor decisions."

"It got us this far. Well, it worked out for me. For you, you may be locked up, but you seem at peace for the first time. At least you gained something from having to deal with that guy for a few months."

"The crazy thing is, when he first got here, he asked me to teach him. It told him, that's not my deal. I already have one student, you. Yet, in the long run, watching him from afar and up close gave me the lessons. I guess he became the teacher to me, unwittingly, but still." That's the Frank I know, backhanded compliment.

"Frank, I'm glad you have found some semblance of direction here. Not just for you, but also for me. I know its selfish, but it'll make it easier for us to work through this stuff together. Knowing that you want to make a difference, you want to grow from it. Otherwise I just assume you're messing with me, trying to make it hard on me."

"Fair point, since that's what I've done most of the time we've known each other. I think it's time we finally grow our relationship. The variables have dramatically changed; so should our approach."

"I couldn't agree more."

The next couple of hours were some of the most productive time I've had with Cappelano. I reluctantly started this journey with him as a favor to Maria, to Mike, and now I'm going to have to finish it without Maria. Knowing that each day won't feel like a chore will help tremendously. We went back over the first couple of murders between him, killing his nephew and friend. Then going on his cross-country trip of finding himself and murdering along the way.

Cappelano and I left with the idea that he would start journaling so that he would have better access to information at our meetings. This should be doable; he's of no risk to himself or others in here, and the warden is a friend of Gaines who has a man crush on Cappelano. There shouldn't be any objection to him utilizing some notebooks and a pen.

"Frank, this was fun. For a change, we accomplished a lot. If this is how it's going to be, I might make fewer trips but stay longer. It'll be easier to manage, plus you can work through your thoughts better as you write out, then we can go over things."

"That sounds perfect, maybe just once a week. That way we can both find a schedule. Since I'm stuck in here, you tell me which day works best, and we'll plan on it."

"Sounds good. Have a good day, Frank."

"See you, Neil."

Walking out of the front doors of that prison, for the first time I didn't feel like I needed to remove a hundred-pound weight vest. It was a refreshing feeling to come to terms with Frank, have a plan, and have common ground. Did it take losing Maria and all of this other stuff for me to slow down and work through things? Similar to Frank being in prison, did it take me losing someone so close to realizing the destructive behavior I had? I guess only time will tell. I'm still grieving and hyperaware of all my emotions and thought processes.

Walking outside, I noticed my phone was playing catch-up from the weak signal. Sometimes I get stuff, and sometimes I don't. Today I didn't mind, so I never went outside to grab a signal, nor did I turn on Wi-Fi. Ken had called me and left me a few choice messages concerning the media coverage of the embassy drop-off. Apparently the embassy didn't take too kindly to it. He didn't like getting an earful at eight in the morning from someone halfway around the world when we're doing them a solid by bringing in a rogue spy.

Nicolette had messaged me saying she is in play, no one is the wiser, and she's at work. TJ gave her what she needed for them to pull off the TV switch-over. Things are lining up, falling in a row, and getting ready for the spectacle in a few hours. It's a little after noon, and I need to head back to town, grab that gift for Jason, then get dressed for the occasion. I want to look for Jason on this joyous day of his. It's the least I can do. I should be supportive of his big day. Can you sense the monstrosity of sarcasm? On the road, heading back to town, I'm ahead of schedule, which feels good. Let's see how today goes.

30

THE NAME THEY ARE UNVEILING TO THE WORLD IS . . .

With my package in hand, I even splurged and got a lovely gift bag for it. I think Jason can appreciate the sentiment. I know you guys will when you see what I got him. For now I have to be careful, though. I don't want to drop it or break it. It's a bit fragile, but the way they packaged it, we should be okay. I swung by the house, took a quick shower to freshen up. What I lack in long showers I've replaced with quick ones; maybe they add up to the same effect. Dressed up, dressed to impress my woman, I want to look good for Maria when we lock up Susie. When I put her brother, Jason, on notice that I'm coming for him.

His first stint in federal prison was just the appetizer; I'm coming for him. I'm coming after him, but not bluntly like before. No, I'm going to mess with him strategically. I'm going to let him implode on himself. Then when Pompeii is crumbling around him, I'll close the door. In the car and on my way over to the warehouse to grab Ken, I can see he's calling.

"Hey Neil, are you on your way?"

"Yes I am, Ken. Is everything in place? Mike, ready to show up at three to arrest Susie?"

"He is, which we weren't sure why you wanted to wait. Then we heard what you asked TJ to do. Added that with the surprise media coverage at the embassy this morning and Mike and I put it all together. Nice move; it's a true Baggio finishing touch on a case."

"Only one of them is coming to an end, and the other is just beginning. I know Jason is going to go nuts that we made a skeptical of his big day. Which might slow down the whole process with all the dealers? They are concerned about heat, about the loss of funds."

"Yeah, I get that, but how do you figure any of that should come from this stunt?"

"Perception and reputation are some of the biggest factors any of these gangs look at. Money is great, but they aren't going to trust you if you have a dirty reputation. If they think dealing with you is going to bring them heat, they are going to ask for a bigger piece of the pie. If Gaines is going to push through and try to force it, it'll cost him. One way or another, we give his operation a body blow. He is either cut off while he has to rebuild reputations, or he has to start over and build a new network once he rebuilds trust."

"I should know by now you're thinking a few lanes ahead. Mike and I knew you had a purpose, but we didn't come up with that."

"Did you think I merely wanted to embarrass them?"

"Not in so many words, but yes. We thought it was a bit of revenge."

"It is, don't get me wrong, but there's a purpose to it. I'm almost there, about to pull in. Come outside, and we can get going."

As Ken got in, he noticed the gift bag on the seat. He looked a bit perplexed, handed it to me, then got his seat belt on and I handed it back. I was wondering how long before he was going to say something.

"Okay, what the hell is this?"

"A gift for Jason on his big day. You can look if you want." He peeked in the bag through the tissue.

"Neil, you have a hell of a sense of humor. I'm so glad I get to be there for his shit."

We made our way over to Gaines Chemical and pulled in a little after two. Ken and I noticed all the media already there. Not surprisingly, Jason loves attention, and he is announcing to the world what he feels is a drug to revolutionize the world. He might leave out the part where he is going to sell an illegal version on the street, getting kids addicted.

The building was decked out in banners and signs of the new drug all over. This one didn't say R-1209; it didn't say Requiem, either. The name they are unveiling to the world is Trustia. Oh yeah, you are reading that right. This arrogant prick is naming his drug that will addict people, Trust. I want to punch him so bad right now, but I can't; I have to fight the urge and be on my best behavior for Maria's memory. As we got out of the car, Ken made a wiseass comment about me being dressed nicely. I was wearing a suit, something of a rare thing in our lives. It was from the trip to Argentina, Maria loved it, and I thought it would be fitting for the day.

As we made our way inside, we were greeted by a lovely dressed woman and man. They looked like they were rented out of a catalog; I mean damn, they were beautiful. I know it seems weird, but sometimes you meet people that just don't fit in; they belong in Los Angeles, not here.

"Mr. Baggio and Mr. Chamberlain, it's a pleasure. Mr. Gaines would love to meet with you before the big unveiling in his office. Can we show you the way?"

"Is it in the same place it was last time it was here?"

"Yes, sir. The elevators are right this way."

"You two are fine; we know the way."

Making our way up the elevator with Ken seemed a bit surreal. Since the last time I was in this building, I was trying to save my girlfriend. The level of anxiety is pretty close. The difference is I'm not expecting gunfire. Then again, maybe I should. I didn't pack a gun; I hope Ken did. He usually does, he's always prepared. He's the kind of dad that wears a fanny pack; you might be embarrassed, but you want what's in that fanny pack.

Walking out of the elevator, I noticed they fixed all the damage; not surprising. I don't know why I would have thought that there would be turned-over desks and bullet holes still. Sometimes your brain can play tricks on you. He changed the office a bit, a new color scheme, no couches this time, just some chairs and a big table in the middle of the room. Knowing him, it makes me think he's going for a "knights at the round table" effect. As we walked in, I found myself looking for a coat of arms on a wall somewhere.

"Hello guys, nice of you to join me. Thank you for taking me up on my invitation." Jason spoke with a smile.

"Ken, this is why you said, 'Don't worry,'" I muttered under my breath.

"Yup. Surprise," he muttered back through a smile.

"Thank you for your kind gesture, Jason. I brought you a gift on this big day for you."

"Neil, you shouldn't have, you didn't need to. Thank you so much." As he grabbed it, Ken whispered,

"Here we go in three . . . two . . . one!"

"Charming Neil. A small fishbowl and a small fish." Jason took it graciously.

"I figured now we're even. It's not just any fish; the lady said it's a fighting fish. So be careful." Ken was trying not to laugh.

"I just wanted to say hello to you guys before the big event. Thank you, Neil, for the kind gift."

"I love what you did with the place; the remodel looks great. Glad we could help."

"On that note, Jason, we'll let you get situated. We'll be down there waiting for the big event.

We made our way down to the big conference room where they are doing the press conference. TVs lined up on the wall, one behind the podium. Oh, this is going to be great. I could see Nicolette off to the side. We made eye contact and smiled, left it at that, didn't want her to blow her cover. Who knows? I might keep her gainfully employed there full-time. If Jason is there working through the chaos, the FBI and other agencies are about to rain down. It will be good to have someone on the inside.

"Hey Neil, it is almost showtime," Mike texted me, saying that he and the others are outside ready to go. "It's almost two forty. Are you sure Larry is good to go at two forty-five?"

"He said if there were an issue, he would have let me know early. We should be good to go. Larry has always pulled through. No reason to worry now, plus it's just icing on the cake to the show when the FBI raids this place."

"Good point. I'm glad we have a front-row seat to this. Do you think she's going to run?"

"I'm not sure. I'll bet you twenty dollars that she blames her brother in the first minute of getting handcuffs on."

"That's a bet. Running is hard since we're inside, and there isn't an easy way out of here."

As Ken and I were sitting there talking shit and enjoying the moment, we watched as the Gaines siblings walked in, almost to a perfect cue of two forty-five. I think they're trying to make me look good today. The TVs all kicked onto CNN, cutting to Larry at the anchor desk, introducing a story about the agent killed earlier in the week. Then it cut to the video footage of Erin being walked into the embassy. It was then that Larry dropped this amazing nugget, unprompted; he knows me so well.

"Sources, according to the investigation, have confirmed that the person being brought into the embassy is cooperating fully and has information that may lead to a larger arrest in the coming days."

As that bit of information dropped, Jason and Susie shot each other a look and tried to power on and start their press conference. Jason stepped up and played the fool quite well, making it look simple or like a gaff.

"Sorry about that, everyone, we were watching the news in the back, and it looks as if the show followed us out here. Back to why we are here, the unveiling of R-1209, or as we will forever know it, Trustia!" Jason said, smiling for the cameras.

He went on for a good three minutes about the drug and all its amazing qualities. It was then I felt my phone go off, with a message from TJ saying, "This one is for you, boss." I wasn't sure what he was talking about until I looked up and saw the screen change from their presentation to a clip of the video Maria took. It showed Susie talking to the girl on the news clip and a drug cartel leader, Ms. Choike. TJ outdid himself. He added some graphics to help people know who was in the scene, as if they were watching the news. Just as Jason was about to lose his shit, the FBI came in, crashing the party.

"FBI! Everyone stay seated!" Mike commanded the room.

For a moment you could see Susie contemplate running as she turned toward the doors, but two agents were waiting for her. As they handcuffed her, Ken looked down at his watch and started timing. "Come on, Susie, make me twenty dollars."

"And one minute. Sorry, Neil, you lose."

"Oh shit, wait for it. Here it comes."

"Jason, this is all your fault, you and your crazy, greedy plans!" Susie screamed across the room.

"Sis, shut up! Wait for our lawyer to get here. Just shut up."

"Ken, come on. I think you started timing too early."

"You know I didn't. I probably gave you an extra minute or two."

"Good point, but so close. Damn it." I handed him twenty bucks.

As we were sitting there, enjoying the circus around us, Mike shot me a look and a thumbs up, something out of a beer commercial. Jason, on the other hand, looked pissed. Among the fish, his sister getting arrested, and ruining his party, he's having a shit day. I can relate to having a bad day, what it feels like, and how it can throw you off-center. Hell, yesterday he just got out of prison, though he worked his plan to perfection. He even thought his sister got away with killing an FBI agent, since the killer had left the country.

Ken and I sat there watching the show as it unfolded. Susie was jawing at her brother. Though he wasn't in handcuffs, they had him sitting down and in the corner away from everything as they explained to him the arrest warrant for his sister and the search warrant for the premises.

Jason forgot as a convicted felon he's not out for time served. His lawyer forgot to mention one detail of the deal: the first six months of his freedom were a form of parole. He's out early on good behavior; that comes with some less than favorable freedoms compared to those of us that haven't committed multiple felonies.

Mike came over and sat down with us as the three of us shared a bit of a moment about the case and everything going on. It was nice to just breathe after getting sucker-punched earlier in the week. It took a solid minute or two for Mike to say anything; we just sat there, enjoying the circus around us—the agents working systematically to gather information, take computers, paperwork, and everything between.

"Hey guys, this doesn't take away from the way the week went, but it helps." Mike said, smiling.

"I'll second that one, Mike. How about you, Neil? You've been quiet during this whole thing."

"I'm good. I'm just thinking about how Maria would be enjoying this moment right now."

"You mean because you're dressed up for a change?" Mike said with a laugh.

"Very funny, Ken. You two are giving me shit just a few days after all that mess. Then again, that's why we're friends. Do you think I should go talk to either one of them, or should we just sit here and watch them sulk a bit?"

"I'm enjoying the view. Aren't you? This is the most fun I've had in a long time. I've always wondered what it would be like to be at the end of a movie like *Die Hard* or something, and I feel like this is it."

"Should one of us says something catchy?"

"Do you have anything in mind?"

"Only one thing seems fitting right now."

"I know exactly where you're going with this."

"Cluster-Fuck!" we said, laughing in unison.

31

REST IN PEACE.

"Well, where do we go from here? I would like to tell you that everything will be perfect. That we can get through almost anything and that Maria would want us to live on with her memory in light, not darkness. I would like to tell you many things about Maria, but I can't—those are for her family, her loved ones, and her colleagues. They will speak to you about all of the memories they shared and the things that will be missed. What I'm going to talk to you about is justice, perseverance, and overcoming odds to be a great inspiration to many.

Maria was an inspiration to me, pushing me to be a better man. Though it has been nearly two weeks now since she was taken from us, I find myself talking to her. Still, I find myself looking for her to hand me a cup of coffee or a drink. Though these days I no longer drink, I still look for it in that routine, that calmness she would give me at the end of the day. I know it won't be there, I know it's gone, but my heart still longs for it, forces me to try and search for it.

I remember being a kid and thinking if I don't try and see if I have superpowers, how will I ever know if I have them? It's the inner seven-year-old in me having faith that she is going to come walking through that door tomorrow. Though the adult in me knows she is not going to, under no circumstances. I know the only time I will get to see her again is when it's my time to pass on. Though right now I want to be selfish and cry to her, I know many people need me here, and in time I will be with her again and all the others in my family that have passed on before me.

Those are what make days like today tough, but also joyous. Just as Father Roberts spoke earlier about the passing from life to the next. To be reborn in the life of God among the heavens. I must have faith that this journey isn't over for me; it isn't over for any of us. We must live in her honor, make the hard choice, do what is right, and make a difference. I miss you, Maria, I love you, Maria, Rest in peace."

Out at the gravesite, giving a eulogy to a woman that touched me in a way that Maria has, broke me. The last week has been tougher than expected, without the drive to engulf me, I flew out to Santa Fe for a few days, knowing the funeral wouldn't be for a week. I hiked, took some baths, and hiked some more. It was the most introspection I've ever had in my life. I had great company and support from Sister Irene and some other familiar faces from our trip.

I had to make sure I had some positive memories again of that place; I couldn't leave it with Maria's death. Though we had great memories prior to her being taken from us, that lasting memory was what stuck with me. I wanted to go back out, visit with Sister Irene, and lay to rest the memory of her death. Now back in Detroit, at the cemetery, I am calm but still broken.

"Neil, that was moving, I've never heard you speak like that, or that long. Are you going to be okay?" Sheila gave me a big hug.

"I will. I think I'm finally moving through it, accepting it, and working past it. Where is Carol Lynn?"

"She's with Uncle Ken. They went to grab something to drink. She was thirsty, and Ken said he had water in the car."

The funeral had ended with my final eulogy. Once we laid Maria to rest, I felt a change inside me, just a small one, but noticeable. It was as if we collectively let go of uncertainty. We all got to watch together, the finality of it all. I know death is something that happens, I've been around it for so long, but when it hits home like this, damn. It's a reminder of all the times you glossed over something to cover it up. It's as if I covered a hole in the wall with a poster. It solves the visual issue, but not the structural one. Eventually you'll have to deal with it.

"Hey Mike, how you holding up?" He gave me a big bear hug.

"Neil, I hope she was here to hear you say those kind words. I know she would be touched."

"Thanks, Mike, remember this is the only day I will allow touchy-feely sappy stuff. After this, we go back to bro stuff, okay?" I said, trying to lighten the mood.

"When are you going to get back to work? The bureau guys and I have plenty of work piling up, could use your help. Even some stuff with Gaines."

"The Gaines stuff. Feel free and send it to Ken. If it's worth my time he'll send it on to me. I'm going in for my weekly meeting tomorrow at FCI Milan with Cappelano. It's better now that we have a set schedule and routine. Every Wednesday, I'm there at nine in the morning."

"We're glad to have you back from Santa Fe; some of us weren't sure if you were going to stay out there. I may have checked to see if you had a return ticket to New Mexico." Mike smiled.

"What if I decided to drive it again?"

"Shit—good point, Neil. All kidding aside, we're here for you. Anything you need, just call."

"Thanks, Mike."

The next hour went on like this until I and Maria's parents were exhausted. We had met only a few times, but under the current state, we had bonded over their daughter and gotten to know each other quite well. It's not how I would have planned to get to know her parents, but I'm glad I did just the same.

Sheila left with Carol Lynn as well as a few others. As people started to go, I noticed it was only me and Ken sitting in silence when I saw someone walking up in a dark suit, approaching me slowly.

"Mr. Baggio, I presume, and Ken Chamberlain?"

"Yes. What can we do for you?"

"There's a gentleman who would like to speak to you in his Town Car over there. He said you know him as Mr. Johnson."

I looked to Ken, and we shared a quick moment simultaneously, saying, "Erin." As the two of us slowly followed the well-dressed suit to the car, we kept looking at each other. Through body language, we were asking if either of us packed a gun or if we should stay outside the car. The whole thing was surreal, and I didn't think the week could get any odder. As I had told Christian weeks ago, I prepared myself for some news that Erin wasn't locked up.

The meeting in the car went as expected. Sorry, you didn't think I was going to let you in on a covert meeting with some guy using a fake name at the end of the book now, did you? Sorry, that's just not going to happen. Ken and I didn't even want to hear him out, but he offered to put our kids through college and pay for it. I'm just kidding. He didn't offer to pay for anything, but he did offer to get them into any school. By now you can sense that I'm stalling, not giving you the details you want. That's true, but why, I'll tell you. It's because by now I am in my car driving up the freeway, to FCI Milan.

I know I'm supposed to meet with Frank tomorrow, but I wanted to take a moment out and talk to him. I think I might skip tomorrow, and I wanted to get some notes from him. See where he was at with everything and tell him the great news about the warden. With all the case files the FBI seized, they were able to pin the warden to enough illicit activities that he stepped down and walked away.

Getting Gaines's buddy out of there will allow me to operate with Cappelano without the prying eyes of Gaines on me. You may ask who has filled that role. It is none other than Officer Colby. We may have pulled some strings, but he has proven himself worthy. He even was going back to school to get his master's degree, which helped us push that along. Sitting in the room as Frank walked in, Colby looked at me strangely. Almost like a dog does when they are confused, and they turn their head to the side.

"Neil, we aren't supposed to meet until tomorrow. Is everything okay?" It was then he noticed how I was dressed.

"I just needed a bit of distraction for a bit. You game for doing it a day early?"

"It's understandable; let's start."

32

I BET YOU DIDN'T THINK YOU'D GET TO HEAR FROM ME.

Hello, how are you guys doing today? I know Neil is a bit distracted right now. He's reading over my notes. He needs the distraction. I bet you didn't think you'd get to hear from me, but this is just the beginning. This is just the start of my voice being heard. I can't wait to share my story with you in its entirety. The past couple of weeks have been hard on Neil, so I took time and put a lot of work into this. Giving him the detail, he needs to take a week or two off and just review everything he already has. I figured it was the least I can do. Plus it will allow me some more one-on-one time with you, my audience.

Don't you want to know why I did it? What it was like on the run, leaving the FBI? Wouldn't it be great to know the other side of the story, the part you didn't get? The part no one ever tells?

About the Author

Charles D'Amico is a husband, father, writer, and business owner. Having grown up in the Metro Detroit Area, he acknowledges much of his success to his upbringing and schooling at St. Mary's Prep in Orchard Lake. He graduated from Ball State University with a bachelor's degree, where he studied Criminology and Psychology. Charles is continuing to write, as well as publish other great authors through Blue Handle Publishing, LLC. He currently resides in Amarillo, TX.

FOR MORE UPDATES SIGN UP AT

WWW.BHPUBS.COM

THE NEIL BAGGIO UNIVERSE

 NEIL BAGGIO SERIES

 **MARIE PERDITA**